WRATH OF THE UNDEAD

By Eric Moreno

CHAPTER 1

Hello. My name is Doctor Madeline Monreal, the new head of research here at this Center for Disease Control and Prevention. From this day forth, my team of scientists and I will be working toward the development of a permanent cure for the UD Virus. Sorry, excuse my shortness of breath and watery eyes, I'm just nervous to be here. As you stand there, locked inside this small empty room made of glass walls, staring at me with a blank expression and locked jaw, I wonder if anything I say will make sense to you. In any case, you're here. You're real. And you'll be treated as a human being, a real patient, not just a test subject or lab rat. That I promise you. But before we begin, I want to sit with you and share a little of myself so that you know *exactly* who I am and what I've come here to accomplish. Gosh, I'm so nervous. My hands won't stop trembling. I've practiced this speech a million times, and suddenly my mind has drawn a blank and my voice is shaky. There are so many things that I've been wanting to say to you, but I can't find the words… perhaps it's the shock of finally being here in front of you. After all these years. Anyhow, I digress.

As I stated earlier, I have been assigned to work down here as head of our medical research. Actually, I put in the request. After a bit of pleading and a few pulled strings, my wishes were granted. Behind me is the newly installed lab where my team and I will spend most of our time conducting research and development. Being in close proximity to you, I feel will encourage us to work toward an attainable goal. So, every morning you'll see me walk through that sliding metal door to the left of me and every morning I'll drop by to say good morning and see how you are doing. I'll share with you a little of my story and then I'll conclude my day with our work in the lab.

I'd like to start our first session with what I call 'human interaction' by telling you the story of how I got to be in this position and then dive into the backstory. I'm hoping to find that cognition is possible by re-telling a story that may spark a memory or trigger some form of recognition of what you were, or rather I should say, *who* you were. This of course is another form of research, but one without serums injected into your body. Although you have been a huge contributing factor with progress made in the past, toward the development of the first ever cure for the old virus, I thought we'd try an alternative method this time, until we find a new vaccine that will permanently eradicate the mutated virus. Once we do, we can begin clinical trials again. Let's start, shall we? I've brought this chair and a cup of hot green tea for myself. I figure we'll be here for a while, so we might as well make ourselves comfortable. I'll have a seat now and you can too, if you'd like... or not. I'll begin by telling you the story of what drove me to become a Biochemist and pursue a career in medical research.

It started when I was a senior in high school, almost twenty years ago, and it was the first day of the semester. The morning clouds were gray, and the weather was chilly. A typical day in Los Angeles. Long gone were the days of a warm and sunny morning. Escalating global warming saw to that. I arrived at school at seven fifty-three a.m. and by the way things were looking, I was going to be late for class again. The long line of students including myself sluggishly marching to the front door reminded me of cattle in a slaughter house. We formed a line in front of the main building and every student had to walk past a large blue door then go through wide, black, full body scanners. The body scanners, which looked like metal detectors, were used for detecting traces of the Undead Virus, or as we call it, the "UD-Virus." Although I was a senior and had walked through the scanners for almost every day of the past four years, I still could not get used to the cold stare coming from the two-armed security guards that were stationed on each side of the scanners. The *executioners* as we called them, stood tall wearing a black face mask, outfitted with black tactical gear.

Their itchy finger which rested on the side of a fully automatic rifle waited to scratch one of us off with a bullet to the head if we triggered the virus detector. As I took another step forward, the bright red alarm mounted on one of the scanners went off. The red-light spun and sounded off an ear-piercing beep followed by commotion coming from the front of the line.

That's when I saw Jake, a sophomore, forcefully pushing his way through the line. His thin face painted with fear screamed for help as he maneuvered through the line. "Move!" he cried, desperately shoving people aside trying to escape. Seconds later and without a warning, the loud cracking sound of a rifle echoed through the hall and Jake's scrawny body fell forward onto the steps of the front building. His face bounced up as he hit the steps. A few that were standing in front of me gasped and the girl behind me let out a high-pitched scream that rattled my ear drum. She must have been a freshman who had never witnessed something like that before. The virus usually appeared in teenage years, that is, once you entered high school, which could explain her loud hysteria.

Specks of Jake's blood splattered onto my hoodie and black Vans. *Great*, I thought to myself, it meant I'd have to check into the hazard-center for sterilization. At least now I had a valid excuse for being tardy. As the guard's cautiously approached Jake's lifeless body with their rifles steadily pointed, I stood over his lifeless body, watching as blood dripped out of his golden-brown head. I then experienced a strange and unsettling feeling. I felt perturbed by my own selfishness. Instead of feeling sorry and crying over Jake's death, like the girl behind me, I was relieved to give my first period teacher Mrs. Jenkins a real excuse for being late to her class. I asked myself, *What's worst? The fact that Jake's death didn't even bother me or the fact that we grew accustomed to seeing our friends or the people we know, killed at school on a regular basis?*

Thirteen years prior, the world would find out that the virus mutated and would reappear in a child once it grew into its teenage years. If a woman was pregnant during the initial outbreak, the child had a high probability of developing the UD-Virus, much like the chickenpox.

George Oremor was the first of his kind. On the day the virus resurfaced, he fell ill at school and went to the nurse's office. He lay on the bed with a violent cough and a high temperature. The nurse phoned his mother to pick him up. George's mom picked him up, took him home and gave him medicine. That night when she went up to his room to check on him, she found him wide awake with white eyes and pallid skin. He had turned into one of the undead and savagely killed his mother. Blood splats were found across the wall and ceiling. Neighbors heard the mother's cries and called the police. When the officer's arrived, they found the boy and his mother eating the remains of his father, her husband. They immediately shot and killed them both and put a bullet in the father's head to prevent him from turning. The entire block was quarantined off and top scientists from around the world were flown in to investigate the matter. After their findings, the news of the virus reappearing in teenagers caused a wave of panic. People lived in fear again and Congress raced for a solution. That's when the Strike Down bill was introduced and later passed into law.

Ever since Congress passed the Strike Down Law, which gave an armed official the right to legally kill a kid on sight if they were carrying the UD-Virus, like poor Jake, our society including myself accepted the death of a student at school as the norm. Back when the bill was introduced, thousands of protesters turned out for rallies in Washington DC and hundreds of cities across the United States to abolish the bill. They futilely marched down our nation's capital with big colorful banners and signs that read, "We Are Not Un-Dead Yet," or "Let Me LIVE," but their loud voices fell on deaf ears. Supporters of the bill stood on the opposite end chanting, "Kill the dead," or "Prevent UD-Day Repeat." Bandana-wearing protesters would snatch banners away from supporters of the bill, rip them apart and stomp on them. They got in the supporters' face and screamed at them, shouting profanity and even spitting at them. Fights would break out between the supporter's and protesters. Men would punch women. Teens would physically fight with adults. Mobs would throw rocks and bottles at each other. Things got so bad that the police fired tear gas into the crowd to disperse the unruly mob. Over time, the bill was voted into law.

Years later, there I was walking past Jake's body getting escorted through the scanners by security and led into the hazard-center just one door down from the building's entrance.

At the hazard-center, a woman wearing a white bio-suit greeted me with a pleasant smile, like an employee at a tea shop cheerfully greeting a customer. She took me by the hand, sat me on a wooden chair covered with disposable white paper in front of her desk, and began to ask a ton of questions. I listened as she spoke, but the glass picture frame sitting on her desk grabbed most of my attention. It was out of my view and faced towards her. I wondered whose picture was in the frame. My guess was of her family. Or just a picture of her kids, if she had any. Or maybe of her cat? Although she didn't strike me as a cat person. More of a golden retriever type person. I became annoyed with her ridiculous questions, not to mention the squeak coming from the black leather chair she sat on. No, I was not traumatized. No, I did not want to see the school psychologist. I just wanted to get into the shower and get the whole ordeal over with, so I could get to class. After the long questionnaire, she took my clothes, gave me a towel, and led me into the shower room enclosed with glass doors. It had a high-pressured rainfall shower head and four liquid dispensers on top of the shower caddy affixed to the tile wall. She instructed me to use all dispensers, starting with the weird slimy green lotion that was to be used all over my body and hair. "This special compound will disinfect and kill all the bacteria," she said. "So be generous with it," she added.

After my bath, she handed me a humiliating burgundy school outfit to wear throughout the day. As for my blood-stained clothes, not to mention my new cute outfit for the first day of school, into the fire it went. My new unstylish fit for the day was a sweatshirt with the school logo printed on the front and sweat pants with black slipper shoes. I hated being the kid with the uniform that everyone stared at. Quiet whispers of ridicule and teasing laughter were what I had to look forward to all day. And then it dawned on me that Andrew, the boy whom I had a growing crush on, was going to see me in that hideous outfit during our fourth period history class. I grew red and embarrassed at the thought. The woman with the bio-suit then gave me a handwritten note with her signature on it and sent me off to class.

During fourth period, I sat in my history class minutes before it began, staring at the door, dreading the moment that Andrew would walk through it. I felt nervous and tried to distract myself by looking over a large map of the U.S pinned onto the wall, but I kept looking back to the door as students walked in. Just as the bell rang, Andrew, who I managed to avoid all day so that he wouldn't see me in that god-awful uniform, stormed in. He swung off his backpack, sat next to me and whispered, "hey, I heard what happened. Are you okay?" He was sweet to ask. His cute smile and genuine concern had reassured me that he really didn't care of how silly I may have looked. I told him that I was okay and briefly went over the incident.

"Shhh!" Mr. Anderson loudly said and continued his lecture on the Second Cold War. Mr. Anderson, a lively and passionate teacher that talked with his hands, was the kind of teacher that made learning fun and kept your attention with his projecting voice. His lectures were far from boring. "After Undead Day or UD-Day, which we discussed last week in chapter ten," Mr. Anderson went on to say, "the wheels were in motion for uncovering the truth about what happened that day in what is now the worst day in American history. In today's chapter, chapter eleven, we will learn of Russia's attempt at getting its hands on the most dangerous bio weapon this world has ever seen and the beginning of the Second Cold War." His words flooded my mind with memories of my brother and the events that occurred on that horrible day and my face went blank.

"Maddie," Andrew strongly whispered and shook my arm. "Where did you go?" he asked with a strange look.

"Sorry, I spaced out," I replied and redirected my attention to Mr. Anderson who was a word away from shushing me again. As the teacher carried on, I tried taking notes, but I drifted away again. I have vague memories, but I've been told by several people stories of what transpired on that horrible day. I pieced the stories together like a jigsaw puzzle. I sorted them out on a timeline and then played them in my head like a movie. A horror flick that I would have rather not watched. But it was something that I had been doing over the weekend to prepare myself for the personal statement we had to write.

After fourth period, Andrew walked me to my next class which was upstairs in the same building. "Have you started working on your personal statement yet?" he asked adjusting the strap on his backpack as we slowly walked down the crowded hall. Locker doors slamming, inaudible conversations, and sneakers squeaking were the soundtrack of our walks to my fifth period.

"Not yet," I replied. "But I plan to do start it tonight. How about you?"

"Me neither," he said in disappointment. "I've been putting it off, but I'll start it this weekend for sure. Any idea on what you're going to write?"

"I have an idea. I just don't know how I'm going to put it together."

"Well you're a smart girl, I'm sure you'll figure something out."

We stopped at the door of my next class and were rudely greeted by my best friend Ashley. "Just kiss her already," she blurted and walked into class. Andrew and I awkwardly stared at each other. "Alright- well, I'll talk to you later," he said in an uneasy voice and walked off. I rushed into class past the first two rows and planted myself into the chair desk next to Ashley and began to berate her for embarrassing me. "Oh lighten up," she said while setting the hologram keyboard on her phone to take notes. "You should be thanking me. He's taking way too long to ask you out. You both like each other so I'm just acting as a facilitator, enabling him to make the first move."

"Well your role as 'facilitator of romance' hasn't worked out so well in the past. Remember what happened with Alan?"

"Okay, that's different. I didn't know he was gay. Besides, you guys are good friends now thanks to me."

"I'm just not sure if Andrew's into me is all."

"Well the guy sits next to you, walks you to class, texts you almost every night to talk about whatever. Of course he's into you. He's probably scared that you'll reject him if he asks you out. I think he's playing it safe. Too safe. If I were you, I'd ask him to hang out after class. I bet he'll get the point. And if he still doesn't, then he's a big dummy."

"I can't, I'm going to start writing my personal statement tonight."

"Oh yeah, have you decided if whether or not to write about your brother and what happened that day?"

"Yeah. I've decided that I am going to focus on that. I mean, it is the sole purpose of why I'm going to college, so that I can graduate with a degree in biochemistry and one day find a cure."

"Good luck friend. I still haven't decided on what I'm going to write myself."

After school, Andrew was standing in the hallway by the red doorway of the front building waiting for me. The executioners stood close by, guarding the doors. The red door was used only for exiting the building. If anyone exited and had to go back in, they would have to use the blue door and pass through the scanners. From afar, I could tell Andrew seemed a bit nervous. Not his usual self. He dried his palms on the side of his pants and smiled as I walked down the hall. He passed his fingers over his slick hair making sure it was neatly combed. He then quickly reached into his pocket and popped a gum. "Hey," he greeted me and quickly chewed the gum to mask the odor of his breath. "I was hoping to walk you home so we can talk?" he asked. I was excited to say the least and relieved. I thought he was in some sort of trouble. "Of course," I replied with a big smile that ran across my face.

The executioners stared us down as we passed them by on our way out. The stairs where Jake bled out had been pressure washed and sanitized as if nothing ever happened. Soon to be a forgotten memory like several before him.

I then turned my attention to Carol, one of the popular girls in school as she got into her AI self-driving car, one of the older models, handed down from her older brother who went off to college in a different state. The sleek car with sliding doors came with carbon fiber panels and a hologram touch screen with voice command. I could hear her giving it instructions to drive home as she comfortably sat in the back. The seats, which came equipped with automatic seatbelts, were made of leather and reclined with voice command. It had some of the latest technological advances and didn't come cheap. Her family was better off than most of the kids at school and could afford that kind of luxury, whereas the rest of us still had to manually steer the wheel or worse, walk home, like me. Andrew and I stared in admiration as Carol's car sped off. "Man, one day I'll own a car like that," Andrew said with confidence. "One to drive me everywhere while I nap in the back seat like a boss."

"Give me call when you do and pick me up so you can take me around the city in it," I said. He turned at me and smiled, "absolutely, you'll be the first person to sit in the passenger seat. We'll take a trip up to San Francisco, cross the Golden Gate Bridge, make a U-turn, and drive right back home," he said and laughed as he envisioned the fun road trip in his future sporty car. As we walked, we discussed other things that we wanted out of life. He shared his dream of being part of the first crew to fly up to Mars. As a child, he had an admiration for astronauts and spaceships. His room looked like a planetarium, adorned with rocket ship toys, a solar system ornament that hung from his ceiling, a telescope and a colorful outer space bedding set. He dreamt of traveling through space on a big rocket ship. As he grew older, he made plans for making his dream a reality by going to college and getting a degree in engineering. Then he'd get a job at SpaceX and join their Astronaut program with the hopes of flying to Mars someday. "I want to be part of a team that starts a new civilization in Mars," he said with enthusiasm. "A new way of life. Away from all this… this mess," he said with revulsion. "Where people won't have to live in fear. Where the Undead Virus doesn't exist. No more executioners. No more death."

I admired his passion and shared his vision. I liked him even more. "While you're up there, I'll be down here trying to find a permanent cure for the virus," I said and shared my own goals. I told him that I also wanted to go to a University and get a degree in biochemistry, with the hopes of working for the CDC and finding a cure that would permanently do away with the UD-Virus. He raised his eyebrows with an impressed look at hearing my ambitions. Our goals were sort of aligned with one another, in helping other people but in a completely different way.

"Maybe we'll end up going to the same college," he said with a smile. "That would be cool," I replied.

"So, what did you want to talk about?" I asked as we came to a stop sign. He looked both ways before crossing and said, "Oh, yeah, uh, well… I actually made something, but I kind of feel silly showing you now," he said scratching his head. "Oh you've got my curiosity now, so you *have* to show me." I entreated for him to show me what he made. He looked down with embarrassment and hesitated for a second before finally giving in. "Okay, okay, but promise not to laugh?" he asked and swung his backpack over to his chest and unzipped it. "I promise," I replied and anxiously waited. He pulled out a large piece of black card board paper, unfolded the paper and held it up over his head. In large yellow letters it read, "My name isn't Han, but don't let me go to prom Solo." He held a big smile as he watched me read it, then asked, "Maddie will you go to prom with me?" My face beamed with joy. I was ecstatic with happiness. "Yes!" I joyfully cried out and gave him a tight hug. As we embraced, our eyes met and I could feel the warmth of his lips close to mine. I stared up into his light brown eyes and he looked into mine. That moment which must have only been a second, felt like it could last forever. It was as if we were the only ones in the street. He drew closer when suddenly a car honked its horn as it drove past us. We got startled and wondered why he had honked if we weren't standing in the middle of the road? It must have been an immature jerk behind the wheel who knew how to kill a moment. We laughed it off and kept walking. As we reached my block we stopped at the corner. I didn't want my dad to see him yet so we said our goodbyes. I gave him another hug and felt brave enough to kiss him on the cheek. He blushed and smiled. "See you tomorrow," he said with rosy cheeks and waited as I walked to my house. I quickly walked home and ran upstairs to my bedroom because I couldn't wait to tell my best friend what happened. She would have jumped out of her bed at hearing the news. As soon as I got in my room, I threw my bookbag on the bed, put on my virtual-reality headset and virtual-dialed my friend Ashely. I wanted to see her face when I told her the news.

Later that evening, when I started working on my personal statement, I thought of ways to introduce myself and the first paragraph. Something that would capture the reader's attention right away. The hook. I sat in my bed with tablet on my lap staring at a blank screen with a blank mind. I reflected back to the day when it all began to draw inspiration. As thoughts flashed through my head, I began typing on the hologram keyboard. I once read that if you get in the "zone" just keep writing as the ideas and thoughts rush through your mind. Worry about editing later. So that's what I did. And by midnight I had over ten pages. A lot of it was really good, but I also deleted some stuff. I felt some of what I wrote wasn't necessary or didn't fit in with what I was writing about. By the end of the night I knew I had a solid introduction and at least three strong paragraphs.

The next morning, I went to school a few minutes earlier this time, and when I got to the front of the building, I saw the biohazard team, the cleanup crew, carrying out a black body bag. They wore white biohazard suits and were responsible for cleaning up the mess left by the executioners. They lifted the body bag onto a stretcher and into the back of a truck, or "death wagon" as we called them. *Another poor soul,* I thought to myself as I kept walking. My friend Ashley was standing by the front door waiting for me. Her nose was red and her eyes were watery. She held tissue in her hand. I could tell she had been crying. Her face was gloomy and when she saw me, she frowned and gave me this apologetic look. She took in a deep breath and went down the steps. As she walked toward me, I looked at the death wagon driving off and something inside me knew who was inside that body bag. "Maddie," she softly said in a somber tone and placed her hands on my shoulders. "I'm so sorry friend, but … they killed Andrew." She began to weep again and pulled me in for a hug. As she held me, it hadn't quite hit me yet, not until I saw his face in my mind and remembered him holding up the banner asking me to prom. I pretty much lost it after that. I felt my legs go weak and even got light headed. She had to help me from falling over. I never knew a person could hold so many tears. I cried so much. I wanted to die. I was inconsolable for over a month. I took a few days off from school and locked myself in my room. I cried every day and every night thinking about him. He was the first boy I ever cried over. It wasn't fair I thought to myself. Why did it have to be him? Shameful actually; now when I think about it. Wishing that it were someone else in that body bag. No one deserved to die like that. Specially not a beautiful young soul with big dreams. I still think about that boy from time to time.

I wonder how prom would have turned out. I used to imagine myself shopping for a dress and trying them on, one after the other. I pictured him showing up to my house in his dapper tuxedo with corsage in hand and his hair neatly combed back. I saw myself being held in his arms as we danced the night away. Laughing at something funny he might have said. I imagine our first kiss would have been something out of a romantic movie. The lights dimmed low with soft romantic music playing in the background, serving as the soundtrack to our first kiss. But in reality, I didn't go to prom. I ended up staying home that night, reading up on the virus, educating myself on the effects of it. I'll tell you this, his death made me to work harder toward my goal. I told myself that I would go to a University and one day find a permanent cure so that young people like Andrew would never have to die again. After his passing, I got myself together and finished my personal statement. I applied to the best Universities for Biology and Biochemistry like Harvard and Stanford and got accepted into U.C Berkeley where I got my degree in Biochemistry with a minor in Behavioral Science. I then transferred to Harvard and got a PhD in Biochemistry. My father works here as head of security and helped with getting my foot in the door. In time, I worked my way up and finally got to be in a position where I can make a difference. Where I can focus all of my energy in finding a permanent cure and put an end to the Strike Down Law.

Andrew's unfortunate death has been a major influence in my life's work and helped in achieving my goals, but it wasn't the only driving force that led me here. He was just that little extra push I needed to keep climbing higher. Tomorrow I'll tell you the story of how Undead Day began and the ultimate reason of why I'm here.

CHAPTER 2

Hi. Good morning. Yesterday when I got home, I ordered a new caramel tea flavor from my local market and I've been dying to try it ever since the drone dropped it off on my door step last night. Well I just tried it as I walked in and oh my God, it is amazing. So delicious and it smells wonderful. This will be my new tea, every morning, well at least until the pack runs out. Alright, let's begin our session. I would like to start by giving you a little history lesson, but before we get into how Undead Day started, I thought it important to go back a little further. A lot further actually.

Back to the year 1942, when Germany along with the Axis powers were at war with the Allies. During this period, several German physicians conducted unethical, deadly, and painful experiments on numerous concentration camp prisoners including children. The macabre experiments, which were meant to aid with the survival of German military personnel and to treat their injuries and illness, were done for research. Thousands were forced to undergo grisly experimentations that for many, led to their agonizing death. In one such case, naked prisoners were left outside in the freezing cold with temperatures as low as -6 °C to study the physical effects of being exposed to the cold. They were later thrown into boiling water to rewarm.

Hitler, seeking ultimate power and control, demanded of his top scientists to develop a new master weapon that would render all of Germany's enemies powerless and under his control. Hermann Hirschfeld, the infamous scientist, led a secret team of scientists and physicians to develop the Fuhrer's secret master weapon that would win them the war. They collected data from every torturous and inhumane testing administered and spent several years analyzing it. Their analysis, research and evaluations would lead to the discovery of a lethal agent that would later be developed for biological warfare. Facing heavy pressure from the Fuhrer to create his weapon, Hirschfeld and his group hurried to finalize Hitler's weapon as the curtain began to fall on the axis powers. The inchoate biological agent that would take two years to create was formulated to control the Allied soldiers. Hitler's intent was to manipulate the minds of Allied forces and create his own army of mindless soldiers. With the use of this weapon, Allied soldiers would lose cognition, emotion, and conation and ultimately surrender to Hitler's command.

In April of 1945, the Soviet army advanced deep into Berlin defeating Hitler's army. Facing a certain and imminent death, Hitler and his wife ultimately committed suicide and the prospect of winning WWII by means of biological warfare died along with him; moreover, the imperfectly formed biological agent would remain idle.

Hirschfeld hid in his laboratory before trying to flee the country but would later be captured by American troops who uncovered his work and found gallons of the biological agent. The American army covertly shipped the barrels containing the biological weapon to the U.S. and for a short time would remain a secret from the rest of the world. During the first Cold War, the Soviet Union learned of Hirschfeld's biological weapon and conjured up a plan to steal it from the U.S. but after learning of the Russians intent, U.S. military commanders secretly ordered the barrels to be placed in a highly guarded military bio-defense research facility. Following several years after the Cold War, Hirschfeld's weapon would be brought back into light when a classified biological defense program was created to begin its research using new technological advances in hopes of applying its findings toward the development and treatment of diseases. Years later and events leading up the Second Cold War, the barrels would be transported to another facility and sit in a warehouse for a week until a warehouse dock worker by the name of Fred would accidentally come across it.

Who is Fred you ask? Good question. That brings us to our next story. The beginning of Undead Day.

It was September 26, 2017 and I was five years old. I lived in a small, yet cozy, humble apartment. It had one tiny restroom and two small bedrooms that were positioned at opposite ends. The apartment complex was in a rough neighborhood in Central Los Angeles, surrounded by gangs, thieves, drugs, and the homeless.

There, in a small bedroom of a single window, morning daylight crept through the dusty drawn shades. My twenty-year-old brother Fred laid flat on his stomach on a twin bed, wearing shorts with his face buried in a worn-out pillow. He had a black digital clock on top of an old, brown, two-drawer night stand next to his bed that would go off every day at six a.m. Without fail, the pulsing and annoying sound of his alarm clock went off and woke him. He stretched his arm out and slapped the off button. His fingers then felt around for a black lighter and crystal blue pipe that were set on top of the night stand. With a loud yawn, he threw off the blanket and sat on the edge of the bed with his eyes half shut. He scratched his buzz cut head and give himself a moment to fully wake. He opened the top drawer and pulled out a small green plastic container with a label that read O.G Purple Cush. It contained cannabis, a powerful ganja strain. Fred was a big pot head. The wake and bake type of person. The kind of person that needed marijuana in order to carry on with his day. He'd wake up and smoke before breakfast. Smoke before lunch. Smoke before dinner. Smoke before a snack and smoke just before going to bed.

In those days, when marijuana was illegal, he'd get his weed supply from our fat drug dealing neighbor across the street, so he always had easy access to it.

Fred packed a bowl with a large nugget of cannabis, lit it up, inhaled and let his lungs fill with smoke, then slowly exhaled. The smoke swayed side to side before vanishing into the air, leaving behind its distinct odor. He packed the pipe again and puffed it another four times, before setting it down to get ready for work.

In front of his bed was a single door closet where he pulled out a pair of faded blue jeans and a black tee-shirt that hung from a plastic hanger. He liked wearing baggy clothing which made his skinny and tall frame look thinner. From underneath the bed, he brought out a pair of old, worn out, beige steel toe boots with an almost visible metatarsal guard. He tied his boots, grabbed the lighter, keys, phone, wallet, and walked out, closing the door behind him.

I remember that morning, I was laying down on our stained sofa, watching superhero cartoons. I wore my favorite pink butterfly pajamas and closely held on to my most prized possession, a soft plush teddy bear that I called Berry. He was my best friend and went everywhere with me. Wherever my imagination took me, Berry was there by my side. If I was a super hero, he was my side kick. If I flew an airplane, he was my co-pilot.

What made Berry most valuable to me was that Fred had won it for me at the street fair a few months earlier.

At the fair, I remember him throwing a soft rubber ball at three stacked old dirty milk bottles and knocking them down. After he won, the old carny with hair white as snow leaned down and asked, "Which one do you like little lady?" "That one," I said pointing up at the row of stuffed animals.

Fred walked in the living room and sat next to me. "Hey, good morning little lady," he said. I looked up, staring at his goatee and asked if he was going to work as he brushed my tangled curly brown hair away from my face. He looked down at my big brown eyes and softly poked my little round nose. "Yes, I have to go to work now," he replied. "You and Berry be good and listen to mommy okay?" I nodded and he leaned down to kiss me on the forehead. He got up and peeked into our mother's bedroom which was a few feet to the left from the sofa.

"Ma' going to work now. I'll be home by five," Fred said softly standing in the doorway.

She was lying on her side facing the wall on a full-size bed, which she and I shared, and didn't respond. A strand of her curly hair slid down her shoulder which had a tattoo that read 'Frederick' in cursive letters; a tattoo that she got of my brother's name when he was two years old and she was nineteen. Our bedroom was a little bigger than Fred's by only a few feet but was dark and didn't have windows. The lights were turned off, but the light coming in from the living room revealed the bottle of painkillers set on top of the dresser next to the bed. Fred shook his head in disappointment. He leaned against the doorway and in deep thought stared at the front door next to the TV. He slowly paced from the front door back to the sofa where I was laying. He looked at me and then glanced at our mom and sighed heavily. With apprehension, he opened the front wooden creaky door and held onto it for a few seconds. He looked back at me and faked a smile. "If you get hungry, there's milk in the fridge for cereal and the cereal box is on the table okay?" he said standing in the doorway holding the door knob. "I'll be home as soon I can after work. See ya' later little lady." I waived my teddy bear's arm goodbye as he closed the door behind him.

He walked three blocks from the apartment to catch a bus to work. As he leaned against the bus stop sign waiting for the next bus, he stared at a candlelight vigil that was held in a boy's memory who was shot two days earlier. Next to the glass candle of the Virgin of Guadalupe lay a bouquet of flowers and a framed photo of a smiling kid taken on photo day at his junior high school. It was a raw image of the life that surrounded the city, but one that Fred grew accustomed to. Unlike myself, Fred grew up in a rough neighborhood where drugs and gang life were an everyday fact of life. Buildings and alleys were spray painted with graffiti, gun shots were heard through the window almost every other night, and police helicopters buzzed over the streets nightly.

Two nights earlier, a rival gang member had driven into our neighborhood and shot at three teenagers that were standing on the corner by the bus stop. The boy from the photo, age fourteen, took two bullets to the chest and one in the stomach. His older friend of age fifteen, ducked and hid behind a car and recalled seeing his friend on the ground. He said the boy looked like a roach does when it's lying on its back desperately trying to get up. His white tee was soaked in blood as he struggled to get up. He tried pushing his chest forward with his arms in the air, taking hard breaths. A minute later he was dead and the never-ending violent cycle of young males killing one another would once again make the evening news.

When you grow up in a neighborhood that's filled with violence and death, you learn to accept those things as normal and become immune to the sadness of it all. As was the case with my brother who blankly stared at the vigil and felt nothing. He then redirected his attention at the end of the street and saw the bus approaching.

For the duration of the bus ride, Fred sat in the back gazing out the window. He stared at several cars and people on the street and imagined that they all had a different story to tell. He observed a young woman behind the steering wheel of an electric car use the visor mirror to apply makeup. A man in a pickup truck turned the radio knob searching for a station. A mother in a SUV dressed in business attire drove her teen daughter to high school. On the street, a group of friends laughed as they walked to school. A homeless man slept underneath a bench on the street corner. A woman wearing an apron walked back from her minivan rolling a stainless-steel cart filled with food and supplies to start her long day at her family owned Chinese restaurant. Fred's own story was just beginning.

Monday's were his day off, but the warehouse supervisor Hector approved Fred's request for extra hours and called him the day before to ask if he could work a Monday shift. Fred who was in desperate need of the extra money happily agreed. After my biological father, Fred's step dad, walked out on us and with our mother recently fallen ill and medical expenses mounting, Fred jumped at every opportunity he could to make additional money to support us. He felt it a heavy burden and big responsibility to go from being a young man to the man of the house. But he also felt that he couldn't let us down no matter what, for much depended on him.

He arrived to work a few minutes early, but before clocking in, he walked over to the liquor store down the street from his job. "Let me get some zags," Fred asked the plump clerk at the counter of the liquor store who was wearing a brown tee-shirt that was one size too small. Outside the store, behind two green garbage containers that reeked of urine and food waste, Fred rolled a zig-zag, a type of rolling paper used for rolling tobacco. He of course rolled it with marijuana. With the freshly rolled joint rested on his lips, he felt his pockets for a black lighter. He felt it right below his keys in his left pocket, pulled it out and sparked the joint. After his smoke, he walked back to work with his head in the clouds and drank a mango flavored energy drink he bought at the liquor store and savored every sip.

Once at work, he popped a gum and went in through the side door where all warehouse personnel entered. In front of the large warehouse was a tall office building of two floors with several windows. There was a flag pole out front holding a faded American flag. Below that flag was another blue flag with the company name that read *Worldin Logistics*. The back of the building was the warehouse where Fred worked, roughly the same size as a Costco Wholesale retail company. The warehouse was used for storing cargo imported from different parts of the world. It could be any type of freight, from tires and cars, to barrels filled with propane, although chemicals like propane were stored in a special area called the Dangerous Goods Area, or D.G for short. There, Fred was employed as a warehouse dock worker. His duties ranged from receiving and unloading cargo brought in by trailers, to sweeping the warehouse floor.

After clocking in, the warehouse supervisor Hector, a short bearded stocky fellow walked up to him with a grimace look, "clocked in?" he asked.

"Yeah," Fred replied in a definite tone.

"On time this time? Because according to my watch it's ten after seven and your shift started at seven."

"Yeah, I was in the bathroom."

"But you clocked in at seven o'clock sharp?"

"Uh-huh," Fred nodded.

"You sure, because I 'm going check the time card."

Aside from being a big pot head, Fred was also notorious for being late to work. It was a bad habit that he picked up in high school. He'd show up late to school almost every day, and almost every day he would get detention. Hector already had given him a verbal warning for being late a week earlier. Another warning would be a write up and two more strikes after that, he'd get fired.

"Yeah, I clocked in at seven o'clock sharp," Fred said. "But I think the time clock is broken."

"Oh, it's broken?" Hector sarcastically asked and rolled his eyes. "Okay sure. Well, find a forklift and load Jose's trailer. He's at door number eight and he's got a hot shipment." Hector handed Fred documents containing the cargo information and the cargo's location. Fred walked down to the export side of the warehouse, found a forklift, jumped on and secured the seatbelt. He started racing down the middle of the warehouse which occupied twelve aisles of three shelf pallet racks that held imported cargo. The top of the racks on each aisle were labeled with an inventory location like A-12 which help to locate stored cargo. Fred would race back and forth from the trailer to the racks. He'd grab a shipment, load the trailer and repeat the process. On the last load, he sped down the warehouse, which on several occasions he was warned by Hector not to do, and as he picked up speed, the documents rested on his lap flew off into the air. The loose papers scattered as they fell to the floor. Fred kept his foot on the gas and turned back to see where the documents fell.

As he turned his head back around, he slammed hard on the breaks after ramming the forklift blades straight into a metal green barrel that was staged in the dangerous goods area. In those days, a dangerous goods area was out in the open with no chain or secure fence around it. All that would change after that day. Fred had accidentally punctured two large holes on the bottom of the barrel which immediately began to ooze green liquid that was spilling onto the floor. "Fuck!" he shouted under his breath, staring in disbelief at the blades inserted two inches deep into the green barrel that was labeled with yellow hazardous stickers. He panicked and jumped off the forklift. He rushed over to call his supervisor who was working on reports.

Jose, the driver standing at door number eight, was waiting for Fred to finish loading his trailer when he saw the accident. He laughed hysterically at Fred's blunder. "What an idiot!" Jose mockingly shouted at Fred while laughing and holding his pot belly. Jose had never really been liked by some of the warehouse crew. He could be an annoying and rude person. Simply put, he was a total dick. His dry laugh irritated Fred even more so. With Hector at the scene, Fred explained what happened and could tell from Hector's facial expression that it would probably be his last day working there due to the gravity of the situation.

"Ughhh, we might have to evacuate the whole damn building," Hector told Fred while staring at the leaking barrel with his head in his hand. His face turned red and he breathed harder. He shook his head and took in a deep breath to calm himself. "I have no idea if this is toxic or not, so do me a favor, run and ask Laurie inside the office to give you the log sheet for cargo that we have stored in the D.G area, the dangerous goods area. We need to know what's in the barrel, toxic or not, so we can inform the fire department. I'll finish loading Jose's trailer so he can get out of here and drop the load at the airport."

As Hector carried on with loading the rest of the cargo into the trailer and Fred retrieved the Dangerous Goods log sheet from inside the office, Jose walked over to the barrel and inspected the punctured hole. He crouched down and examined the depth of the hole with his fingers. "Ouch!" he grumbled, quickly yanking his bleeding fingers out of the hole after cutting them along the sharp metal edges. He walked back to the door rubbing off the green liquid from his fingers on the side of his pants.

After loading the last piece of freight into the trailer, Hector called over two other warehouse dock workers and instructed them to pour sand over the leaked substance and to open every warehouse door to let any possible toxic fumes out. As Jose shut and locked the door on his trailer he began to feel a tingle in his nose and sneezed uncontrollably. Larry, a dock worker came over to ask what happened and Jose sneezed directly into his face. "Oh God I'm so sorry, I can't help it," Jose apologetically said followed by another sneeze. "It… it just came out. I'm sorry." Larry gave Jose a stern look. "What the fuck man?" Larry said in anger as he wiped Jose's saliva off his face. "I had my fuckin' mouth open."

"I'm so sorry," Jose ruefully stated walking backward and sneezing irrepressibly.

"Just get in your truck and cover your damn mouth next time. What's wrong with you?"

Fred ran back with the log sheet in hand and handed it to Hector. "I don't' see this barrel listed anywhere on here," Hector told Fred as he studied the log up and down with a perplexed look. "And the barrel itself doesn't have any numbers or labels from where it came. No airline stickers, nothing. Strange, how the hell did it get here? And why didn't anyone log it in? Well, either way, I'm calling the fire department and see what they say."

"Do we still have to evacuate the building?" Fred asked.

"Not yet, at least for the time being. First, let's see what the fire department has to say about this."

Outside of the warehouse, Jose kept sneezing as he walked down the metal stairs connected to the warehouse entrance. He stopped and grabbed onto the rail to keep his balance. He felt dazed and short of breath. He felt an abnormal rise in body temperature. He paused for a moment hoping to clear his head as sweat formed and slowly dripped from his forehead. His face was burning up and his body felt weak. He decided to go back inside the warehouse to use the men's restroom and wash his face. He took a couple of deep breaths and stumbled back inside the building using the walls for balance.

He reached the men's restroom and walked to the sink. He washed his face with cold water to cool him down and thought the cold water would rid him of the strange illness that plagued him, but it didn't help. He cupped his hands together and took big gulps of water from the faucet in hopes of finding relief. Larry walked in, the man Jose sneezed on. Their eyes met through the wide mirror directly in front of the two sinks and Larry glowered at Jose. He kept silent, then rolled his eyes, used the urinal and walked out without washing his hands. Jose stood at the sink practically bathing in it. He soaked his neck and chest with water. He splashed water on his face repeatedly and ran his wet fingers through his wavy hair. He grabbed a few napkins and patted his forehead. He looked at himself in the mirror and was troubled by what stared back; the light brown hue on his face had disappeared and was replaced with a pale color. He developed puffiness and dark circles under his bloodshot eyes. He struggled to breathe and felt a sharp pain in his stomach that shot up to his chest. He grabbed his chest while gripping the water faucet tight with the other hand trying to keep himself upright. He felt the room spin and go dark. The sound of running water ran off in the distance before it ceased from making a splashing sound. His eyes rolled back, his knees buckled, and his fingers lost their grip on the faucet. He fell back hard on the white floor and laid unconscious. Blood seeped from the corner of his eyes and rolled down the side of his face. Jose would be the first casualty of the deadly virus and he would be the first carrier of it.

That same morning, at 6:50 a.m., an alarm went off in another part of the city. A man that I would later meet by the name of Michael woke up to the sight of his fiancé Kari's long dark black hair covering his face. He gently pulled his arm out from underneath her head, turned over and grabbed his phone set on top of the night stand beside their bed and hit the snooze button.

"Just ten more minutes," Kari softly said as Mike put his arm underneath her head again, hugging her tightly from behind and thrusting his pelvis against her bare bottom. "Gooood morning," she said with a naughty smile feeling his morning erection press against her behind. She threw the covers on him. "Is that your flashlight or are you just happy to see me, again?" "I have to pee," he replied and shut his eyes. For the next couple of minutes, they tried sleeping a bit more before having to let go to begin their day on what several people consider to be the most dreaded day of the week, Monday. After the alarm went off again, Kari turned toward him and stared into his small hazel eyes covered with rheum and he stared back into her green eyes. Her eyelashes were long, her nose was thin and pointy. She had a mole like that of Marilyn Monroe's on her left cheek above the corner of her soft and full lips.

"Get up sleepyhead or James will be mad again," she said and gave him a peck on the lips. "Mmm, morning breath, delicious," he sarcastically said with a smirk. She blew hot breath into his face, "Shut up, get up-get up," she repeated pushing him off the bed. "Did you have a poop sandwich for breakfast?" he asked and laughed at his own joke followed by a punch on his arm which she firmly served. "I'm joking honey. Jeez, no need for violence. Or was it a sardine protein shake?" She followed his insult with a kick to his rear. He got up and turned the alarm off on his phone and sat it back down next to a silver framed picture of the two which was taken at a trendy high-end restaurant in celebration of their second-year anniversary. During his shower, Kari got up and put her black panties on and pink striped pajama shorts that Mike pulled down and tossed over the bed at night before going to sleep. She walked to the kitchen to make coffee. As she grabbed her mug from the cupboard, she looked out the kitchen window and saw James pull up in the driveway.

She unlocked the front door to let him in. "Good morning James," she said and waved him in.

"Good morning Kari," the bald thirty-eight-year-old James replied as he wiped his black boots on the welcome mat. The barrel-chested and beefy man towered over Kari and shortened her appearance even though she was five-foot-five. James could have played football and may have gone pro, had it not been for running with the wrong crowd during his adolescence. The sleeves on his blue U.S. Customs Border Protection uniform fit tight over his bulging arms. The former Marine carried a tattoo on his right forearm of an eagle flying over earth with a long dagger through it and a banner wrapped around it that read, 'Death Before Dishonor U.S.M.C.' James was a former Staff Sergeant in the U.S. Marine Corps who retired and later found a career as a U.S. Customs and Border Protections officer. Mike, who was assigned to James' squad in the Marines before James retired, was looking for a job once his Marine Corps enlistment contract of five years was over. He called his old friend James upon his return to Los Angeles and asked if he knew of a place that was hiring. James suggested to apply for a career with his agency who tended to highly favor qualified veterans. Mike followed his advice and submitted an application. James put in a good word to his superiors at U.S.

Customs and Border Protection and helped Mike to become a CBP Officer. Ultimately, Mike would be assigned to partner with James and their bond grew stronger.

"Would you like a cup of coffee?" Kari asked.

"Yes please," James replied and took a seat at the round kitchen table.

"No cream, no sugar, right?"

"That is correct. Hey, please tell me my partner isn't in the shower still, barely getting ready?" he sarcastically asked adjusting himself in the seat.

"Nope!" Mike shouted as he came out of the bedroom with slippers and dressed in his U.S. Customs Border Protection uniform. "Ready partner, I just have to put my boots on."

"So how was the weekend you two?" James asked as Kari set his coffee down on the dark walnut table.

"It was good; a fun weekend," Mike replied as he pulled up a chair beside him. "Saturday, we had dinner at an overly priced restaurant in Downtown L.A. and then we went to go see that new zombie movie."

"It sucked!" Kari commented shaking her head with wide eyes as she poured Mike a cup.

"The restaurant or the movie?" asked James holding the mug to his lip.

"The movie. The restaurant was okay. What we really paid for was the ambiance more than anything. But the movie was something else. It was supposed to be scary, but I was scared of how bad the acting was. How did a 'C' type movie make its way to the big screen? This movie played inside of a movie theater? Really?"

Mike chuckled, "Yeah, we almost walked out, that's how bad it was. Some of the scenes were incredibly ridiculous. And I know you're not big on horror flicks like we are, but if you were, I'd say don't even bother with waiting for it on Netflix. Anyway, and yesterday morning we went for a hike at Runyon Canyon. This one over here was dying and couldn't even make it up the last hill."

"My legs are killing me," Kari said while massaging her sore legs. "It's been a while since we've gone on a hike and Runyon Canyon is a tough one. Plus, I haven't gone to the gym in a while, so going on that trail probably wasn't the best idea."

"Well that's what happens when you stop exercising for over two weeks," James replied. "Once you begin to work out again after having stopped from your regular workout routine, even if you stopped for just a short while, it can really set you back and hurt. But it's a good hurt. Just your muscles rebuilding and getting stronger."

"I know, it's been hard for me to get back into that workout routine. After work, I just want to crawl into bed and go to sleep," Kari said with her eyes shut mimicking herself sleeping.

"It's all those late hours that you've been putting in at work that's got you drained," James replied.

"I know," she sighed holding her coffee mug that read, 'Shhh… there's wine in here.' "But there's so much work, I can't seem to get caught up on things."

"Well, try your best to find some time for yourself, maybe three days out of the week for at least thirty minutes and slowly get back into a routine. Aside from keeping you healthy, exercise can also raise your energy level. It sounds weird but it's true." James looked at his silver wrist watch, "We should get going brotha'," he told Mike. They both took one last sip of coffee and got up from the table.

James opened the front door, "I'll wait in the car," he told Mike. "Thanks for the coffee Kari."

"You're welcome," Kari politely replied. "And I think I'll take your advice. Starting tonight, I'm going back to the gym." James nodded with a smile and gave her the thumbs up and walked out the door while Mike laced his boots.

"Okay my love," Mike told Kari as he held her by the waist in front of the doorway. "I'll see you tonight and we'll go over the list for the reception?"

"Yes, finally," she answered with a smile as she looked up at Mike who stood at 5'10. He embraced her and gave her a gentle kiss. Her lips were moist and warm. They kissed again as he grabbed her from behind and pulled her in closer. "I Love you," he said while caressing her behind.

"Me or my ass?" she asked with a frown.

He paused in deep thought. "Both," he answered affirmatively and squeezed her butt cheek.

"I love you too, creep-o. Have a good day at work."

"You too honey," Mike said as he looked back before walking out the door. She locked the door behind him, walked back into the bedroom and took a shower.

After showering she got dressed and put make up on to get ready for work. She stood in front of a gray six-drawer dresser with mirror and finished applying blush to her cheeks. Her phone, which was set on the dresser, vibrated from a text message. She looked down at the screen in disbelief with her mouth agape. The message came from an unsaved phone number that she recognized all too well. The message read:

> Hi Kari, this is Chris. Hope you are doing well. I'm back in town and was hoping to get together during your lunch today and catch up?

She looked confused and was at a loss for words. She couldn't believe what she read. She feared the moment would come, when her past would come back to look for her. She hoped that Chris would have moved on with his life so that she could be free to peacefully live hers. She picked up the phone to reply, paused for a second, shook her head and set it back down. She backed away from the dresser and sat on the bed to put her heels on. The phone vibrated again with another message:

> I moved into an apartment in Downtown L.A. close to where you work and I can swing by to meet you if that works best. Are you still working at that Insurance building on 7th street?

She gazed at the phone with an angry look, huffed, got up and picked up the phone. She squinched up her eyes in revolt at reading his message and replied:

> Hi Chris. I'm getting married in two months and I don't think it's a good idea for us to meet up, but I hope all is well. Take care.

She grabbed her purse from the bed, picked up the keys and walked out of the house. As she opened the car door, the phone vibrated with another text message from Chris:

> I was really hoping to speak with you in person. It would be nice to see you again and I promise not to take up much of your time.

She rolled her eyes at the screen and tossed the phone in her purse, slammed the car door shut and pulled out of the driveway. During her drive, she contemplated on replying, periodically gazing over at her purse rested on the passenger seat. A memory of her time spent with Chris flashed through her mind. She gave in and decided to reply. She reached into her purse and felt around for the phone. She took her eyes off the road for a split second to look in the purse. *Hiding from me,* she said to herself as she pulled out the phone. As she redirected her eyes onto the road, she saw yellow headlights from a blue pickup truck coming straight at her.

She gasped and realized that she was on the wrong side of the road. The truck flashed its headlights and loudly honked its horn. She jerked the steering wheel to the right swerving back into her lane, nearly swiping the truck as it passed her by. The alarmed truck driver blared his horn. "Stupid bitch!" he furiously shouted as he drove on. *Oh my god,* she thought, tightly gripping the steering wheel with both hands. Her palms were sweaty and her heart was beating fast. "Fuck you Chris!" she shouted and chose not to reply. She couldn't believe that she almost got into an accident and could have died all for digging in her purse to reply to a man who wasn't worth a damn. Someone who was lower than scum and didn't deserve a good woman like her. "Stupid, stupid, stupid," she repeated as she concentrated on the road. Chris' surprise message gave her an uneasy feeling. *What could he possibly want?* she thought. *Freakin' psycho stalker! I hope he gets the point and stops sending me messages.*

James sat in the driver's seat of a white van with a logo that read 'U.S. Customs and Border Protection' and equipped with an x-ray machine. Mike was in the passenger seat holding a silver clipboard with documents. "Next on the list is 'Worldin Logistics' in Hawthorne," Mike said reading off the clipboard. "You know which one right?"

"On El Segundo Boulevard, right?" James replied as he steered the wheel.

"Yeah, that one. Your girl works there, remember?"

"Oh yeah," James replied with a big smile. "The cute receptionist at the window with the glasses."

"Yeah her. You should talk to her. Ask her to get together sometime over coffee or maybe dinner? You never know, she might be interested. The worst she can do is say no."

James simpered and looked over at Mike. "Yeah, then I'll feel like an idiot every time we go there if she does say no."

"James, you have to meet someone new. It's time to get back on the saddle. Get out there and start talking to women again. You're never going to meet someone new if you don't at least try and it begins with talking; sparking a conversation."

"A conversation about what?" he asked while waiting to make a left turn at the yellow light.

"I don't know man, anything. Talk about global warming. Girls love that type of intellectual conversation. Who doesn't like a smart man that knows about global warming?"

"Get the fuck out of here. Is that the conversation you had with Kari when you two met? Global warming?" James sarcastically asked. "How the hell did you get her number anyway? Because I don't see how that beautiful woman could have ever given a guy who looks like Sloth from the *Goonies* the time of day. God only knows why she agreed to go out with you."

Mike laughed, "Hey come on now, I'm handsome, at least my mother always said so and I'll tell you how we met in a second. Wait, I never told you how we met?"

"I know where you met, but I don't recall you telling me what cheesy pick up lines you used on her to get her phone number."

Mike straightened out in his seat and recounted the day he met Kari. It's a tale he's told several times before to different people whenever someone would ask, but every time he re-told the story, it was as if it were the first. He narrated the story with great enthusiasm like an old retired boxing legend re-telling the story of one of his greatest victories in the ring.

Their story would begin on a cool Saturday morning. Mike started the day with a two hour hike up Runyon Canyon, next to the famed Hollywood sign where several tourists and out of towners go to take pictures. He drove up the hill to Griffith Park and parked his black truck alongside of the road. He threw his leg up onto the hood of the truck and stretched for a few minutes. He shook his leg out, took in a deep breath, inhaled the misty morning air, put on his headphones and started the long hike up a steep, and precarious hill on a narrow path surrounded by trees, bushes, and tall grass. Kari was already at the top of the hill catching her breath.

She placed her hands on her hips and admired the beautiful and awe-inspiring view of Los Angeles and its surrounding cities. The sky was painted with the golden rays of the sun. The skyscrapers of the city were blurred by the morning fog. Dewdrops covered the green grass atop of the hill and birds chirped nearby. As Mike went up the trail, Kari was making her way down. As they drew closer, they came to a halt on a narrow path. Mike pleasantly smiled at her and she smiled back showing her pearly white teeth. "Good morning," she said. "Morning," he replied and stepped to the side to let her through.

Later that afternoon, Mike stopped at a coffee shop in downtown Los Angeles. The aroma of fresh grounded coffee filled the air. Next to the counter was a bakery display filled with warm and colorful pastries such as croissants and fruit tarts. On the back wall was a mural painting of an African American playing the trumpet with music notes coming out of the instrument and human figures dancing across the golden-brown wall. Above on every corner of the wall were little black speakers playing soft jazz music. Mike sat beside the entrance, on a polished wooden stool, resting his elbow against the counter top. He wore black running shorts, dark gray running shoes, and a fitted gray tee shirt.

As he drank a vanilla latte, he turned his head at the sound of the front door opening, and saw a woman walk in. She immediately grabbed his attention.

"I saw her walk in and man oh man, I said to myself, she's a goddess of a woman," Mike told James with an amorous look as he carried on with the story. "And just like in one of those overly dramatic scenes in a movie where a breathtaking woman walks in, time seemed to slow down."

She was dressed in black tights, a gray muscle tee, and pink running shoes. She stood in line to place an order and removed her sunglasses. Mike discreetly checked her out. He looked her up and down, admiring her curvaceous toned figure as she read the menu above the barista counter.

"*Je-sus Christ!* I thought to myself," Mike told James, *What a beauty.* Then it dawned on me. This was the same girl I saw on the hiking trail earlier that day."

"That's funny," James said as he drove. "Fate."

"Absolutely. Here she was again. It was meant to be. I knew I had to talk to her or spend the rest of my day regretting and kicking myself in the ass for not seizing my second opportunity."

Mike rested his foot on the base of the stool, and restlessly shook his knee up and down pondering what to say to spark a conversation. He slowly built courage as he thought of a good pick up line. Just as he was about to make a move, Kari walked over to him. "Hi, can I get a napkin?" she asked.

"Wow, she beat you to the punch," James said and pressed on the gas pedal as the stop light turned green. "You wuss."

"I know, she completely caught me off guard. I got nervous and panicked. I almost ran out of there with my tail between my legs. But I pulled through and handed her a small bundle of napkins."

As Kari waited for her order, Mike seized his opportunity.

"'You were at Runyon Canyon earlier this morning, right?" Mike asked seated on the stool.

"Stalker?" Kari replied with a strange expression. "Kidding," she joked. "Yes I was. You were also there, weren't you?"

"Okay who's stalking who now? I've been here at this coffee shop long before you," he joked back. "But yeah, I was going uphill as you were going down, uh coming down."

She caught how he corrected himself and grinned. "I thought I recognized you as I walked over for the napkins. I said to myself, hey that guy looks familiar."

"Yup, that was me. Beautiful view up there isn't it?"

"Amazing. It's so peaceful and relaxing, I love it there. And the weather was great this morning. Not too cold, not too hot."

"Yeah I like being up there too. It's nice being away from the busy and noisy distractions of the city. It's also a great workout and stress reliever. Definitely, one of my favorite hiking trails. So, what are you having?"

"I ordered an iced green tea. And you?"

"A latte, vanilla. It's my favorite."

"Looks good. Have you ever had the iced green tea here before? I'm curious if they make it as good as it looks on the picture."

"No. I'm actually not a big fan of tea. I guess tea is not my cup of tea." *Tea is not my cup of tea? Smooth Mike, smooth,* he thought.

"Then I guess you don't know what you're missing. Green tea is delicious."

"Iced green tea!" the barista at the counter shouted.

"There's my order," Kari said. She reached for her drink. "Do yourself a favor and try it sometime," she said with a smile. "You might enjoy it. Well it was nice talking to you, enjoy the rest of your latte."

"Yeah you too. Nice meeting you," Mike replied holding his hand up in a motionless wave. He panicked and knew his chance of getting her phone number was walking out the door. He rolled his shoulders back, rose up from the stool with newfound courage and chased after her. Outside the door, he stopped her by her car and said, "Hi again. I don't mean to come off as a creep here and I swear I'm really not stalking you, but I was wondering if it would be okay that I call you sometime? Possibly get to know each other a little better and maybe we can go out and have a drink someday?"

She took a step back and leaned against her car with drink and car keys in hand. "I don't know, I'm barely getting over a really, really bad break up and I usually don't give my number out to strangers ya' know." She was fearful of getting hurt again and held her guard up. But she was also very attracted to Mike and thought he seemed like a nice guy.

"Well, in that case, my name is Michael. I like working out and enjoy going on hikes. I was in the Marines and did one tour in Iraq. I'm currently employed as a U.S Customs and Border Protection officer, I'm a Sagittarius, Catholic, and enjoy trying new things including iced green tea. Nice to meet you." He extended his hand and hoped that she would shake it.

She laughed and shook his hand. "Nice to meet you too Michael, my name is Kari."

"And the rest is history," Mike said to James concluding the story. "I asked if she would like to go back inside and talk to get to know each other a little better, which we did and at the end of our conversation she asked for my phone; I handed it to her, and she saved her phone number under the name 'Cup of tea' ha, ha."

"I bet you were dying to know if she gave you the right number."

"Oh man, it was the longest two days of my life."

"Two days!? You waited two whole days to call her?"

"Yeah, don't you know the rules of dating? You have to wait at least two days before you can text or call someone after meeting them. You don't want to seem too desperate."

"That's a stupid rule," James countered shaking his head. "If you like someone or they make a good impression on you, why do you have to wait? You should just be able to call that person whenever you like, not two days later. You kid's these days don't make any sense."

"Yeah I hear you old man. Well, when I finally did call, she jokingly asked what took you so long?"

Suddenly James slammed hard on the brakes in the middle of the road, stopping from plowing into a group of teenagers that dashed in front of the van. They were dressed in skinny jeans, black skate shoes, hoodies, and rock band tees. The five teenagers looked like a punk band from the 70's crossed over with a hip hop group. They flipped James off as they sped away on their skateboards. "Fucking kids!" James shouted as he drove off.

Well that's enough story time for today. Tomorrow I'll tell you more about those ill-behaved teens but for now, I have to get some work done. As always, it was a pleasure talking with you, even if I am the only one that does the talking. But that's okay, one day we will change all that and I'm sure you will have lots to say. Hopefully you remember some of the things I've said during our morning sessions. Alright, talk to you tomorrow.

CHAPTER 3

Hi. Yesterday was a good day. We made a lot of progress. Some real exciting things developing in the lab. You probably saw me working late last night. I tend to get that way sometimes. When I get into this mode, I just keep working. Which explains the bags under my eyes, you see? I'm a bit sleepy today. Which is why instead of my usual tea, I'm having coffee. Alright, let's get into it shall we? Where did I leave off? Oh yes, those mischievous boys.

Two blocks away from where James nearly ran them over, the group of five adolescents in their senior year in high school came to a stop in front of a liquor store and huddled in a circle. Within the circle was Robbie, considered by his friends and others at their high school to be one of the popular kids. He was slim and tall with long black hair that covered his thin face. He wore his favorite black tee shirt with 'The Ramones' written across, skinny blue jeans, black vans, and a black bandana that hung from his back pocket. He was the best skater out of the group with a unique aggressive style and was leader of the crew. People gave him respect. Guys would try and copy his style of dress and girls at school liked being around him. Standing next to him was Flaco, a nickname in Spanish given to Pedro which translates into skinny.

He was a chubby kid and the butt of everyone's joke. They'd joke about his belly and rub it for good luck. Or they'd crack a joke and throw Flaco in it for the punch line. Although mocked at times, but only within the group, he remained loyal to them because they were the only ones who let him into their circle when no one else at school would want to talk with him. He was particularly fond of Robbie who was the first to carry a conversation with him in algebra class at the beginning of their ninth-grade semester. Standing beside him was Jesse, a goofy looking kid with a fade and curly hair that looked like an afro. He was the follow up joke guy. The guy who follows up a joke with another joke. Just by looking at his goofy face and style of dress would make you chuckle, but he was a great friend to them all. Next to him was Joey. He was Robbie's best friend and had been ever since the two were in middle school. Joey was the kind of guy that always had something funny to say and was liked by everyone much like Robbie. He had a fun and wild personality. He could be a bit of a daredevil at times even if it meant getting in trouble. Like the time when he jumped off the top of the stairs on his skateboard inside the school building and got caught by security. Closing the circle was Henry. He was the smart one of the crew and usually kept quiet, but when he had something to say, everyone listened.

"Alright, we got to hurry," Robbie told the group holding his skateboard at his side. "The bus is on its way, but we can catch it down the street at the next stop. So here's the plan, Joey and I will grab the beers. Jesse, you grab the tea. Henry and Flaco, you two look out for the cops. Henry- keep your backpack open."

"Grab some chips," said Flaco. Jesse calmly walked into the liquor store, casually making his way to the beverage freezer, followed by Robbie and Joey. Jesse picked up three lemon flavored ice tea bottles and a large bag of chips and walked them to the register. Robbie and Joey briskly made their way to the freezer that held an assortment of beer as Jesse distracted the clerk at the register. They each grabbed a forty-ounce bottle of beer and immediately ran out of the liquor store. Jesse grabbed the teas and bag of chips and scrammed out the door behind them. They tossed the stolen drinks and chips into Henry's backpack and made a run for it. They hopped on their skateboards and chased after the bus that rolled passed them headed towards the next stop further down the street. The store clerk ran out and chased after them. He cursed in Spanish waving his fist at them. The bus came to a stop and they quickly boarded one by one, pushing their way in with Flaco hopping on last. The winded store clerk gave up the chase as the bus drove away. The boys took a seat in the back and talked with excitement and laughed about what they had just done. Joey, or 'Three-way' as his friends mockingly called him after they found him at a house party making out with two girls at the same time, reached over to Henry's backpack and asked, "Let me see what we got?"

"I just got whatever dude, which one did you get?" asked Robbie.

"The first one I saw, but I think it'll get us fucked up," replied Joey. He took out his phone and took a picture of the stolen beer bottles and posted them on Snapchat with the caption, 'Cali drought, save water, drink beer!'

Eleven stops later, the five boys exited the bus and skated toward a popular donut shop close to their high school where a lot of the kids hung out. Behind the donut shop, in an alley, Henry squatted next to a garbage container and emptied out the three bottles of ice tea. Jesse stood as a look out and Flaco took video to post on his Snapchat. Robbie and Joey then poured the beer into the empty ice tea bottles to make it appear that they were drinking tea and not beer.

"Dude, you're spilling it all over my fucking hand," Henry told Joey as he held both empty tea bottles watching Robbie and Joey pour the beer inside.

"Well keep your hand steady," Joey retorted as he carefully tipped the beer bottle.

"You can't spill a drop Three-way, this shit is liquid gold," Robbie told Joey. He poked his tongue out in between his lips with a concentrated look and a steady hand as he poured.

After pouring the remaining beer into the third bottle of tea, Robbie threw the beer bottles into the garbage container. "Who's first?" Henry asked.

"Me!" said Robbie and snatched a bottle from Henry's hand. Joey grabbed the other one and Henry picked up the third bottle to make a toast. "Cheers muthafuckas!" Henry said before bringing the bottle to his lips. He made a sour face and gagged. He hadn't developed the taste for beer yet but kept drinking. They all shared the three bottles and practiced tricks on their skateboards in front of the donut shop.

"Hey is Sheena coming?" Joey asked Robbie as he balanced on his board.

"Yeah, she just text me that she's on her way with Lily," said Robbie looking down at the screen.

Sheena was Robbie's girlfriend who attended the same high school. She was captain of the softball team and their strongest hitter. Her friend Lily, who also played for the softball team, agreed to ditch class with Sheena and meet up with Robbie and get introduced to Joey. Their school didn't have gates back in those days, pre- UD-Day, which meant skipping out on class was easier. They could just walk out, assuming security patrolling the area in their golf carts weren't around at the time. The two seventeen-year old girls giggled and spoke quietly as they approached the boys.

"Hey bae," Sheena said and embraced Robbie. They kissed for what seemed like an eternity to Joey as he awkwardly stood next to them waiting to be introduced to Lily, whom he thought looked way better in person than the picture that Robbie showed him.

"Hey Joey," Sheena said brushing a strand of her red hair away from her lip. "This is my girl Lily," she said and turned to her friend standing beside her.

"Hey what's up Lily?" Joey said.

"Hi Joey, nice to meet you," Lily replied with a blushing smile.

Lily, who was a little shorter than Sheena, extended her hand to shake Joey's. Flaco looked on from the back, ogling over Lily's wide hips as he ate chips out of the bag. "Let's hangout inside the donut shop," Joey said to Lily. They walked in while the rest of the gang stayed outside and continued to practice their moves on their skateboard. Robbie and Sheena took a seat on top of the hood of a white car parked in front of the donut shop.

"So, what are you guys up to today, besides ditching school and getting drunk?" Sheena asked holding Robbie's hand.

"Just hanging out," Robbie replied twiddling his thumb against hers. "We're going to Muir Park later. You guys should come. We'll probably get some more beer in a bit."

"Eww, beer smells and looks like piss. How can you guys drink that stuff? But if you can get me one of those strawberry flavored drinks, that would be nice?"

"Oh yeah for sure; so you guys will come?"

"Yeah. I'm sure Lily will be down to go, she thinks Joey is cute."

"Cool. Yeah, he wasn't too sure about her at first, but it looks like they're getting along well huh?"

"Yeah they look cute together," Sheena said as they looked through the window at their two friends seated inside the donut shop chatting and smiling.

"Cool Chucks," Robbie said looking down at Sheena's new pink shoes.

"Thanks, got them in the mail on Friday. You like them?"

"Yeah, they look nice on you. I'll trade you for mine."

Sheena laughed, "Oh you would wear my pink shoes?"

"Yeah, I think they'll look better on me."

"Oh really? Well I don't think they'd fit your big feet." He stretched his legs out and placed his feet next to hers, "Yeah probably not," he said. "You have practice later?"

"Yeah. We have a game Saturday morning at eight."

"Are you going to hit a home run?"

"I always do," she said with confidence. "Are you coming to watch me play?"

"I don't think so, that's super early."

She frowned and grew upset with him. Silence followed and Robbie suspected that she was bothered. She let his hand go and turned her head away staring off into the distance. "What's wrong?” he asked. “Nothing,” she replied and rolled her eyes. He sighed heavily and also rolled his eyes. They stayed quiet for two minutes until she broke the silence. “I think it’s funny how I go to your things, but when it comes to me, you can’t get out of bed a little early and come to my game?” “But you have games like every week,” he said and shrugged his shoulders. “Am I supposed to lose sleep every weekend?”

Their quarrel escalated into louder words. Jesse sat on his skateboard next to Henry watching them argue. “There they go again,” he said and passed the ice tea bottle to his friend. Henry twisted the cap and swigged the bottle. “Bet you three bucks that they’ll be sucking face again in the next ten minutes,” Henry said. “Fifteen minutes,” Jesse countered. “You’re on,” Henry replied and shook Jesse’s hand. Flaco sat on his board behind them and kept an eye on the time.

The young couple argued back and forth with one another for the next ten minutes and came to a compromise which was that Robbie would attend Sheena’s games that were played after nine a.m. and if she had an early morning game, he would attend at least one morning game out of the month. In turn, she would go to his parties and get together only if she didn’t have an early morning game. “Okay that’s fine,” Sheena said. Robbie kissed her and she was smiling again.

“Where’s my money?” Henry asked with his palm out. “I’ll pay you tomorrow,” said Jesse. Flaco laughed and stuffed another handful of chips into his mouth. As the hour passed, the young lovers were joking and laughing again while the boys cracked their skateboards against the pavement as they practiced moves and drank the rest of the beer. Before the next class would start, the girls said their goodbyes and walked back to school. The half-intoxicated boys skated off to the park, but not before stopping at another unsuspecting liquor store for a refill.

Meanwhile, in nearby downtown Los Angeles, a dapper gentleman walked through the automatic sliding doors of a twelve-story building and approached the young receptionist seated behind a marble counter.

"Hi good morning, I have a meeting today with Kari Rodriz," said the man with slick back hair and charming smile.

"Hello, good morning," replied the receptionist. "Kari, okay and your name sir?"

"My name is Steve and I'm owner of B.A.S. My company manufactures aircraft parts and Kari is setting me up with insurance for my new company."

"Okay Steve, let me give her a call to let her know you are here. You can have a seat in the lobby if you'd like, while you wait?"

"Perfect, thank you very much."

The man took a seat and picked up a magazine from the glass coffee table while he waited. Linda, the receptionist gazed at him, awestruck by his handsome features while he flipped through pages. She picked up the phone and called Kari to inform her of the client waiting in the lobby.

"Hi Kari. Steve from B.A.S is here for your meeting."

"Steve from B.A.S?" Kari asked in wonder. "That's strange, I don't recall scheduling a meeting today with any Steve."

"He said you're setting him up with insurance for his new company."

"And he's there in the lobby?" Kari asked. She was baffled. She checked her email calendar, combing through the day's agenda. Perhaps she forgot to make a note of it, she thought, but his name just didn't ring a bell.

"Yeah, he's here sitting in the lobby," Linda replied as she stared at the man, studying his square chin and fine attire.

"I don't see that I have a meeting scheduled for today," said Kari with a perplexed look. "It's okay, I'll be down in a minute. Thanks Linda."

"You're welcome."

Linda hung up and called out to Steve, "Sir, she'll be down in a few minutes."

"Thank you," he replied putting the magazine down.

Minutes later, the elevator beeped opened and Kari walked out. Her high heels echoed off the marble floors and granite walls of the elevator hallway as she made her way toward the lobby. She greeted Linda with a smile before coming around the corner to meet her unexpected client standing in the middle of the lobby. She turned the corner and her mouth dropped. She felt paralyzed with fear. Her heart was beating faster. She took in deep breathes through her nose to control her breathing as she locked eyes with her ex-boyfriend Chris who stood across from her in the lobby.

She searched for the courage to confront him. She dropped her shoulders back, held her head up high and walked toward him. Her face was red with anger and her fists were clenched.

"Chris!? What the hell are you doing here?" Kari demanded boring into his eyes.

"Hello Kari, it's really good to see you too," Chris sarcastically replied with a big smile. She cautiously approached him so that Linda, the receptionist, wouldn't hear their conversation.

"Are you the supposed 'Steve' who's here to be set up with insurance!?" Kari asked in a low angry voice.

"Guilty," Chris teasingly replied. "Come on, if I gave the receptionist my real name, you would never have come down to meet me, right? So, I had to give a fake name. Can you blame me? Kari, men have done crazier things than that just to get close to a woman, especially one as beautiful as you. While I'm on the subject of beauty, may I add you haven't changed a bit; still breathtaking as ever. Why, I nearly fainted just now when you walked in," he teased in a humorous tone. "In fact, I might need mouth-to-mouth CPR."

"First off Chris, I told you I didn't want to see you and second, cut the shit already and save it for someone who cares! And last, but certainly not the least, need I remind you that there's a restraining order on you from the last time I saw you when Mike kicked your ass out in front of my old apartment?"

Chris looked appalled. "Goodness," he said with his hand over his chest. "You would think that after so many years and after several apologies, a guy would be forgiven by now and that we, as two mature adults, could have a decent conversation, but I understand that old wounds don't heal easily, which is why you sound so upset. And just for the record, you told me it wouldn't be a 'good idea' to see each other, but I think it's an excellent idea which is why I'm here. So, can we sit and talk or perhaps go up and have a chat in your office? Please?"

"Goodbye Chris."

He gently grabbed her by the arm, "Just so you know, I am also here on business. I wasn't kidding about needing insurance for my new company, which by the way is soon to be a multimillion dollar company. You know the government is one of my clients. We make parts for some of their aircraft engines. Big customer. Big money. Therefore, I seriously doubt that your boss would pass up on the opportunity to insure my business. Now, either we further discuss this in your office or I call your boss and see what he has to say?"

"You know something Chris, you also haven't changed a bit- you're still an asshole! Linda," she called out to the receptionist, "If this man doesn't leave in the next thirty seconds, please have security escort him out." Kari forcefully removed Chris' hand from her arm and walked away.

"I don't know how many times I have to ask for forgiveness? Look I am on my knees begging please forgive me and please for the love of God insure my company," he mockingly pleaded. Kari speedily walked back to him, "Get up, you're embarrassing me!"

"Seriously though," Chris said as he stood up. "I know I messed up and broke your heart, and for that, I am truly sorry, but that was a long time ago. The old me; I'm a new man now. Yes, I was an asshole, but people change, can't they? And if they can change, can't they be forgiven?"

"Chris not only did you cheat on me with another woman, but you also slept with my best friend. And I forgave you for that a long time ago because there is no peace without forgiveness, but I didn't erase the memory."

"You know the memory of losing you is still fresh in my mind. So many sleepless nights, countless sleeping pills just to be able to go to bed. Drinking myself to sleep. Close to committing suicide. It's true what they say that you truly don't know what you have until it's gone. Losing you was the hardest thing I've ever had to deal with. People tell me to move on and leave the past behind me, but no woman can ever truly stay in the past when you constantly think of her in the present. I've dated, tried to move on, tried to love again, but no one could ever fill my heart with joy and love the way that you did. Which is why, I'm here to tell you that I am sorry. I do regret the mistakes I made back then, but those mistakes helped mold me into the man that I am today. A better man than I was yesterday. If you would just let me show you. Let me show you that I really did love you. That I still love you. That I am willing to do anything it takes to get you back. Absolutely anything," he said with sincerity.

"Chris, I think it's best you go now. Before security shows up. Our chapter closed a long time ago and I'm writing a new one with someone else now. If you truly are sincere, then I do hope you find love again and are smart enough to know when it's in your face. If you find it, and you feel that you can't live without that person, then hang on to it because that's real love and it's not something you come across too often. Don't let it go and don't fuck it up again. Take care."

His eyes began to water so he bit his lip to hold back the tears. The pain of losing her was an old wound that was still fresh and had just re-opened. Realizing and accepting his loss, he quietly left with his head hung low. The sight of her again reawakened a strong desire for her love and affection. One that he yearned for over several years. Unwilling to accept total defeat, he headed back to his apartment to gather his thoughts and scheme a plan that would win her over.

Across town, fire truck sirens blared from down the street as Hector and Fred waited outside the warehouse for the fire department to arrive and inspect the spill.

"Hey, why hasn't Jose left yet?" Hector asked staring at the trailer docked at door eight.

"He's got a hot delivery on that load. Go check and see where he is please? Let him know that he has to take off ten minutes ago."

Fred rushed back inside the warehouse and asked around for Jose.

"Last I saw him he was in the restroom," Larry told Fred as he walked away coughing.

Fred walked to the men's restroom adjacent to the office and placed his hand on the door to push it open. "Hey, so what happened, did you guys find out what that barrel is?" asked Laurie walking out of the women's restroom across from the men's.

"No, we don't know what it is or where it came from," Fred replied standing at the door. "And it wasn't marked down on the log sheet either. Hector's outside waiting for the fire department. I think they just got here because we heard them coming down the street."

"Do we have to evacuate the building you think?"

"I'm really not sure. Depends on what the firemen say. That's what we're about to find out once they inspect the spill. But Hector will let everyone know."

"Oh, I see. God, I hope it's not too serious. But if we must go home for the rest of the day, then that is totally fine by me. I could use a three-day weekend. Long as we still get paid," she said with a short huff.

"Yo Fred!" shouted Larry from down the warehouse, "Hector said to come outside, the fire crew wants to talk to you." Fred ran back to Larry who was leaning against the wall. "Hey, do me a favor yeah?" said Fred. "Can you look for Jose? Tell him he's got to deliver that trailer load ASAP." "Got you," Larry said in a hoarse voice as Fred ran outside the warehouse to meet with the fire crew.

Larry waived down his co-worker Nick who was driving a forklift. "Hey Nick, do me a favor and look for Jose," Larry told Nick who was sitting on the forklift. "Hector is flipping out that he hasn't left yet and they need him to deliver that trailer ASAP. Hector said he might miss the cut off time. Last I saw Jose, he was walking to the restroom."

"Alright I'll go tell Jose. Hey, you feeling okay man?" asked Nick. "You look real pale and you're all sweaty. Did you pop a pill or something?"

"Nah man. I don't do those type of drugs. But honestly, I do feel weird. Like dizzy and shit. I can feel my heart beating real fast."

"You should go see a doctor. Seriously man, you aren't looking too good right now."

"Yeah I think I am. I'm going to talk with Hector once he comes in and ask if I can use a sick day."

"Alright, well I'll see you. Feel better," said Nick and drove away in search for Jose to pass on the urgent message. Larry's eyes grew puffy and turned red, as if suffering from severe allergies. His face kept losing color and sweat steadily dripped from his head. He leaned back against the wall breathing heavily and waited for Hector as he tried to make sense of why he felt in such an unusual way.

A few minutes later, Hector hurriedly walked into the warehouse accompanied by Fred and four members of the Hawthorne City Fire Department. Hector discussed the incident with the firemen as he led them toward the dangerous goods area where the spill occurred. Larry reached his hand out in an attempt to grab Hector's attention but he passed him by. Larry then felt a sharp pain in his stomach and grabbed his belly. He wailed in pain.

He dropped to one knee and let out a violent expulsion of puke. The splattering vomit accompanied by gagging sounds echoed through the warehouse. The fire crew heard Larry's cries and gags and quickly ran to his aid. Larry collapsed and fell face down on the puddle of his own vomit. One of the firemen called for an ambulance while another rolled Larry over and checked his pulse. A loud and eerie screech was heard coming from the men's restroom just a few yards away. The firemen turned their heads toward the noise and glanced at the restroom. Their faces puzzled by the odd sound. Hector and Fred looked at one another just as confused as the firemen. "What was that?" Hector asked. "I don't know," said Fred with a baffled look. "Sounds like it came from the men's restroom. I'll go check it out."

Fred ran to the restroom to inspect. He placed his hand on the door and slowly pushed it open. As he held the door half open, he saw blood scattered across the floor. He pushed the door further and saw Jose, the driver, crouched over Nick's lifeless body, clasping Nicks head and tearing off a piece of his throat with his teeth. Fred gaped in utter shock and horror at the sight of human flesh dripping with blood, dangling from Jose's mouth as he chewed and swallowed the warm flesh. Jose continued to tear away at Nicks skin, unaware of Fred's presence. Fred was struck with fear and stood numb. His light brown color drained from his face. He stared wide-eyed at Jose masticating human flesh. As the shock wore off, adrenaline shot through his body, "WHAT THE FUCK

ARE YOU DOING!?" he yelled down at Jose. With the jugular vein gripped to his teeth, Jose stretched it out as he turned his head in Fred's direction. Their eyes met and Fred could tell from Jose's aggressive stare that he had lost his mind and it gave Fred a new level of fear that he'd never known. Jose's eye colors were cloudy and the vessels at the surface of the white portion of the eye were swollen and turned red; his skin turned pale and transparent, exposing his artery and veins. He snarled at Fred like a wild animal and lunged at him with deadly intent. Fred reacted and pushed him down with force. He reached for the door to run out.

One of the firemen got concerned and walked over to the restroom to check out what was going on. As he opened the door, he saw Fred grappling with Jose. "Get back!" Fred shouted. Jose turned his attention and attacked the fireman. The fireman put his arm up in defense and Jose bit him on the wrist. The tall fireman tackled Jose to the ground where both men fought for dominance. Fred grabbed Jose's legs and tried holding them down while the fireman buried his knee into Jose's chest. Jose kicked and screamed while attempting to get free and snapped his jaw up at the fireman.

"What is he on?!" shouted the fireman as he held Jose pinned down. "Bath salt?"

"I don't know," Fred shouted back with a tremble in his voice as he held Jose's legs down. "I came in and saw him eating Nick." The fireman hadn't realized the severity of the situation until he got a good look at the mutilated lifeless body of Nick. "JESUS!" shouted the fireman in disbelief. "Call the police. I'll hold him down, call the other guys in here too. Go call 911 now. Hurry!"

Fred ran out of the restroom while the fireman stayed to hold Jose down until the police would arrive.

A week before the toxic barrel spill, Nick, accompanied by his girlfriend along with his mother and father, sat in the booth of a family restaurant with decor remnant of a 1960's diner. Nick would frequently eat at that diner and had been since he was five years old. He and his family would dine there on several occasions; like his brother's high school graduation. On that particular Friday night, all four were celebrating Nicks' dad's 60th birthday. They talked, laughed, and shared memories and stories of the past and present. Nick, like his father, ordered the New York strip steak, well done. At the end of the night, Nick kissed his mother goodnight and hugged his father tight; wished him a happy birthday and gave him a little wrapped box with a silver bow placed on top. Inside was a gold watch engraved Happy 60th Birthday Dad, love Nicholas. That night would be the last time Nick ever embraced his parents again. It would be the last time he ever went to his favorite diner. It would be the last time he ever ate a well-done New York strip steak. But it wouldn't be the last time he ever ate meat.

Inside the men's restroom of one stall and two urinals with white walls and white tile floors, the ensuing struggle between the fireman and Jose continued. Behind them, a few feet away from the door, lied Nick in a puddle of blood, bordered by the remains of his mutilated body. Nick's eyes began to twitch and his fingers jerked. His eyes blinked open and Nick slowly brought the room into focus. He turned his head toward the ceiling staring at the lights. His eyes were cloudy and skin had gone pale like Jose's. He sluggishly sat upright and heard the tussle going on between the two men behind him and turned his head in their direction. He got up and staggered toward the fireman who was unaware that Nick had risen from the dead. Nick caught the fireman by surprise and pounced on his back. He grabbed him by the shoulders and sank his teeth deep into the fireman's veiny dark neck. The fireman screamed loudly in pain as Nicks teeth tore into his flesh and ripped out a quarter sized chunk of meat. Blood squirted out from the open wound and the agonizing fireman quickly grabbed a hold of his bleeding neck. He turned his hips and used all of his might to shove Nick off. Distracted with the undead Nick, he lost his grip on Jose who broke free from his hold. Jose sat up and tore into the other side of the fireman's neck. Nick scuttled across the floor and savagely attacked again. They forcefully pushed the fireman to the ground and held him down as they ferociously tore apart his face and neck like a pack of starving wolves. It wasn't' long before the fireman abandoned his struggle and took his last breath.

Inside the office, employees sat in front of their double monitors, typing on their keyboards, replying to emails, answering phone calls, shuffling papers and conversating amongst each other. Some shared stories about what they did over the weekend and others talked gossip. A girl stood by the copier making copies. Managers ran reports, the operator at the front desk answered incoming calls and the receptionist assisted customers who walked in. The break room in the back of the office smelled like coffee. Miguel prepared his usual morning breakfast which consisted of peanut butter and banana slices spread over toasted wheat bread. As everyone in the office continued their day, all were unaware of the ongoing grisly attacks taking place just a few feet away from the office, outside in the men's restroom.

Fireman Smith was in the middle of giving Larry chest compressions when two paramedics arrived at the warehouse with a defibrillator in hand and took over. They checked Larry's breathing and checked his neck for a pulse. They pulled Larry's shirt up and attached the electrode pads from the defibrillator to his chest and waited as the AED analyzed the heart rhythm. After a few seconds, paramedic Jones pushed the shock button to send an electric shock to Larry's heart so that it could restore the heart beat to a normal rhythm. Larry's body jolted from the shock, but the attempt failed. They tried it again, but Larry still had no pulse and the heart monitor flat lined. Fireman Smith, along with Fireman Gables and the warehouse supervisor Hector anxiously looked on as both paramedics attempted to revive Larry.

"HELP! I NEED HELP!" Fred shouted with a terrified look on his face as he ran out of the restroom with blood smeared on his shirt. "Jose's in the restroom biting and, and, and was eating his flesh."

"Who? What? What are you saying?" fireman Smith asked in an incredulous tone.

"Hurry!" Fred pleaded. "Come and look for yourself. Your partner has Jose pinned down. Hector- call 911 and tell them to send the police here right now! Jose lost his fuckin' mind. He killed Nick and was eating him; Nick's dead!" Hector tried to rationalize all that Fred had just blurted while keeping his focus on the paramedics who continued to try and save Larry's life. Fred along with fireman Smith and fireman Gables ran inside the restroom to help. As they cautiously opened the door, they were shocked at what they found. Nick and Jose were both on their knees gobbling on the dead fireman's body. Their faces were smeared with blood. Thick warm blood dripped from their fingers as they savagely tore through the fireman's flesh.

"Nick?" Fred fearfully cried out in disbelief. He couldn't comprehend how Nick, who moments ago was murdered at the hands of Jose, was now alive with an enormous hole in his neck and participating in the barbaric act. Fred tried to analyze and explain everything that had occurred up to that point. He thought that perhaps it was all a practical joke being played on him and recorded like several of the prank videos he had seen on the internet. He was sure that everyone was in on it and that the video would go viral with millions of views. It would be the best prank of all time. He was instantly brought back into reality when the three firemen shouted at Nick and Jose to get off their partner. They shoved the undead men off and started to grapple with them. They would go back and forth trying to keep their balance on the slippery blood-stained floor. During their struggle, the fireman whose lifeless corpse lay on the floor, awakened and bit fireman Gables on the ankle cutting through his tibial artery which immediately brought the hefty fireman down on his back. He screamed in agonizing pain as he held his ankle. Smith, who was six foot-two, picked Nick up over his head like a wrestler, let out a loud roar and slammed him to the ground head first, splitting his skull in half. Blood splattered across the wall and small skull fragments scattered on the tile floor from the forceful impact that killed Nick. Immediately after, Smith reached for Jose and put him in a rear choke. Fireman Gables squirmed off his back while trying to defend himself from his undead partners' relentless attack. Fred rushed in to help and grabbed the undead fireman from behind. The undead fireman violently swung his arms in the air and turned his hips trying to escape Fred's hold. Fred slipped and fell backward with the heavy undead fireman landing on top of him. In a quick motion, the undead fireman turned over, grabbed Fred by the throat, opened his mouth wide and lunged in at Fred's neck. Fireman Gabbles reached out and grabbed onto the undead fireman's shirt pulling him off Fred. The undead man went back to attacking Gabbles and Gabbles jerked the undead man's head side to side trying to avoid his snapping jaw. Fireman Smith who was unable to put Jose to sleep continued to struggle with him on the ground. He screamed out to Fred, "Get out of here! Get help!" Fred quickly got back to his feet and ran out. Catching fireman Smith off guard, Jose lifted Smith's arm up to his mouth and sank his teeth deep into his forearm.

As Fred rushed out of the restroom, he saw two men trying to pin someone down. He ran towards them and saw the lifeless body of paramedic Jones face down as blood gushed out of his neck like water spurting into the air from a punctured garden hose. Hector and the other paramedic-Melendez were on top of Larry struggling to hold him down. Paramedic Melendez dug both his knees deep into Larry's chest while Hector held Larry's arms down.

Hector lifted his head and saw Fred coming toward them. "Fred get over here and hold Larry's legs!" he screamed.

Fred immediately dropped his weight down onto Larry's legs.

"What the fuck is going on Fred?" Hector asked in a quivering voice.

"They're coming back to life…the dead, they're… coming back to life," Fred replied with a straight look in his eye.

"What?! What are you talking about? What happened in the restroom?"

"I told you…" Fred replied trying to catch his breath. "Nick, he was dead but, but… is now somehow alive!? And the fireman too. He's back from the dead."

"What the hell is going on here?" Hector said in disbelief mustering all his strength to hold Larry down.

"I told you guys! I ran out of there to come get you guys for help. The other two firemen are in there fighting with Jose, Nick, and the other dead fireman. I … I couldn't believe it. They were dead," Fred said with a bewildered look. "I saw them die and then, they just came back to life. How –I don't fucking know. But I saw it with my own eyes. Is that what's going on with Larry?"

"This man was clinically dead," paramedic Melendez said as he forced his knee down onto Larry's chest. "We did everything we could to revive him but his respiratory system failed. Then this asshole wakes up and takes a large chunk out of my partners neck like some kind of… animal."

"I called 911 already. The police should be here any minute now," Hector stated holdings Larry's arms.

Minutes later, two police units arrived at the scene. Officer Hauser parked the cruiser in front of the warehouse next to the ambulance. She was joined by her partner of four years, officer Rhodes who quickly surveyed the area and saw commotion coming from inside the warehouse. The other two officers were officer Chan, who was serving on the force for over twenty years and his partner, a recent graduate from the police academy, officer Nguyen. The four officers jumped onto the dock from outside of the warehouse and immediately grabbed a hold of Larry. He ferociously fought back as the officers struggled to turn him over face down on his stomach. "Stop resisting!" officer Chan yelled at Larry. They ordered him to obey but Larry continued to attack and snarled like an animal. Officer Hauser felt left with no choice and pulled out her yellow taser and shot him. Larry was momentarily stunned but long enough to be subdued. "What happened?" she asked. Fred paused and gave her a worried look. He patiently waited for them to restrain Larry so that he could explain what occurred and also tell them of the ongoing incident taking place inside the men's restroom. Hector and paramedic Melendez cut in and recounted the incident with officer Hauser while her partner officer Rhodes managed to cuff both wrists behind Larry's back. She put them on tight while officer Chan applied pressure with his knee down onto Larry's face.

"Do you know if he's taken some kind of drug?" officer Chan asked while examining Larry's pupils. "His eyes look weird. Different than normal drug use."

"No, he hasn't," Hector replied. "But officer, there's something else," he said with his hand pointing towards the restroom. "There are three firemen inside the restroom who need help too. I think these men are suffering from some type of disease that's making them act crazy. I have two other employees in the men's restroom right now with the same problem and the firemen are in there trying to detain them."

"Officers, be careful. These men don't die," Fred warned.

The officers gave Fred an odd look after hearing his comment. Officer Hauser and Officer Rhodes quickly walked toward the restroom with Officer Nguyen closely behind. Officer Chan stayed watching over Larry. As they reached the door, fireman Smith stumbled out with blood and bite marks all over his body. He fell into Officer Rhodes' arms. She struggled to hold the large man up and gently lied him down with Officer Nguyen's help. "Is anyone else inside?" Officer Rhodes asked. "Don't go in," fireman Smith warned in a soft voice.

"Hang tight for me, we'll get you some help," Officer Rhodes said in a soothing voice. She waived paramedic Melendez over and then signaled to the other two officers to draw their weapon. She told Officer Nguyen to kick open the door while she and officer Hauser readied themselves to go in. Officer Nguyen firmly planted his feet and kicked the door open; all three rushed inside and the door closed behind them. Fireman Smith looked on with a blurry vision staring at the door as he lay on his side quickly losing blood. "No…" he softly murmured. "I told you."

He heard several shots fired followed by shouting that echoed from wall to wall. Officer Hauser's high-pitched scream was the loudest and slowly faded into gurgling sounds. All he could see from the bottom crack of the door were shadows moving in all directions. He heard someone's boot stomping the floor and another gun shot.

Officer Chan, who had Larry pinned down with Hectors help, heard officer Hauser's painful screech and called for backup with his radio. From the corner of his eye, he noticed the dead paramedic Jones slowly rise. Paramedic Melendez also noticed and left the fireman's side to check on his partner. Fred saw Melendez and pulled him back.

"Jones, are you ok? Paramedic Melendez asked his partner. "Lie down for a sec, let me take a look at you."

"Sir, please lie down and let your partner take a look at you," Officer Chan said to paramedic Jones after he noticed something strange about his behavior.

"Get back!" Fred warned as he saw Jones move in the Officers Chan's direction.

Just as Fred shouted his warning, the undead paramedic Jones tackled officer Chan down and landed on top of him. Chan held him off with his left arm in an attempt to protect his face from Jones' vicious attack and snapping jaw. Jones sank his teeth deep into Chans forearm with ferocity. Chan yelled out in pain and reached for his weapon. He aimed it up into Larry's chest and squeezed the trigger two times knocking Larry back. Chan wiggled out from underneath and scooted back pointing his gun at Jones. His arm was bleeding profusely which gave Fred an unnerving feeling. "Stay down!" Chan yelled out as Jones slowly got back up. Fear of the inexplicable froze the officer's motor functions as he watched in astonishment Jones get back up. Officer Chan shook his head and snapped out of it and fired two more rounds that echoed loudly through the warehouse. Jones was hit in the stomach, but he kept moving forward. Chan shot him again in the chest and neck. The fifth bullet struck Jones in between the eyes piercing through the brain killing him instantly but Chan kept firing. The sixth bullet, which was shot off immediately after, missed Jones by an inch as hell fell backward. The bullet shot past his head and straight into the toxic barrels behind him causing an explosion that sent everyone flying off their feet.

Dark smoke filled the air and small flames by the barrels were dying out. Officer Chan, Fred, Hector, and paramedic Melendez woke up coughing with a loud ringing in their ear that slowly started to fade away. They gradually regained conscious and suffered minor burns and scrapes. Plumes of black smoke spread through the warehouse that flowed out through the open dock doors and up to the sky. The warehouse began to smell of thick smoke mixed with a putrid odor. "Everyone out," Officer Chan said choking through his words. Fred and Hector acted quickly and staggered into the office to evacuate the building while paramedic Melendez tended to officer Chan's bite wound.

"Oh my God, what happened?! Are you guys ok?" Laurie from inside the office frantically asked.

"There was an explosion in the DG area," Hector replied in a loud voice. "We'll explain later, but for now, we need for everyone to please evacuate the building immediately. Quickly get your belongings. Quickly, quickly. This is not a drill! Everyone evacuate the building now!"

He waved his arms forward and gently pushed people toward the emergency exit which lead to the parking lot in front of the building.

Fireman Smith struggled to breathe and coughed out blood followed by heavy breaths. Black smoke filled his lungs and he gasped for air. He then saw the restroom door open. His vision was hazy, and the smoke made it difficult to see, but he could make out the silhouette of three people sluggishly walk out of the restroom. It was officer Hauser, Rhodes, and Nguyen. Their eyes were bloodshot and cloudy, and their skin turned pale. Officer

Hauser's right arm was torn off and veins that dripped with blood dangled from the shoulder socket. Officer Rhodes' left eye was gouged out and pieces of flesh were missing from his wrist. His pinky finger was detached from his left hand and he gimped with a broken left ankle. Officer Nguyen's body was left unmarred but sustained a visible deep bite wound on his lower back which bled down his leg. Fireman Smith's eyes grew wide as he gasped for air and clutched his chest before taking one last breath.

From afar, officer Chan saw his colleagues through the thick smoke and called out to them. "Hey, are you guys alright?" he asked. Paramedic Melendez hurriedly walked toward them. The three undead officers rushed toward Chan and Melendez and tackled them both to the ground. Officer Chan soon realized that they were suffering from the same bizarre condition as Larry when they started to viciously attack him. He struggled to unholster his weapon while shoving them off. Their relentless attack overpowered him, and they began to bite down. Chan screamed out in agony as they tore into his flesh. Melendez quickly got back on his feet and ran out of the warehouse as they gorged on the officer. The undead officers ripped through Chan's guts, swallowing intestines and savagely tearing him apart.

Outside the office building, Fred and Hector spoke to the confused crowd in the parking lot. "It isn't safe here," Hector loudly said. "I suggest going home and wait for management to call you and let you know when it is safe to return, but at the moment we don't know when that may be." The crowd of people standing in the parking lot grew concerned and began to whisper amongst themselves. "Do we have to leave right now?" Laurie asked. "Yes. There are possible toxic chemicals in the warehouse that can be very harmful," Hector said. "It is not safe to stay."

Several of the employees heeded Hector's advice and got in their cars. Others stood outside to wait for their ride home. Managers from the office discussed the incident with Hector and asked if it was necessary for them to leave. Hector urged them to leave and work from home. "Your work is not worth risking your health, more importantly, your life!" Hector exclaimed. He walked away leaving them to talk amongst each other.

"We have to check back with the officers and see what's going on," Hector whispered at Fred.

"Yeah fuck that, I'm not going back in there. Did you see that shit? What those people did? Hector -that officer in there pumped that paramedic dude full of lead and he kept coming after him. After getting shot like 5 times he still wouldn't die. That's not normal. You saw it! And I saw Nick, with a huge hole in his neck but he was somehow still alive? Those aren't drugs that they're on, that's something else. Something straight out of a horror movie. We have to get the fuck out of here. I need to get to my family and be with them. So, if you want to fire me then go ahead, fuck it, but there's no way I'm going back in there with you, hell no!"

"Alright, alright calm down. Go home. I'll call 911 again and tell them what happened here and to send backup. The hazardous material team should be on their way too because also I called them when I called the fire department. They can take care of the toxic chemicals."

"Are you going to stay here?"

"I don't know," Hector said scratching his head. "People are still here and I have to wait for the hazmat team to arrive so I can explain the chemical spill and explosion."

"Are you going to tell them about the undead people too? How the hell are you going to explain that one? They'll think you're fucking crazy like you guys thought I was when I ran out of the restroom to tell you about Jose and Nick."

"I don't know okay, but I have to tell them something. I-I-I still can't understand why they couldn't didn't die? How? What caused them to come back to life and then attack like that?"

Fred looked up in deep thought and saw the black fume of smoke rise out of the warehouse and darken the sky, and then it dawned on him. "Jose touched it!" Fred exclaimed.

"What? What are you talking about?"

"The spill, the chemical spill; before I ran into the office to get the D.G log, I saw Jose walk over and touch the barrel. It looked like he cut himself on the barrel when he touched it. Maybe that's what made him sick. There must have been something inside the barrel that made him sick and caused his death, then somehow was brought back to life.

"What about Nick? I didn't see him touch the barrel."

"Well Jose was the one who started eating Nick and then Nick came back to life. Nick must have gotten infected with the same virus when Jose passed it through his saliva. But I can't explain how Larry got sick? He didn't touch the barrel or was bitten by Jose."

"Jose sneezed in his face!" Hector replied. "I remember because I thought Larry was going to kick his ass. But Jose didn't mean to, it was an accident. He just couldn't control his sneezing. Could it be? That chemical actually infected them like that?"

"I honestly don't know, but right now that's all I can think of. I mean what else could it be? After the spill, all this started to happen. And it must have spread through saliva. That's how the firemen and paramedic got infected, through saliva when they were bitten, just like Nick."

"But Jose didn't get it through saliva, he actually touched the chemical. So, I guess you can get the illness both ways through the blood and saliva?"

Office personnel that were waiting for a ride home began to sneeze and cough almost uncontrollably. Fred and Hector turned their heads and stared at them with confusion then looked back at one another with dread in their eyes. They feared the virus somehow spread to the office staff. They would soon learn that once the liquid from the barrels fused with fire from the explosion, the virus would go airborne and infect millions of people.

"Okay, I'm getting the fuck out of here now," Fred said as he backed away. "Good luck boss."

CHAPTER 4

Thirty minutes into their drive in route to the warehouse, Mike remembered that there was a donut shop where they made one of the best ham and cheese croissants he's ever had, just a few blocks from their destination. A few months back they had stopped into the donut shop for a cup of coffee. Mike ordered the ham and cheese croissant after salivating over it when he saw a customer sitting at the yellow table enjoyably munching on one.

"Hey man we have stop at that donut shop," Mike said. "You know which one right?" he asked and James nodded his head with a grin. "I have to get one of those bad boys."

"Alright, I think I'll get one too," said James as he steered the wheel. Mikes phone vibrated from a text Kari sent that read, 'Call me ASAP please!' Once they arrived, Mike stayed in the van to give her a call.

"Hey, can you order one for me, please?" Mike asked with his phone in hand. "Kari sent me a weird text. I'm going to call her and see what's going on."

"Ok, ham and cheese with a medium coffee, right?"

"Yeah, thanks," Mike said holding the phone to his ear as it rang. Kari answered in a panicky voice and Mike could tell that something was definitely wrong. "Hey, is everything okay?" he asked.

"Hey… no, it's not," she replied in a tremulous voice. "Chris is back, and he came to my job. He just showed up out of nowhere."

"What!? What did he want? What did he say?"

"He came unannounced and talked a lot of nonsense. I'm scared babe. I don't know if he's going to be waiting outside of the office for me or if he's going to be waiting at the house. I'm freaking out right now. I'm in the bathroom right now. I'm carrying mace with me. If I see him again, I'll spray it right into his eyes."

"Yes! Do that but stay calm. We've already gone through this once. We'll just do the same thing again. We'll go to the police station, report him, and make sure that the restraining order is still in place. And if he dares show up to our home, I'll put a bullet in him for trespassing. Or I'll just kick his ass again. Don't worry, everything's going to be alright. So, what did you tell him?"

"I pretty much told him to fuck off and told Linda the receptionist to call security if he didn't leave. I stayed in the lobby to make sure he left the building. I saw him walk out but I'm scared that he may come back."

"Alright, when you leave tonight have Linda call security to escort you to the car. I'm going to hurry up with what we have today and rush home. I'll be home before seven, so stay at work a little later because you usually get there before I do. I'll rush home after work and we'll talk tonight and go to the police station. Okay? Stay calm honey, everything's going to be okay."

Mike kept a positive attitude throughout their conversation which seemed to calm Kari, but deep inside he was furious and wanted nothing more than to get his hands around Chris' neck. Years ago, when Mike and Kari started dating, Kari shared her story of her crazy ex-boyfriend that would stalk her and at times show up out of the blue. Under different circumstances, Mike would have immediately stopped dating a woman with that type of drama in her life, but by then, he was already too romantically involved with Kari and cared deeply for her. One night, Chris unexpectedly showed up to Kari's old apartment, drunk and belligerent. That night, Kari and Mike planned to have a romantic dinner at a restaurant by the beach with waterfront views. Upon arriving at Kari's apartment, Mike saw a drunken man screaming and pounding on her apartment door which alarmed Kari's neighbors, prompting them to call 911. Mike knew it was Chris and without hesitation walked up to him and punched him square on the chin, knocking him out cold. Chris lay on his back in a stiff position with his eyes rolled back. The police arrived at that moment and placed Mike in handcuffs. Kari went over the incident and explained to the officers what Chris had been doing. Her statement would be backed up by the neighbors who were peeking out the window watching all the drama unfold. They later released Mike and took Chris to jail. Kari filed a report and Chris was ordered to stay one hundred yards away from her. He would never look for her again until that morning when he showed up to her work.

"Nice and fresh my man," James said as he opened the door to the van and handed Mike the croissant and coffee. "What's wrong?" he asked. James could tell Mike was fuming by the heated look in his eyes.

"Chris is back," Mike replied in an angry voice. "He went to Kari's office looking for her, can you believe that? I can't believe that son of a bitch, after all these years, he would still go looking for her and harass her. I swear if I see him …"

"You'll keep your cool partner," James said cutting him off. "Now I know this guy has been a pain in the ass for you both, but you can't let him get the best of you. And I don't want to see you end up in prison for doing something in the heat of the moment. So, if you see him, you'll keep your cool."

Mike nodded his head. "But this guy isn't all there in the head," Mike said pointing at his temple. "What if he shows up to my house? What am I supposed to do then?"

"If that's the case, then you do what you have to do to protect your family. You have the right to defend yourself with a reasonable response. But if that is not the case, don't take matters into your hands. Should you have to face him, compose yourself and think with a clear head. Rid yourself from thoughts of anger and hate because it clouds your mind and judgement."

Mike listened and followed his advice. He thought of James as an older brother who always had his back and gave him sound advice. James knew of Chris from previous conversations and he knew that this ordeal would bother Mike throughout the day. He tried to get Mike focused and level-headed by assuring him things would work out and that everything would be alright. "Try and stay positive, because any negativity will rub off onto her and make matters worse. Now stay focused. We have long day ahead," James told Mike as he bit into the croissant. The small pep talk calmed Mike down a bit, but he couldn't stop thinking about it. Different thoughts and ideas ran through his head that took his appetite away. The croissant in the little donut bag that was placed on top of the vans gray dashboard would remain there untouched for the rest of the day.

"I hope that receptionist at the warehouse is in today," James commented trying to lighten the mood by changing the subject. "If she is, I'll talk to her for a bit, throw some bait out there and see if she bites; let you deal with the paperwork while I do my thing know what I'm sayin'?"

"No, I don't what you're sayin'. Please elaborate. What's your 'thing'?"

"Well first I'm starting off with the basics. Questions like how's your day? How's work going so far, etc. Then get into some personal stuff like, what city do you live in? What does she like to do when she's not at work? Hobbies? If I feel that the conversation is moving in a positive direction, I'll keep going deeper."

"Yeah I bet you'll go deeper."

"Then, I'll ask questions like what type of food do you like? With each question getting more personal. What do you like to do for fun? Do you have kids?"

"Wow, that's really deep."

"Oh, I'm just getting to the climax. Finally, if after all these questions are asked and during this whole conversation, if she hasn't asked me a single question, I'm simply walking away and not even bothering in asking for her phone number."

Mike was confused. "And why is that?" he asked.

"Because if all she does is talk about herself and ramble on and on and not care to ask me anything in return, then I'll know that she's really not interested."

"Ahhh, I see. So the bait, are the questions, and the bite would be the questions she asks you back which shows interest, am I following correctly?"

"Si. And I know some girls like to talk a lot, especially about themselves, which is fine with me, but I feel it's the one's that ask genuine questions and show interest in you, that you'll have better luck at getting a call back from and eventually developing a deeper connection with. When I start dating again, that's what I'll be looking for. Because I'm too old for games. Don't want to deal with someone who seems interested but is only playing me for a fool. If she seems interested and asks me some questions, then I'll ask for her number."

"Sounds like a plan my man. I think she'll be interested. I mean who could resist this chocolate man with a head shaped like a milk dud. But what if she asks- how deep can you really go? What then? Ha ha."

"Well, then I'll just tell her that I can go deeper than the Pacific Ocean and can get it wetter than Niagara Falls."

When they arrived to the warehouse, they gave each other an odd look and stared at the abandoned fire truck, ambulance and police cruisers parked outside of the warehouse. James slowly drove past the vehicles and backed the van up on one of the loading-dock ramps. They got out of the van and scanned the deserted area. They stood by the back of the van looking inside the warehouse waiting for someone to walk by or to make a sound, but the warehouse was strangely quiet. There was no sound of a forklift beeping. Or the sound of chatter and shouting. No sound of boxes getting loaded onto pallets. Only dead silence. They also found it unusual that all the dock doors were open. "Where is everybody?" asked Mike looking in all directions. "No sign of anybody here. Not a warehouse worker, or an officer? Nobody."

"They're probably all gathered inside the office having a meeting," responded James with his hand rested on his pistol. Mike wondered if they should go in and inspect or if they should check in with receptionist first, as normal procedure. His instinct told him to go in and check the place out. He walked through the open wide door and quickly saw blood splattered across the floor. James also noticed the blood and both men immediately pulled out their weapon.

They slowly walked further in, examining their surroundings and followed the trail of blood that lead them to the office. They stopped at the door where the trail cut off and James slowly reached for the handle. He nodded at Mike to confirm if he was ready to go in. Mike nodded back and firmly gripped his gun. James softly grabbed the metal handle and pushed the door open. Mike darted in, pointing his weapon with James following behind checking the rear. They found the office empty. The large office had several workstations grouped together and each station was abandoned. All the computer monitors were turned on, but with no one seated at their desk. The two men stared at each other with confusion. Mike picked up one of the half empty coffee mugs and felt the warmth of it in his hand. To the left of the office was a long and wide window where the receptionist sat. There was a pile of documents laid in front of the keyboard with a smaller pile next to it and a half eaten bagel next to the mouse. It was plain to see for both men that everyone went into work that morning and that it was business as usual, but extremely bizarre and unnatural that no one was around.

James decided to call to his supervisor Martin and ask about the odd situation while Mike walked around the office inspecting people's desk.

"Hello," said James holding the phone to his ear. "Hey Martin, it's James. I'm at the Worldin Logistics warehouse in Hawthorne. We're inside the office, but there's no one here. Seems like everyone just up and left. Have you received any type of notice about what's going on?"

"What's that James?" replied Martin. "I can hardly hear you."

"I said we're inside the office and it's abandoned. Do you know what happened here?"

"Oh yes. There was an incident that led to an evacuation. Listen, ughh..."

"Hello? Hello?"

"What's wrong?" asked Mike.

"Line cut off," replied James with an odd look. "That was weird." James redialed but the call wouldn't go through.

"All of this is weird," said Mike pacing around the desks. "Feels like I'm in one of those Twilight Zone episodes. You ever see that show? Of course you did, you were around when it first aired on TV. Hey, how was it to watch television in black and white back in the fifties?"

"Fuck you, I'm not that old," James said rolling his eyes at Mike with the phone to his ear. "And no, I've never seen it."

"What? You've never seen the Twilight Zone? Wow! It's a cool show. My favorite episode is of a bank teller that loves to read. Everyone including his boss and wife always gives him shit about it. Anyway, one day at work during his break, he goes inside the vault to read a book when all of a sudden, a bomb goes off killing the entire world. When he opens the vault and walks out he…"

Mike paused at noticing James looking at something behind him. Toward the back of the office, a police officer slowly limped toward the two men.

"Oh, hello officer. Is everything okay?" asked Mike walking toward the officer. "We were wondering why there's no one here?" James was standing by the receptionist area still on the phone trying to get his supervisor back on the line. He noticed the officer's limp and saw a trail of blood on the floor left behind from the blood that dripped down the back of the officer's leg.

"Officer are you hurt?" asked James with a suspicious look on his face.

The round-faced young officer with short black hair and blood splats on his arm kept approaching. "Officer Nguyen?" Mike called out after reading the officer's badge. The officer snarled and darted toward him. Mike was shocked by the officer's attack and wrestled with him, careful not to hurt him and pushed him against the desk. They swirled around before Mike flipped him to the ground. James ran over and helped to restrain the officer.

"Officer calm down, we are U.S Custom's officers!" James shouted as he held the officer's arms. "I don't want to hurt you," Mike said as he held him to the ground. "Please calm down and let us help you!"

They battled on the ground as Officer Nguyen repeatedly tried to bite them both. He made growling sounds and snapped his jaw. James managed to secure hand coughs on the officer while Mike tied up his feet with a telephone cord. The officer whirled around the floor while James called his headquarters. Mike caught his breath and watched over the officer, occasionally stepping back, away from him as he jerked side to side.

"Yes sir. Will do," James said over the phone after a brief conversation.

"What'd they say?" Mike asked.

"Martin said there was a chemical explosion and that everyone was evacuated. Which is why the fire department is here.

Or at least was because I don't see them. He said we have to stay here until a HAZMAT team arrives to inspect the area."

"Hazardous-Material unit is on the way? Okaayy, but where is the fire crew and why is the police department here and why did this fucking asshole attack us? And what the hell's wrong with his eyes and skin?"

"I don't know partner, they didn't answer a lot of my questions. All they said was to hang tight. This is all really strange. I say we check out the rest of this place. Maybe we'll find someone from the fire department or anyone that'll give us some answers."

"Copy that. Let's start with the back of the office then make our way out to the warehouse."

They searched through the office and opened every door. They opened the men's restroom and found it empty. James knocked on the women's restroom and announced himself before going in. He looked under the stalls and didn't find anyone. They moved toward the back of the office and came to the breakroom. Mike pushed the door open and James went through pointing his weapon with a finger steady on the trigger. The break room had another door at the rear that lead into the warehouse, which the warehouse staff used to enter and exit when they took a break. James held the door open as they both exited the breakroom and stepped into the warehouse. At the end of the wall that separates the office from the warehouse, they heard footsteps getting closer. "Hello?" James called out. The remaining undead police officers emerged from behind the corner and started running toward Mike and James. They snarled and growled at the men as they furiously ran toward them.

"STOP! Customs officers, we will shoot if we have to!" Mike yelled and let off a warning shot. The undead officers pressed forward. "Final warning! Stop where you are!"

Undead officer Hauser was at the lead of the attack. James and Mike both held their ground and ordered the officers to stop again. Mike gave another warning but the undead kept moving forward. Mike shot the legs out from under Officer Hauser causing her to fall forward which tripped Officer Rhodes who was behind her. Immediately officer Rhodes got back up and officer Hauser crawled forward using only her arms. James took aim, breathed in and shot right through officer Rhodes open eye socket blowing a hole through the back of his head. Rhodes fell back.

What the fuck is wrong with them James!?" Mike screamed. "Look at her- she's still moving. Her fucking legs are shot up and she's still crawling towards us? Please tell me I'm not imagining this."

"I'm seeing it, but I'm still not believing it. Look at her, if she got a hold of you, she'd bite your dick right off, swallow it and keep eating your ass. Mam… officer… can you hear me? Can you understand anything that I am saying?"

The undead officer stretched her arm out reaching for Mike and growled. She kept pulling herself toward him. The two men slowly inched away with their guns pointed at her. The undead fireman Smith appeared from the corner and started running toward them. The men pointed their guns and shouted "STOP!" Fireman Smith continued running at full speed and James pulled the trigger hitting the fireman twice in the chest which knocked him to the ground. The fireman sat up and got back on his feet. Mike took aim and paused, but before the fireman could take another step, Mike shot him in the head.

"Well there's the fire department," said James. "I think this is why headquarters told me to hang tight. They probably think we're infected with the same disease or illness as them and want us to stay here."

"Well, I can't sit around and wait to be a lab rat James. I have to get to Kari and you know it."

"Well I'm not stopping you brotha', let's get out of here."

Nearby, Fred sat on a bench at the bus stop and rolled another joint to calm his nerves. Images of what took place in the warehouse flashed through his head. He took in a deep puff to shake the thoughts. Once the bus arrived, he sat in the back and tried piecing everything together. He tried making sense of the impossible. *How and what caused it?* he thought. He recounted the conversation he had with Hector and thought about the office personnel who showed similar symptoms as Jose. They coughed and sneezed uncontrollably. He stared out the bus window and looked up at the dark clouds. The black plume of smoke from the warehouse spread and it worried him. *If the chemicals inside the barrel got my co-workers sick, the firemen, and everyone else that was infected by toxins inside those barrels, could it get other people sick too if it's airborne?* he thought. *Could the fire from the explosion have caused some sort of chemical reaction activating an airborne type of virus that's spreading in the air through the smoke? Oh God,* he thought of the possibility if his theory were true and imagined the worst. He sat nervously during the ride back home and shook his knee up and down like an impulsive twitch. He was afraid of dying a horrific and grueling death from being eaten alive. He feared turning into one of them and hurting people. Fear crept up his spine and gripped his body. His hands began to tremble. Images of him being eaten alive and torn apart flashed through his head. He then thought of his mother and sister and began to panic. The painful thought of losing them disturbed him. Guilt began to settle in as he soon realized that it was all his fault. *Had I been focused on driving the forklift, I would've never punctured a hole in the barrels. Fuck it's all my fault, fuck!*

During the ride, passengers in the front rows sneezed and coughed wildly. Fred stared off into the sky tormented by his thoughts. He hadn't noticed a handful of passengers showed symptoms of infection. An older woman wearing a long brown coat with frizzy white hair seated at the front had built a violent wet cough. She gagged as if to catch her breath, then grabbed her chest with a shaky hand and fell off the seat. A young girl seated across from her quickly got up to aid the elderly woman. The bus driver pulled over and Fred noticed the commotion going on in the front. He got up from his seat and saw the old woman on the floor with the young girl holding her hand over the old woman's nose to check for breathing. As he walked slowly through the aisle, he began to realize that others around him were sick and experiencing symptoms of the infected. He cautiously walked backwards noticing the symptoms of several people seated. As he reached the back door, he kicked it open and jumped out. He looked back at the bus and saw a frantic crowd standing over the old woman. A pale faced man stared back at him, covering his mouth as he coughed. Above the pale man was an open window. Fred took another look up at the dark sky and ran home.

Across town, in a luxurious high-rise apartment with fine modern furnishings that overlook the Downtown Los Angeles area, Chris walked back and forth from one end of the living room to the other, talking to himself while holding a glass of whiskey in one hand and his phone in the other. He composed a long text for Kari but wasn't done writing it. In the unsent text, he wrote:

> I wish I could say more. But all I can do is write and then delete as I'll probably never send this message. Maybe you were the one for me or maybe you weren't. Who knows. But what I do know is that I've missed you and good times we had. The tight hugs and the way your hair smells. I miss love and in it I miss you. I could go on and on about what I miss and I'd have an entire book about it. I just wish I had a day with you like we used to. A day in which I could hold your hand. And blah, blah, blah, fuck you, you cold hearted bitch!

He threw the phone against the wall in a rage. The phone made a loud thud as it cracked and bounced off the wall. He felt an increasing and uncontrollable rage. He was angry with his cold-hearted ex for humiliating him in front of everyone at the lobby and for not giving him another chance at making things right. He held anger towards the son of a bitch Mike for taking her away from him and filling her head with his bullshit. His thoughts grew darker and his eyes turned deadly. Old pictures of him and Kari were scattered over the mahogany wooden floor. He picked one up and lit it on fire. He shed tears as one by one he watched them burn in a trash bin. He took a seat next to a round lamp table. On the table was a half-empty bottle of whiskey. He picked it up and put it to his lip. He held up the last picture and deeply stared at it for a while. It was one that he took of Kari sitting on a boat when they took a trip to Florida during the summer several years ago. "I'll always love you, in life and in death," he said holding the picture with tears rolling down his eyes. He titled the bottle and took a big gulp.

At Muir Park, a few miles from Downtown L.A, there was a sign posted at the entrance that read: NO Skateboarding, Bicycle Riding, Roller Blading, Roller Skating and Scooter Riding. Next to the sign was a wooden bench where Robbie sat drinking an iced tea bottle filled with beer which he passed to his best friend Joey. Robbie's other friends, Jesse and Henry practiced tricks on their boards while Flaco sat on his board eating another bag of hot chips.

"For sure they're coming?" Joey asked and flipped his board with his foot.

"Yeah that's why I got this shit," Robbie replied holding a tall can of strawberry margarita liquor.

"What if they want to hang out after the park? Where can we go? What time does your sister get home from work?"

"She gets off at 5:30 and usually gets home after 6. So, we can go back to my house 'till my sister gets home."

"Okay cool. Hey, you think the girls smoke?"

"I think Lily smokes, but I don't think Sheena does. Maybe she'll be down to smoke if Lily does it. I still got some Kush from last time so we'll see what they say. I gotta' fuckin' pee though. Im'a pee on this sign, watch."

Robbie stood up on the bench, unzipped his pant and urinated on the No Skateboarding sign. Flaco took video and laughed hysterically.

"Look, the girls are coming," Joey pointed out to Robbie as he quickly zipped up.

Sheena and Lily's hair blew with the wind as they ran toward the boys with a panicky look on their face.

"Hey, did you guys here about all the schools getting out early?" Sheena asked.

"No- what?" asked Robbie.

"Yeah, they're letting out all the schools early because of an airborne disease going around that's quickly spreading from city to city."

"People are getting fever and cough like symptoms," Lily commented. "Peter from 2nd period threw up blood and had to be rushed to the hospital. It's all over the news, you guys haven't heard?"

"Nah, we've been skating here all day since we left the donut shop," Joey replied.

"What kind of disease is it or where did they say that it's coming from?" he asked and pulled out his phone to search online for what the girls were talking about.

"Before they dismissed the school, Mrs. Andres turned on the TV and the news people said that it's an airborne disease or virus spreading all through the city of L.A and that it could spread all across the world. They said it's probably coming from an explosion that happened at a warehouse this morning, but they don't know what caused the explosion or what's spreading in the air to make people sick," Lily commented.

"Holy shit guys come check this out," Flaco said and waived everyone over to look at his phone.

They huddled around Flaco's phone and saw a video posted on Facebook of police officers surrounding a skinny black teenager with braids. He was fired at multiple times but continued to get back up despite getting shot.

"Oh shit, they keep shooting at him," Robbie loudly remarked. "Fuckin' pigs, why are they still shooting? The dude doesn't even have a gun or a knife, what the fuck!?"

The girls gasped as they witnessed the young teen rise. "Stay down!" an officer loudly commanded, but the teenager rushed the officer and bit him on the arm. The group of officers swarmed in on the teenager and began beating him with their batons. Robbie looked on with an angry expression as Flaco held the phone. The teen managed to grab one of the officer's baton and yanked the officer down. He wrapped his arms around the officer in a bear hug and chomped on his neck. The other five officers struck the teen with brutal force, repeatedly striking him on his back, arms and legs, but the teen held onto the moribund officer as blood gushed out from his neck. A crowd of onlookers screamed and yelled at the officers, pleading with them to leave the teenager alone. "He's just a kid!" screamed a woman. The crowd grew hostile and threw bottles and trash at the officers. Additional units with booming sirens rolled in to provide back up. The officers jumped out of the patrol cars and pushed the crowd back. Others that arrived stepped in to help and hold the teen down. The teenager kicked and growled as they forced him face down and put him in cuffs. The angry mob held their phones out to record the incident and yelled vulgarity at the arresting officers. Lily looked away. She couldn't stomach the graphic nature of the video. Robbie and the others were left in shock after watching the video.

"How is that even possible? That kid should be dead. Does it have anything to do with that airborne virus you said that's going around? What are we supposed to do?" Robbie asked.

"Well the news anchor said that it's recommended to stay home, lock all your windows, doors, and seal everything that has an opening," Sheena replied.

"So, we're not supposed to be outside right now? Shit, we've been out here all goddamn day. Wait, how come you didn't go straight home?"

"Because I wanted to see you and make sure that you were okay."

"You're sweet, but yeah I'm okay. Does your mom know that school was cut short today?"

"I don't think so. I've been trying to call her after being told that they were going to let us go home early, but she hasn't answered my calls or replied to any of my texts."

"Maybe she's busy at work?"

"No she always replies when I text her; at the most within ten minutes. I even called her job and no one picks up. Lily's mom doesn't answer either. I'm really starting to get worried."

"It'll be alright," Robbie said and placed his arm over her shoulder to comfort her. "I'm sure she's just a little busy at work right now and can't get to the phone. But she'll call you soon."

He kissed her on the lips and handed her the tall can of liquor. Flaco and the others searched through Facebook for more videos of the ongoing epidemic. Lily and Joey sat together on the grass as he looked at videos posted online. Lily viewed her friend

Tamara's timeline and saw her video posts of the day. Her last post was of heavy traffic congestion on the 110 freeway as she sat in the back of her mother's car after getting picked up from school. In her video post, cars were seen bumper to bumper and traffic at a standstill. Sirens were heard approaching. In the next clip, an ambulance passed her window; clear signs of an accident up ahead. To her left, she saw an old woman with a wrinkly face who looked to be in her late seventies, sitting in the driver's seat of a burgundy Buick coughing violently. They both made eye contact and Tamara quickly turned away with embarrassment and stopped recording. A few seconds later she discretely pointed her phone back at the old woman and began recording again. This time, the old woman was slumped over the steering wheel and passed out. Her chest pushed up against the steering wheel which caused the horn to blow nonstop. A tall man in the car in front of her became annoyed and flung his door open. He stepped out and made a hand gesture at her, asking what her problem was. Tamara kept recording. The tall man walked over to the Buick and knocked on the old woman's window. He noticed she was unresponsive and opened the door. He gently pushed her head back onto the seats headrest. "Ma'am, are you ok? Ma' am, wake up," the man said. He leaned in to check for a pulse and felt the old woman's cold breath on his neck as she woke up and bit him. He screamed out in agonizing pain as he tried to pull away, but her wrinkly hands were tightly gripped around his neck. Her long nails were sunk deep into his skin as she held on. He shook his head back and forth so that she would loosen her grip, but she only bit harder and ripped his throat open as he yanked away. Tamara shrieked in horror and the video was cut.

"Oh my God!" Lily screamed and covered her mouth as she held her phone.

Seconds later Tamara posted another clip. The new clip was shaky as Tamara recorded with a trembly hand. Onlookers stepped out of their car and rushed to the man's aid who was on the ground holding his neck. His hand was covered in blood as he placed it over his gushing wound. A gray-haired man took off his blue shirt and applied pressure on the neck with it. A woman in black tights was on the phone with 911 as she stood in front of the Buick and watched as the gray-haired man applied pressure. She kicked the door closed on the old woman who was still strapped down by her seat belt. The old woman growled and viciously pounded on the door. The tall thin man who tried to help the old woman gasped for air. His eyes rolled back and his arm went limp, and the video stopped.

"Fuck this is intense," Joey said as everyone stood over him and Lily watching the video on Lily's phone.

"Check if Tamara posted another one. Swipe the screen down to refresh," Robbie said.

Lily swiped down and another video popped up on her timeline. This time, the tall thin man who bled out from his neck and died, snarled as he slowly opened his foggy eyes and came back to life. He got up and attacked the elder man who used his blue shirt to help. He grabbed on and pushed him down as he sunk his teeth and tore out his flesh. The old woman in the Buick continued clawing at the window and growled. She then banged her head and fists against the car window with force numerous times. Blood dripped from her hands as she continued the pounding until the window broke. The crowd of onlookers grew with fear and instead of helping the elderly man, they went back in their cars, locked their doors and recorded the horrific scene on their phone. During the whole incident, vehicles hadn't moved and traffic was backed up for miles. The old woman inside the Buick jerked around in her seat and managed to free herself. She crawled out of the broken window and tore her flesh against the edges of the broken glass. Tamara nervously kept recording. She looked all around, but the old woman disappeared from her view. As Tamara looked far off to the left, the old woman popped out from below and stood in front of Tamara's window. She punched the through window and grabbed Tamara by the hair. Tamara and her mom screamed with horror and Tamara dropped her phone. The video cut off after leaving everyone disturbed.

"Oh fuck! Refresh again, refresh again!" Robbie shouted.

"Oh my god, she hasn't posted anything," Lily fearfully remarked. "I'm texting her now- God I hope she replies."

"That was sick dude," Henry said leaned up against a tree. He gagged and covered his mouth holding in his vomit. "The way she bit into that man's neck like that and ripped out his throat - oh fuck. I feel sick now."

"You're good dude?" asked Robbie with a worried look.

"No dude, that video made me sick to my stomach. If this shit's for real and there's like, like a disease out there making people act all crazy like that old lady in Tamara's video, then we need to get the fuck out of here. It's like the end of the world type of shit. People getting sick and then attacking other people like that. Like zombies. That's fucken real-life zombie shit."

"Seriously, we need to get somewhere safe and we need to get there fast before we run into someone like that old lady!" said Joey. "Like Lily said, we have to lock all the doors and seal everything so that no air or virus can creep in."

"Sheena, your parents work in Irvine, right? So they won't be back in L.A 'til like seven tonight?" asked Robbie.

"Yeah," Sheena replied. "Lily's Mom works out in that city too so she can come with us until we hear from both our parents. But where can we go that's safe and close by?"

"My house. I'll ask my sister to give us a ride home and we can stay there for now. Your parents can pick you up from my place until you hear from them. My sister works at an insurance building close to here, in downtown. She drives a van and I know we can all fit. The girls will probably have to lap it, but we'll manage. Sheena and Lily, your parents can pick you guys up from my place, cool?"

"Okay, yeah that's cool," responded Lily. "How far is your sister's job from here?"

"It's walking distance, maybe like fifteen, twenty minutes from here. But we need to start walking fast and get out of the open now."

The group of teens made their way through the lonely park. The clear skies of the day had turned gloomy. The howling winds breezed through the trees. Sheena tightly held Robbie's hand. He could feel the warmth and sweat of her hand.

"Are you scared?" he asked.

"I'm terrified," she replied. "What if we run into sick people like on the video or what if we get sick?"

"Don't worry. We'll be alright. And I don't think we'll get sick because if we were, we'd be feeling sick by now right? And no one here is sick, except maybe a little in the head ha, ha."

"Well, what about Henry? He doesn't look too good, look at him."

They both looked back and stared at Henry who sluggishly trailed behind holding his board. He had a sweaty face and his skin began to turn pale.

"He's just drunk," Robbie said. "He can't hang. With just a few sips of beer, he gets all drunk super-fast. Don't worry, Henry will be okay once he sobers up a bit. Besides, I think that video made him sick too. He's got a weak stomach for that type of stuff."

"Yeah, I guess." She wasn't too convinced and worried even more.

"God, poor Tamara. I hope she's okay. Hey, did Tamara ever reply or post anything new?" Sheena turned to ask Lily.

"No, she hasn't, I just checked," replied Lily holding her phone. "I called her too but she didn't pick up. And I know her phone isn't off because it keeps ringing instead of going straight to voicemail."

Lily walked beside Joey and reached for his hand.

"Are you scared too?" Joey asked.

"I mean yeeaahh. Henry's right, this is like the end of the world type of stuff. I read about it in the Bible, I just didn't think it would happen now or in my time."

"You read the Bible?"

"Well, I used to back when I was younger and in Catholic school. My mom would take me to church and I did my first communion and confirmation. I'm not like super religious or anything, but I do believe in God. Do you?"

"Nah, I'm not religious. My mom never took us to church, she always worked, even on Sundays."

"What does she do?"

"Cleans rich people's houses. My older brother kind of raised me."

"And your dad? He never took you to church or taught you about religion?"

"No, he's dead. He was a gangster. He got killed when I was four. I don't even have a memory of him, just pictures."

"Damn, I'm sorry to hear that. I don't have a dad either. He wasn't killed or anything, he just chose another family over mine after cheating on my mom. But he's just as dead to me anyway."

"Damn that sucks. Sorry about that."

"It's okay, I've let it go. That's just life I guess."

"Has he tried calling you or have you contacted him?"

"Nope. He hasn't looked for me and I could care less if he's dead or alive so I'm not going to search for him. And I hope he doesn't try to come back into my life to make things right because if he does, I'm going to send his ass straight to hell."

The teens made their way out of the park and into the city. They heard people hollering from a distance and looked at each other with fear. Robbie and Sheena constantly looked over their shoulders as they hustled through the city with their group of friends following close behind. Robbie cautiously approached an abandoned minivan in the middle of the road. He peeked inside through the rear window and found it empty. Both sliding doors were open and the keys were still in the ignition. He opened the trunk to look for a weapon in case they were to run into any of the sick. He found a tire lug wrench. He banged it against his palm feeling the hefty weight of it in his hand. He had found a good weapon. He then noticed a long black sports duffle bag toward the back of the rear seat and unzipped it. He looked at Sheena and waved her over with a grin. She ran up to him to ask what he had found and smiled as she looked in the bag. She reached in and pulled out a thirty-inch aluminum baseball bat. She firmly gripped it with both hands and stared at it with admiration as she looked it up and down. She took a few practice swings. The bat swished through the air as she swung away. Lily smiled at watching Sheela swing and grabbed one for herself. A handful of the undead had come up from behind and ran toward the group of teens. The teens got ready and made a stance. "Batter up," Sheena said as she walked up to the undead. Lily walked beside her with bat in hand ready to fight. Both girls swung for the fences as the undead attacked. Robbie used his lug wrench and rammed it through one the undead's eye socket while his friend Flaco used his skateboard and smashed it over the undead's cranium. They bravely fought on and the girls made good use of their newly found weapon, killing more of the undead than the boys. It was over in less than a minute. "This one was a home run for sure," Sheena said as she stared down at one of the undead. She had swung her bat so hard that she knocked all its teeth out and caved in the side of its head. Her bat dripped with blood. One of the undead moaned as it lay on the floor. Lily finished it off as she whacked away at its head. Blood splattered with every thump. "We have to keep moving before more of them show up," Robbie said. "Okay, I'm done," Lily said tucking her hair behind her ears. "We can go now."

As they turned the corner on Fourth Street and Olive, they saw a large group of people out in the distance, dressed in tattered suits and torn office attire. The teens noticed the ragged bunch surrounding a body on the ground who was out of view. They made hostile movements toward the person, like an angry mob beating on someone. The curios group of teens slowly walked closer to the aggressive crowd to get a better look and caught the attention of a barefooted woman amongst the crowd wearing a muddy skirt. She made a loud grunt and the rest of her group all turned their heads. Lily's jaw dropped when she saw blood dripping from their mouth. Their eyes were foggy, and their skin was pale. Robbie was stricken with fear at noticing a woman's mutilated corpse lying on the ground with most of her flesh torn off. It was the first time they'd seen an actual mutilated body. Chunks of meat were ripped out of her body and her blood was smeared over the groups' face. They looked like a pack of lions as they eat their pray. The woman in a skirt let out a screech and the crowd of undead rushed toward the teenagers. Their bodies jerked and hobbled as they ran. Some of the undead's broken arms and legs flung wildly from side to side as they chased after the teens. "There's too many. RUN!" yelled Robbie.

They quickly turned back around and ran as fast they could. Robbie ran holding Sheena's hand and Joey pulled on Lily. Flaco, Jesse, and Henry skated ahead. They turned right on Ninth Street, which Robbie knew was an incredibly steep hill. He saw two bikes next to a bike post in front of a gastropub and noticed the bike lock was left unlocked. He quickly looked around and undid the lock. He grabbed both bikes and gave one to Sheena and the other to Lily. "Hop on he said," holding the bikes. "Pedal as fast as you can up and over that hill. On Figueroa Street, make a left."

"What about you?" Sheena asked as she mounted the bike.

"I'll be right behind you. Besides, once I get over that hill, I can ride my skateboard down the rest of the way. Trust me I'll catch up, now GO!"

The girls started to pedal away when two men with long beards dressed in skinny blue jeans ran out from the gastropub screaming for their bikes. "Hey that's my fucking bike!" one shouted. Robbie ran behind the girls then looked back at both men who were giving chase. "Behind you!" Robbie screamed at the enraged bearded men and pointed at the large mass of undead chasing after them.

Both men kept their focus on the girls and continued running after them. "Stop!" one shouted just before he got attacked from behind. He fell to the floor as the attacker viciously clawed at his face. His other bearded friend stopped to help but the rest of the flesh-eating mob caught up and pushed him to the ground. "Get the fuck off me!" he screamed as they ripped apart his flannel shirt. He kicked and wildly swung his arms desperately trying to free himself. They clawed and tore their way into his belly. He screamed in excruciating pain as they ate him alive. The undead sank their teeth into his stomach, dug deep into the intestines and ripped them out like weeds. They bit off his fingers and peeled away his flesh.

Flaco, who was chunky, struggled to keep up with his friends as they made their way up the steep hill. He ran with a lazy pace and gasped with every step. "RUUNNN FLACO!" Robbie yelled at him. "Come on dude, run, run, run!" The horde of undead switched their attention back to Flaco and pursued him. Robbie slowed his pace and fell behind to help his friend. He ran behind Flaco and pushed him up the street, constantly looking back at the mass of undead gaining on them.

"Come on dude, you can do it," Robbie said cheering Flaco on. "Almost there," he said and shoved Flaco forward. "Once you get to the top, ride that fuckin' board downhill as fast as you can, got it?"

"Got it!" Flaco shouted in a heavy breath. "We're almost there Robbie!"

Robbie sensed one of them close behind and heard its booming footsteps inching closer. He pushed the pace and shoved Flaco harder. Flaco took heavy breaths as he put one foot in front of the other. He pushed himself harder up the hill. Robbie heard a loud grunt dangerously close to his ear and felt finger tips rubbing against his back. He pressed Flaco forward with all of his strength one last time as they got up to the top of the hill. Flaco hopped onto his skateboard and sped down hill. As Robbie reached the top, he leaped up high and in midair turned one-hundred and eighty degrees like a basketball player making a slam dunk. He had his skateboard firmly gripped with both hands and used it to crack the undead over the head as he came down. The undead man fell flat on his face from the colossal blow and laid motionless. Robbie stood over the lifeless undead man's body as he caught his breath. He had a deranged look in his eye and lifted the board over his head and brutally slammed it down onto the back of the man's head over and again. Blood splattered onto the pavement and skull fragments scattered as Robbie hammered the board into the head, hacking through flesh, bone and brains until the wooden edge of the skateboard cut through the front of the skull, scraping against the pavement. Flaco had made it safely down the hill and shouted up at Robbie to hurry down. Robbie snapped out of his trance and quickly hopped over the corpse and onto his skateboard.

He crouched down on his board, slightly leaned forward and rode downhill picking up speed as he peddled with his hand. The crowd of undead came up over the hill like a tidal wave about to crash down on his head. They chased after him, but several of them lost their balance and tripped forward. They violently tumbled downhill catching speed as they rolled. Robbie turned his hips and maneuvered to the left avoiding the bodies that fell. He pushed his body forward and leaned a bit further to pick up speed. The wheels on his board rolled over gravel with lightning speed. Flaco waived Robbie down to hurry over to Lily who was on the ground bleeding from a gash she suffered after falling off the bike as she sped downhill and lost control. "Get her up on Sheena's handles!" Robbie screamed to Joey. The horde of undead got closer to the group of teens as Joey and Flaco helped Lily up on the handle bars.

"Can you peddle with her on?" Robbie asked Sheena.

"Yeah I got her," she replied.

"Ride two blocks down to Seventh Street and you'll see the big building on the left. Get inside as soon as you get there. I'll be right behind you go! Go! Go!"

Flaco and Joey skated off following the girls. Henry tried mounting his skateboard to follow but fell to his knees. He huffed and tried catching his breath. Robbie crouched down to help him up.

"I'm so dizzy dude," Henry slurred. "I feel super weird. I don't think I can keep going."

Henry tried to get back on his feet with Robbie's help but fell to his knees again.

"Hang on to me dude, I got you," Robbie said throwing Henry's arm over his shoulder. "Come on, we'll run together. The building isn't that far from here."

"I'm not going to make it Rob. I'll just slow you down."

"Dude I can't leave you here. Come on please try."

Robbie tried lifting him up and getting him balanced. Henry desperately hanged on to Robbie's shoulders as he slowly stood up. He sluggishly moved forward with Robbie's help, but lost his grip when all of his strength escaped from his body and he collapsed to the ground. Robbie pulled on his arm and screamed at him, "Get up! Please dude!" he begged. "They're coming! Get up!" Henry didn't move, and his eyes were shut. Robbie checked the pulse on his wrist and didn't find one. He then placed two fingers on his neck and checked for a pulse. His eyes grew watery and a lump formed in the back his throat. "Wake up! Wake up!" Robbie said as he shook his friend with tears rolling down his eyes. Flaco was waiting for Robbie down the street and saw the horde of undead inch closer. "Let's go!" he yelled out. Robbie looked up and saw them approaching. He shook Henry one last time hoping he'd wake up. He didn't want to give up on Henry because he knew that

Henry would never give up on him. They all would never give up on each other. But Robbie felt there wasn't more he could do and hearing Flaco call for him in the distance induced him to leave and to look out for the others. He sighed and took in a deep breath, then gently laid Henrys arm to his side and backed away. He jumped on his board and sped away. As he rolled off, he looked back at his friend and saw the crowd of undead surround him. They didn't pounce on Henry as he thought and wondered why they hadn't touched him. Then he noticed Henry gradually move. Robbie came to a complete stop and looked on with a stunned expression. He was shocked to see his friend reanimated and back on his feet. Henry's face had turned pale and his eyes were white. He fixed his eyes on Robbie and stared at him with a chilling look, grunted and ran toward him. The horde of undead followed behind. Robbie realized that his friend Henry was no longer the same person and that the thing running towards him was infected with the virus that had transformed him into one of the undead. He snuffled, wiped his tears and pushed off on his skateboard at full speed.

That's enough story for today my friend. Tomorrow I will tell you more and introduce another man that I would later meet on that frightful day. I'll see you again tomorrow.

CHAPTER 5

Buenos días amigo. How are you today? Good I hope. As for me, I'm doing well. Gosh, I really wish I could talk with you inside of your room instead of having to talk with you like this, through this glass. But for safety reasons, I cannot. But one day, we'll change that. Alright let's begin this morning's session. Yesterday I told you I'd share the story of someone else I would meet on UD-Day. This is his story.

A thirty-one-year-old construction worker by the name of Saul woke up from a heavy night of drinking and partying that carried on until the wee hours of the morning. He lied in an awkward fetal position on his friend's beige L-shaped sectional sofa. His friend Andres sat on the recliner across from him and flipped through the channels looking for the soccer game that would start at noon. He sipped on one of the few remaining beers from the night's get together. Saul yawned and rubbed his eyes. "What time did you end up knocking out?" Saul asked Andres.

"I don't even remember," he replied. "Like four, four-thirty, I think? A few minutes after you." Saul got up and walked to the refrigerator to grab a beer.

"What time does the game start?" Saul asked.

"In like fifteen minutes," Andres replied.

"I'm hungry!" Saul shouted while rummaging through the fridge. "Let's go to that marisco spot and watch the game there. You down?"

"All right cool; wake up Joe and see if he's down to go," Andres shouted back.

Saul walked over to his friend Joe's room with beer in hand and just before he could knock, Joe opened it from inside with a messy blonde-haired girl standing behind him. "I heard you fools," Joe said. "But yeah, I'm down. Just going to walk Joanna to her car and then we'll get going."

"Walk of shame," said Saul under his breath, deriding Joanna as she walked past him to the front door with her dirty, alcohol stained heels in hand.

The marisco spot was a seafood restaurant that Saul and his friends occasionally liked to visit. The waitresses were beautiful and blessed with curves, the food was delicious, and the liveliness was very attracting. It was located inside of a large venue with an open seating area. Inside of the closed seating area were large televisions that played sports like soccer, basketball, and football. The light blue walls were decorated with sea animals and fish ornaments that hung from the walls. Different bands that played Spanish music would drop by and play every day and night which drew in a large crowd, so the place was always bustling. The musicians set their instruments by the outdoor seating area and played loudly. You could always hear music coming from the restaurant several blocks away whenever there was a band playing. A slim but thick in the waist waitress approached Saul's table with a big tray holding a large platter of aguachile, a Mexican dish made of raw shrimp submerged in liquid seasoned with chili peppers, lime juice, coriander and several slices of onion, cucumbers and avocado. She served them three large micheladas, a Mexican beer prepared with ice, lime juice, and assorted with sauces, spices, and peppers. The beers were served in a large chilled mug with lime wedges and salt on the rim. The boys watched the game and cheered their team on as the band continued to play. They made a toast with every new michelada served and ordered different platters for all three to share. After the game, they split the tab and parted ways to end their Sunday night in the comfort of their own bed. Saul called it a night a little early and went to bed at nine. He was a construction worker and had to wake up at five a.m. to get ready for work at a high-rise being constructed in downtown Los Angeles. That would be the last day he would ever see his friends again.

The next morning, Saul's Monday would start off as normal. He got up at five thirty a.m., got dressed for work, and as routine, stopped at a donut shop a block away from the everlasting congested freeway that he took to get to work. The cute girl at the counter with no makeup and hair in a bun grabbed him a chocolate donut sprinkled with peanuts and a large coffee.

Saul's colleague Juan always brought a small radio with him and let it play as they worked through the day inside the large ten story building. Saul sang along to a song playing on the radio of a broken-hearted man sitting alone in a dark corner of a dive bar, drinking a bottle of tequila, defeated in love and saddened by the loss of his woman. While in the middle of installing a door frame to what would have been a conference room, Saul's woeful singing was cut short when an announcement on the radio interrupted the song. The broadcaster informed listeners of a violent scene coming out of the city of Hawthorne. It was reported that several people with no confirmed link to one another brutally and randomly attacked anyone who crossed their path. Suddenly Saul heard a loud thud. He turned to see what the odd noise was and spotted his manager across the room lying on the newly installed navy-blue carpet floor unconscious. The manager Bob, a bald stout man in his early fifties had fallen off a step ladder after fainting. The construction crew rushed over to check on him and looked for vital signs. "Bob. Bob," they repeated hoping for a response. One of the men knelt beside Bob and placed his ear close to his nostrils. "Dios, he's not breathing," he told the others. He tilted Bobs head back and pumped his chest. He blew air into his lungs and pressed on his chest over and again. He repeated the process for over two minutes but with no success. "I can't get through," Juan said as he held the phone to his ear trying to get a hold of a 911 operator. "It just keeps ringing."

"Keep trying," Saul said as the others looked on with desperate hope that CPR would bring their manager back to life. Mario, the man giving CPR, blew air into the managers mouth again when his eyes grew wide with a painful expression. He gave out a frightful moan. He then let out a deafening cry of fear and agony as the manager woke from the dead and tore Mario's bottom lip off. Blood spurted from Mario's mouth as he tumbled to the floor. "He covered the bottom of his exposed and bloody lower pink gums. "Oh, my God!" Mario murmured with his hand over his mouth. Blood seeped through his fingers and dripped down his arm. The crew feared Bob had gone crazy and was set on savagely harming them. They dropped and held him down. "Stop it Bob!" one of them yelled as he tried controlling Bob's flinging arms. Bob's eyes were wild and pale. Blood was smeared across his face down to his neck. He snapped his bloody jaw at them as they subdued and held him down. Another colleague who was working across the hall ran in with a fury and attacked Juan who was holding the phone. The undead man tackled Juan to the ground and mounted on top of him like a ravenous wolf. He sank his yellow teeth into Juan's neck and ripped out a large chunk and swallowed it hole before biting down again. Two of the men grabbed him from behind. They put him in a body arm lock as the man roared with rage and swung wildly to get free. Juan rolled on the floor from side to side holding the tear on his neck which bled profusely. He then flapped around like a fish out of breath.

"What the fuck's happening!?" yelled out Saul as he applied pressure on Juan's neck. Juan stopped flapping and twitched for a few seconds before shaking uncontrollably. "Someone call 911 again," he asked of the others. The other men were occupied with holding Bob down and the other undead colleague. Saul placed a rag over Juan's neck which quickly soaked up the blood. "No, no, stay with me Juan," Saul pleaded with his colleague as his eyes slowly rolled back. "Juan? Juan! Juan!" Saul yelled. He slapped him on the face to keep him from passing out.

Mario, the man with the torn off lip, was feeling lightheaded and his skin grew pale. He limply sat on the floor with his back leaned against the wall. His vision had gone blurry, but he could see them yelling and frantically attempting to resuscitate Juan. He saw Saul speaking to him and saying something, but he couldn't make out the words. Saul was crouched in front of him and spoke, but the words sounded distant. Mario's hearing was reduced and muffled. His vision was fuzzy like when you try looking out through a foggy windshield on a cold and rainy day.

"Hey, don't pass out on me?" Saul told him. Mario looked at Saul with a dazed look. "I'm driving you and Juan to the hospital," Saul said as he wrapped his arm around him to pick him up. "911 isn't answering so we can't get an ambulance here to come get you guys. Come on get up." Saul tried lifting Mario up on his feet, but Mario was weak and unable to move. "Guys can one of you help me here?" he asked his co-workers who held Bob down and the other colleague that attacked Juan. As Saul tried helping Mario up, Juan sat up straight and faced his colleagues. "Juan- you alright?" asked one of the men with a scruffy beard. Juan let out an eerie animalistic groan and charged at the bearded man. He grabbed a hold of him and tackled him down. His teeth scrapped against the bearded mans' cheek and sank deep into the fat until the upper and lower part of his front teeth cut through and connected. Juan violently ripped off the flesh from the man's cheek. The man let out a loud cry that echoed through the unfurnished space down to the hallway. The manager Bob jerked and set himself free from the tight hold, got up and chased down one of the construction members who tried to flee. He lunged and clung onto his back and sank his teeth deep into his shoulders growling like an enraged animal.

Mario passed out and slumped over. "I'm out of here!" yelled one of the construction workers. He ran out and the others followed him down the hall toward the stairwell. Saul stayed behind to help Mario, but the manager soon turned his attention to him. Saul feared an attack and pulled his hammer out from his tool belt. He brandished the long fiberglass claw hammer with soft rubber grip handle and readied himself to swing it over the managers face. "Stay back!" Saul shouted at Bob who stood over his last victim. "If you take another step, I swear to God I will hit you with this hammer. Stay BACK!" Bob took a giant leap toward Saul but before he could take another step, Saul swung the hammer over his head and brought it thundering down onto Bob's face breaking his eye socket. Bob stumbled back and blood immediately gushed out from his eyebrow. Again, he rushed in and Saul stepped to the side like a matador avoiding the long sharp horns of a bull. He swung the hammer and hit Bob in the back of the head which knocked him to the ground with a flump. At this point Mario came back from the dead and grabbed Saul from behind. He held him in a bear hug with his mouth moving closer to Saul's neck. Saul pushed himself backwards toward the wall. Mario's head bounced off the wall and Saul broke free from his hold. Saul turned around and saw his friends pale face and white bloodshot eyes. "Mario, not you too?" he said facing the man he once used to go lunch with during their breaks. Mario sprang but was met with a square blow to the cheek. He fell face first and Saul stepped on his back and bludgeoned his head until Mario stopped moving. Seconds later after consuming a few pounds of flesh off his co-worker, Juan feasted his eyes on Saul and approached with a fast pace. Saul kicked him down before hitting him on the forehead and knocking him down again. He firmly held the hammer by his side that dripped with blood. He looked down in disbelief as his co-worker slowly started to get back up. "Stay down Juan. Please!" Saul begged his co-worker. "I'm warning you. I don't want to kill you too. Stay down!" Juan got up and lunged at him. Saul swung the hammer over Juan's jaw knocking out almost the entire front row of his teeth out as they flew in the air. Juan fell back on the floor and Saul quickly jumped on top of him. Saul raised the hammer over his head, "I'm sorry Juan," he apologized and swung the hammer down onto Juan's forehead caving it in.

Saul's heavy booming footsteps echoed through the freshly carpeted hallway as he ran toward the stairwell. He was breathing heavily and sweat soaked the collar of his grey tee-shirt down to his portly chest. His palms were moist from the sweat, but he held a tight grip on the blood-stained hammer. *I can't believe I just did that,* Saul thought as he reflected on the men he just killed including Juan. *But I had to or they would have killed me too. I have witnesses. The others know, they saw what happened. But where did they go? They just ran out and left me. Maybe they're downstairs waiting for an ambulance or the police. What is going on?*

At the top of the second floor, he held on to the rail careful not to make a sound. He calmed his breathing. Just as he took another step, he heard a faint sound down in the distance. He directed his ear toward the inaudible noise and barely made out the sounds of whimpers followed by moans of pain. Quietly and with great caution he took a slow and soft step down the stairs. He ducked his head trying to see where the unnerving sounds below were coming from and by who, but there was no one in sight. With each faltering step, down to the first floor he feared that he would find what seemed almost unimaginable just a few minutes ago. On the fourth step, the sound got louder and a bit clearer. He crouched down and took another look.

In front of the automatic sliding glass door exit he saw a whimpering man lying on his back with no movement from his arms or legs except for an occasional tilt of his head down toward his chest. In front of him were two men kneeled over him wildly chewing on large bloody chunks of meat. Blood dripped through their fingers as they ate from their hands. Just as they finished taking the last bite of what they held, they bit down on the man's lower body and tore another piece of meat from his legs and continued eating. With every piece that got ripped apart and torn off, the man who could no longer feel his body, looked down with horror as his former colleagues ate his lower torso. He tilted his head back and saw Saul upside down standing on the steps, frightened and unsure of what do.

Saul feared that if he tried to help, he would end up just like his coworker who sadly clung to life. He could only look at the horror that lied in front of him and wished his colleague a speedy death. At that moment, the man's eyes slowly started to roll back until only the white became visible and his eyelids stopped from twitching. The two undead men stopped from taking another bite and turned their attention to Saul. He was standing on the third and fourth step, wide eyed and frozen with fear. The man who was being eaten alive came back to life and moved his head aggressively. Saul could tell from the color of his eyes that he had also turned into something that was no longer of the living. Saul turned back around and ran up the stairs. The two undead men gave chase and growled as they rushed up the stairs.

Saul tripped on the third step from the top of the second floor and fell forward landing hard on the palm of his hands. The thundering steps from the undead men below got closer. Saul looked back and saw them running up the steps. He pushed himself up and got back on his feet. He hurried to the only safe place that he could think of where he could hide. *On the third floor, there's a restroom that locks from the inside* he thought. He pushed off each foot using all his strength to increase speed as he went up the flight of steps while holding onto the rail to keep himself from falling again. It had been a long time since he ran this fast from anything in his life apart from the time when he was thirteen years old and his neighbors German Shepherd that everyone in the neighborhood hated got out of the front gate and started chasing after him. Back then he was a lot thinner, ran fast and was able to jump over his neighbor's gate without a scratch. Much like the dog, the two undead men were hot on his heels, breathing heavily and making growling sounds waiting to tear into his flesh. On the third floor, Saul raced down the hall toward the restroom and extended his arm in reach of the metal door handle. He pulled the door open as fast as he could, slipped inside and quickly yanked the door back in toward him with all of his might. One of the undead men managed to get his fingers inside the door right before it shut, jamming the door. The undead men pulled at the door back and forth from outside, but Saul kept pulling the door with both hands gripping the metal handle. Using all his power, he gave a strong pull and shut the door, quickly turning the lock above the door handle locking the bathroom door with him safely inside.

He secured the door by using the hammers claw as a door stop. His back was against the door and he slid down to the gray tiled floor. He sighed and put his head in his hands. In front of him were two urinals and two stalls. Underneath the handicap stall were two visible legs stretched out with someone sitting on the toilet. A low, guttural and menacing sound came from the stall and Saul looked up with watery eyes. He rubbed his eyes clear and made out both legs dressed in blue jeans wearing black scuffed work boots. The legs straightened up and moved toward the door.

The stall door flung open slamming against the white wall and an electrician who was on the third floor working on the lights emerged. His skin was pale, and his eyes were foggy like all of the undead. He wore a blue tucked in tee shirt with a lightning bolt logo over the left chest with the words *The Electric Crew* printed underneath. He staggered out from the stall moaning in a belligerent manner until his attention turned on to Saul. He let out a growl and Saul jumped to his feet and frantically tried to pull the hammer out from underneath the door. He pulled on the hammer and shifted the handle back and forth trying to pry it out from beneath the door. The electrician charged at Saul forcing Saul to abandon his struggle with the hammer. He took the undead electrician head on and grabbed him in a choke hold with both hands tightly wrapped around the man's neck. Saul pushed him back with great force and slammed the undead man's head against the wall. The man fell to his knees and hit his head against the urinal on the way down. Saul grabbed the undead man by the back of the head and banged his forehead against the front of the urinal repeatedly splitting it open. Blood spewed out from the man's forehead and splattered over the urinal. His body finally went limp after several blows to the head and Saul released him. The splashing sound from the blood that dripped down the side of the urinal was muted by the two undead men on the other side of the restroom door who continued to growl, pound and claw at the door.

Battering echoed within the restroom as the door jolted with every thump. Saul looked down and saw the hammer slide across the floor. A screw from the lock came undone and with another blow the lock broke off. "Oh fuck," he said out loud. He rushed toward the door picking up the hammer along the way and threw his weight against the door. He leaned his back against the door and firmly planted his feet desperately trying to hold the door shut and to keep them from coming in. He huffed and grunted in a low voice as the sweat from his forehead dripped down his face. Fear crawled up his neck and pushed into his eyes. He feared dying like his co-workers. The door continued to push open and he kept forcing it to close. He knew that he wouldn't be able to keep it up forever. He hit the light switch off and firmly gripped the hammer with his right hand. With his weight pushed against the door he took two steps to the right, waited to get the timing right and yanked the door open. The two undead men fell forward and lost their footing. Saul took advantage and swung the hammer onto the last man who fell in. Saul bashed his head to the ground with a strong blow from the hammer. He swiveled and ran out as the other man gave chase. The undead man let out a bloodcurdling growl as it ran after Saul through the hallway. Saul stopped in his tracks, turned around and whacked him with the hammer against his head. The undead man fell face down. He was still alive and stretched his arm out reaching for Saul's ankle. Saul stepped over him and bashed the undead man's head in. After killing him, Saul raced downstairs and came to a stop at the bottom of the first floor. He had forgotten about his co-worker who was laying in front of the door with most of flesh from his lower body ripped out. The undead man growled and wobbled his head while snapping his jaw. He was paralyzed but very lively. Saul stood over him feeling confused, afraid and saddened for what had become of his former colleague. He ran out through the front doors hoping to find help.

Just a few blocks away, Kari sat at her desk composing an email and paused in midsentence. She looked up and noticed her coworkers quickly walk into the conference room. She found it odd and didn't recall a scheduled meeting for that day. She looked through the calendar pinned on her cubicle but didn't see one noted. "What's all the commotion about?" she whispered at Cindy who sat across from her. "I have no idea," Cindy replied as she got up from her desk to join the others. Kari got up curious to find out what was going on. She caught up to Cindy and walked in with her. Everyone from the office gathered around a large TV mounted on the wall and attentively watched the local news channel. Kari noticed everyone's face struck with panic and fear. The news anchor, Dan Moray, a longtime television news anchor with a full set of gray hair, nervously looked into the camera as he informed the public of the deadly airborne virus.

"At this time, what we know is that it has been confirmed by the CDC that an airborne virus is spreading throughout Los Angeles. It is believed to have been caused by an explosion that occurred earlier this morning at a warehouse in the city of Hawthorne holding highly toxic chemicals. It is unclear at the moment as to how or why this warehouse came into possession of these chemicals. It is also unclear as to what caused the explosion as an investigation into this matter is still pending, but we do know that there were several fatalities inside of the warehouse. Deaths include several staff members that worked in the warehouse, members of the Hawthorne Fire department and Police department. No official number of fatalities have been confirmed. The Centers for Disease Control and Prevention has released the following statement: CDC teams have been deployed from the CDC Emergency Operations Center and activated at level 1, its highest level, because of the significance of this outbreak." He then paused for a few seconds, kept a serious look and continued. "I'm sorry…I am being told by my producers that people who get sick from this virus will quickly show symptoms of the common cold and/or flu. Symptoms include sneezing, coughing, runny nose, headaches, faintness and vomiting. If you show any of these symptoms it is urged for you to get to the hospital immediately. Call 911 or have someone transport you. Otherwise, stay indoors, close all your windows, lock all your doors and seal anything where air might seep through such as door cracks. Christ," he said and paused again with a disconcerted look. "I'm sorry, please hold … I'm getting reports …people that ill are violently attacking one another."

Cindy clasped her hands in prayer as she listened. Kari darted out from the conference room back to her desk. She dialed Mike with her office phone, but he didn't answer. A few of her coworkers stormed out the office while others heeded Dan

Moray's advice of staying inside. Kari's heart began to race, and she feared the worst. *Oh God baby please pick up*, she thought while holding the phone as it rang. Again, she redialed and sent him a text. She went online and searched for more information. She clicked on a video of another news report and turned up the volume on the monitor speakers. She listened to the anchor reporting live updates as they came in. Reports of people savagely attacking one another possibly due to the airborne virus sent chills down her spine that stood the hairs on the back of her neck. She constantly glanced over at her phone hoping to get a call or text back from Mike. *Maybe he's busy checking cargo and can't get to the phone,* she thought. She gave herself several reasons as to why Mike didn't respond. She reassured herself that he was busy with work and couldn't get to the phone, but her nerves were uneasy and dreadful thoughts crept in.

Mike and James hurriedly ran back to the van to evacuate the building. As they opened the doors, they heard noise coming from inside the ambulance parked on the side of the warehouse. They gave each other a nod to inspect and drew their weapons. They cautiously approached the back of the ambulance which still had its emergency warning lights on. Mike grabbed the door handle while James stood ready with his gun pointed at the door. As Mike turned the handle and flung the door open, a voice from inside shouted, "NO! NO! Don't shoot, please! I'm not one of them!"

Paramedic Melendez fearfully cried out. "I'm not infected," he said with both hands raised. He sat at the back of the ambulance dressed down to his white undershirt and black pants. His blood-stained uniform shirt laid on top the gurney beside him.

"What are you doing in here?" Mike asked with his weapon fixed on the paramedic.

With a trembling voice, paramedic Melendez went over the entire ordeal upon his arrival and shared the horrifying events that he witnessed, including the death and revival of his partner. James and Mike went back and forth with questions trying to piece it all together.

"After the cops started attacking their own partner, I ran the hell out of there and locked myself in here. I was about to leave when I heard you guys pull up, so I stayed inside until the coast was clear," Paramedic Melendez explained.

"Well we're glad you got out of their in one piece," James said. "But it's not a good idea for you to stick around here. I got a bad feeling this area is going to be crawling with military chemical biological defense units and anyone found here will be taken in for testing. We're not sticking around to be used as lab rats so we're rolling out, I suggest you do the same."

James was interrupted by the sound of a helicopter that quickly approached overhead. The three men looked up and saw a red helicopter fly over the building. It was part of the local news station who got word of the incident. They were the first reporters to arrive and film the plume of smoke flowing out of the warehouse.

"We better get out of here now," James said. "Before we become part of the evening news."

They helped the paramedic down as he stepped out of the ambulance. "Go back to the hospital and get checked," Mike said.

A red news van from the same station was also dispatched with three crew members inside, news reporter Carolyn Zhen and her film crew. The red van was pulling into the back of the warehouse as Mike and James jumped in their van to leave the area.

Carolyn quickly stepped out with microphone in hand and watched as James drove off following behind Paramedic Melendez. Her film crew stepped out of the van and recorded outside of the warehouse before going inside.

A few blocks away from the warehouse, traffic was at a halt due to an accident involving three cars and a city transportation bus. Paramedic Melendez turned on the sirens and maneuvered through traffic followed by James at the wheel with Mike riding shotgun. At the scene of the accident, they found a city transportation bus flipped over on its side and three severely damaged vehicles faced oncoming traffic. Paramedic Melendez pulled over to check for injuries. Mike and James equally concerned for the people that were in the accident hopped out of the van and rushed over to the bus to help those in need of assistance. The front window on the bus was completely shattered and the bus driver, an African American male, who was still buckled in his seat, bled from an open head injury. James made his way inside and walked on top of shattered glass that crunched with every step. He tapped the bus driver on the shoulder, but the bus driver was unresponsive. He reached over and felt his neck for a pulse. As he looked down, he uncovered the side of his neck was gravely torn as if bitten by an animal. James was reminded of the people in the warehouse and the story that paramedic Melendez was recounting moments ago.

Towards the back, a shadow emerged from behind a seat. As it started moving toward James, the shadowy figure slowly came into focus. Coming into the light was an old woman wearing a long brown coat with blood stains; her eyes were white, skin was pale, hair was frizzy, and she had blood smeared all over her face.

"Ma' am, are you hurt?' James called out.

Right after he called out for her, six other shadows popped up from behind the seats at the back of the bus and they started crawling toward James.

"Mike, get out, now," James told his partner and drew his weapon holding it to his side as Mike exited the bus. James slowly raised his weapon.

The old woman rushed toward him and James let out a round, shooting her directly in between the eyes. She flew back as the bullet pierced through her skull and came out through the back.

Blood and small pieces of brain splattered across the windows and seats. The loud shot echoed in the bus. The other six people furiously crawled over the seats to get to James. James turned around and made his way out of the bus. As he moved forward, he was grabbed by the ankle and fiercely pulled back inside. The bus driver had come back to life and moaned aggressively as he pulled James by the leg and forcefully grabbed him by the belt. A shot rang out and James was able to get free. Mike had shot the bus driver from outside of the bus. He steadily aimed his weapon toward the people coming out from behind the bus. Paramedic Melendez ran over after hearing the shots.

"Oh my God, them too?" Melendez said. "But how?"

"My guess after seeing these people with the same symptoms as the ones at the warehouse — this disease is quickly spreading," James replied.

Mike thought of his fiancé at that moment. Just as he reached in his pocket to call her, he got attacked from behind. The attacker, a recent deceased blonde woman in her mid-twenties who died after flying through the windshield of her car during the accident and landing onto the concrete face first, grabbed Mike from behind. He quickly flung her over. The girl struggled to get to her feet, but Mike held her down with an elbow lock and knee pressed against her head. The six undead people inside the bus were heard inching closer.

"What of the people in the other cars, what's their condition?" James asked paramedic Melendez while helping Mike restrain the girl.

"Well she's one of them," paramedic Melendez said pointing down at the girl Mike was holding down. "She was in that the blue Mercedes. Technically she should be dead. I checked her for a pulse and she had none. The minivan there has three people in it who need to be rushed to the hospital. I saw some minor injuries on two kids and the driver, a woman, has a possible broken arm and legs. And that other car there- the black charger, I didn't see anyone inside, but I did see a lot of blood in the driver's seat."

"Okay, I'm going to back the van up to block off the entrance to the bus and trap the sick people inside. Mike throw her inside the bus while I'm backing it up."

James ran to the van and hurriedly backed it up leaving tread marks on the street from burning tire. Mike held the girl in a bear hug and lifted her up while she kicked and screamed. He threw her inside the bus just as James backed up the van to seal off the front window entrance to the bus. Mike and James then helped Paramedic Melendez get the injured people into the ambulance. The woman, a mother of two boys ages seven and nine, suffered from a broken left leg and arm. They pried open her door without much exertion and removed her from the seat. They carefully lifted her onto the gurney. Her two children who were sitting in the back seat only suffered minor bruises. They sat in the back of the ambulance along with their mother as Paramedic Melendez rushed off to the nearest hospital. News reporters and camera crews arrived at the scene and recorded the incident. The news reporter interviewed a few bystanders. Eyewitnesses shared their stories and gave similar accounts of people walking away from the accident with broken limbs. They saw some of the injured attack innocent bystanders who tried to help.

"We called the police long time ago and they still ain't came," said a woman being interviewed. She wore a vibrant purple head bandana and dirty gray sweats. "Bet if we were in Beverly Hills they woulda' sent the whole damn army."

During the time of the accident, the Hawthorne Police department had received several calls of people being attacked from around that area. Stupefied onlookers claimed to have witnessed two men in uniform violently chuck a woman into a bus and shoot the bus driver.

A police cruiser nearby got the call and quickly arrived with blaring sirens. The officers jumped out of their vehicle and ordered Mike and James to put down their weapons. "Turn around!" ordered officer Franks from behind his door with his gun pointed at Mike. His partner officer Henley had his gun pointed at James. "Put your hands on your head and slowly walk backwards." Both men complied and took five steps back. "Lie face down on the ground and cross your legs!" ordered officer Franks as he cautiously approached Mike and James. Mike tried to explain the situation to the officer as officer Franks placed handcuffs on his wrist. As the officer grabbed Mikes other arm to slap the other cuff on, he looked up and saw a young man wearing a black hoodie with blood stains limp toward him. His shin bone was broken and pierced out of his leg. He hobbled toward the officer and showed no signs of pain from his broken bone. "Hey, hey stop," ordered officer Franks. Mike warned the officer and told him to shoot and aim for the head. "You've been in an accident and you need to lay down," said officer Frank. The young man reached for the officer's hand. Officer Franks stretched out his hand to assist when the young man pulled him close and sunk his teeth into his forearm. "Son of a bitch!" yelled the officer and shoved him off. His partner quickly pulled out his baton and struck the undead young man across the head with it. "Shoot him!" yelled James. The young man fell to the ground and officer Franks whaled in pain as blood poured from his arm. His partner took a knee beside him and radioed for back up. The young man stood back up and pounced on officer Henley. He fell on top of the officer and ripped out his throat. James and Mike got up from the ground. Mike grabbed officer Franks' gun and shot the undead young man point blank in the forehead.

Stay clear from him," Mike warned officer Franks as he pointed with his eyes to officer Henley who had his throat ripped out.

"The hell you say?!" the officer yelled back in disbelief as he applied pressure on his forearm. He crouched next to officer Henley who stopped breathing.

"Officer down, officer needs assistance," cried officer Franks into his radio. Officer Henley's eyes regained conscious and opened his eyes. "Yes, stay with me Henley, come on partner, stay strong, help is on the way," he told his partner in a soothing voice while tightly holding his hand. "No officer," shouted James. "Get back!" Henley then savagely bit deep into his partner's neck tearing off a large portion of flesh. Officer Franks loudly shrieked in pain. Mike and James got up to help when they stopped and noticed their van moving forward. The ravenous undead inside the bus, roused by the commotion incited them to push the van forward.

James pulled Mike, "there's too many of them, let's go."

"What about the officer?" Mike asked.

"It's too late for him, we can't do anything to save him. He's already gone."

"Then let's get moving and find Kari."

James jumped in the driver's side of the police cruiser and Mike sat in the passenger seat and buckled up.

Five miles from the bus accident close to central Los Angeles, a black Prius pulled up next to Fred who was running along the sidewalk.

"Get in! Get in!" Hector shouted at Fred from inside the black Prius.

"Oh fuck am I glad to see you," said Fred with relief as he jumped in the passenger seat of his supervisors car. "This virus is spreading. I saw an old lady on the bus coughing and shit, I got the hell out of there. People all around me getting sick. Some homeless guy came up and tried to grab me. Fucking bum. Luckily, I shook him off. Wait what's up with you? I thought you were still in the warehouse waiting for the fire department?"

"Fuck that! As soon as I saw those chicks from the office getting worse I got in my car and got the hell out of there. I wasn't waiting around to be their lunch. I told them to leave the building but nooo they wanted to stick around and be nosy, well look at them now. Wait what about you? Are you feeling sick?"

"No! Are you?!" Fred answered back holding the door handle ready to jump out.

"I'm not the one breathing heavy."

"Well yeah I've been running since the fucking warehouse back there, I'm tired."

"Well, I feel fine myself so I guess we're not infected. Do you live close?"

"A couple blocks up. By the corner of Gage and Vermont. It's a white apartment building on the corner. And you?"

"An apartment in H.P. I took the streets because the freeways are packed right now. Well, you're on the way there so I can give you a lift if you want?"

"Yeah please, thanks. You live with your wife or kids?"

"No, I'm single. No kids. Just me. You?"

"With my mom and little sister. I hope they're okay."

"Have you called them?"

"No. We don't have a house phone and my mom doesn't have any minutes left on her phone. I haven't been able to add any-not 'til my next paycheck."

"Damn. Well, I'm sure they're okay Fred. We'll get there soon. I'll take the small streets to avoid traffic. Just keep an eye out for any of these crazy fuckers trying to run up on us."

As they drove through the small streets, they saw neighborhoods look like war zones. Cars were on fire and people lay dead on their lawn or on the street. Hector had to jump the curve to avoid stalled cars and bodies in the middle of the road. He nearly hit people that were running and screaming down the street. Hector made sure all the doors were locked and the windows raised. He stepped on the gas pedal, careful to not hit any pedestrians. As he maneuvered through, the situation got worse and gun shots were heard throughout the neighborhood. He drove faster and flew past some of the stop signs. After twenty minutes of driving through residential streets, they safely pulled up to

Fred's four-story apartment building. Both men surveyed the area looking for any suspicious behavior or people acting out of the norm. Although it was Los Angeles, in which nothing is the norm unless you live there to know what normal is, out of the norm on that day would be someone devouring another human being.

"Coast looks clear. Hey, good luck and I hope your family is okay."

"Thanks Hector, appreciate the ride. What are you about to do?"

"Go home, lock my doors, watch the news and wait for things to sort out."

"Be safe and good luck to you too. See ya'."

Fred firmly shook his hand before exiting the car and quickly walked inside the building. The apartment building had poor lighting due to the burned out light bulbs which darkened the hallways that smelled of stagnant must. The burgundy carpet was timeworn and dirty with black spots of old and dried up chewing gum. The old, black gated elevator that smelled of urine was out of order and had been for several weeks. Fred ran up the stairs that cracked with every step he took. On top of the stairwell on the third floor of where he stayed, Fred caught his breath. He saw a shadowy figure standing in front of the doorway to his apartment and he grew concerned. He silenced his heavy breathing and approached the door with stealth. The door was open and the hallway was empty. "Hello?" He called out in a low voice that didn't carry over far enough for anyone to hear. He immediately rushed inside his apartment.

"Mooommm? Maddie!!" he yelled out from the living room. He heard the pitter-patter of tiny feet coming from his bedroom then loud thumping footsteps coming from his mother's bedroom. He turned around and saw his ailing mother standing underneath the doorway to her bedroom.

"Mom, where's Maddie?"

She wore a white nightgown that was covered in brown vomit and held a blank expression. Her eyes were white, and skin turned pale. She staggered toward her son with an aggressive groan.

"Oh no, mom, not you too. Ma' where's Maddie?" Fred pleaded. "Mom, please stop. Where's Madeline?! Your daughter! MOOMMM!!"

She instantly attacked Fred, grabbing him by the shoulders while trying to bite him on the neck. She pushed him up against the living room wall breaking the glass on a picture frame holding a family picture that was taken during one of Fred's birthday parties in the apartment. Fred held her off and they spun around the living room knocking over picture frames and furniture. With the front door to the apartment still open, Fred seized the opportunity and shoved her out, slammed the door, and secured the chain on the door lock. She banged and clawed on the door while Fred leaned on it as tears rolled down his cheeks.

"Maddie!" Fred screamed in desperation as he walked toward the bedroom hallway. "Maddie it's me, Freddy. It's okay to come out, mommy won't hurt you. Maddie are you in here?"

He got startled by a strange noise coming from inside his closet and he slowly made his way towards it. He nervously stood in front of the closet door and wiped his sweaty palms against his shirt before reaching for the door knob. He pressed his ear against the door and firmly gripped the door knob. "Maddie? Are you in here?" he asked. He slowly turned the knob and opened the door with caution. He looked down and saw me sitting on the floor, tightly holding my teddy bear. I looked up at Fred with tears in my eyes and asked if Mommy was still mad at me.

As I reflect back to that moment, I remember nervously sitting inside that closet, hoping that she wouldn't find me. I didn't know exactly what happened to my mother, but I knew she wasn't behaving like normal and I was extremely terrified of her. I was shaking, tightly hugging my teddy. When Fred opened the door, I stared up at him with fear in my eyes, and he replied, "oh sweetie, no mommy isn't mad." He picked me up and said, "she's just really sick right now. But she's not mad at you. Mommy loves you very much. Are you okay though? Did she hurt you?"

"She tried to bite me but I ran away and hid in your closet," I replied.

"You're safe now honey, Mommy won't hurt you, don't be scared. I'll make sure nothing ever happens to you."

"Promise?"

"I promise. Maddie, do you feel sick?"

"No, I'm just really scared."

"Okay sweetie. Don't be scared, I got you."

The banging on the apartment door grew louder and relentless. The battering had attracted several neighbors who had suffered the same fate as our mother. A horde of undead, tenants of the third floor, crowded around the apartment door and hammered away at it. Fred put me down and brought down a shoe box from the closet's top shelf. In it was a handgun wrapped in a black bandana and a small box of bullets. He quickly loaded the gun and checked the front door. The battering at the door was nonstop and the pieces of wood began to crack. Fred tip toed to the living room and pushed the sofa against the door to block the entrance. As he backed away, the first door lock came undone and the screws fell to the floor. The only thing holding the door was the chain which would give way once they broke down the door frame. He ran back inside the bedroom and blocked his bedroom door with his heavy wooden five-drawer chest.

"Listen Maddie we're going to play another game. We're going to hide in the closet and stay quiet. It's going to get very loud, but I need you to stay very quiet no matter what you hear.

Whoever stays the quietest wins. Quiet like a mouse. Can you do that for me?" he said.

"Yes," I said and nodded.

"Ok good, the game starts now so shhh."

We silently sat still and listened to the loud pounding coming from the living room. I jumped and blinked at every blow. The door frame cracked as the nails came undone. We heard wood breaking apart and the door lock chain swung back and forth knocking against the door. Then, we heard the growling get louder. They broke through and the only thing holding them back was the sofa. As they pushed the broken door down we heard the sofa inch back and bodies fall over it. Next, we heard booming footsteps, one after the other running all through the apartment. Their growls and raging moans were terrifying. The footsteps got louder as more of them poured in. Fred gripped the gun with a trembly hand. He struggled to keep calm and not show fear so that I wouldn't be afraid of what was going on outside. He held me tight, "shhh quiet like a mouse," he whispered. Footsteps were heard spreading throughout the apartment and finally into the hallway outside of the bedroom. The heavy breathing that came from the hallway terrorized us as we wished for them to disappear. The undead paced back and forth from the living room to our mother's bedroom. They bumped into the bedroom door which startled me and I let out a soft cry that they heard. The door knob then fiercely twisted followed by heavy pounding. Fred quickly emptied out his storage drawer that he kept in his closet. He threw out the towels and shirts that he kept in it. He then stood me up and said, "you're going to hide in here and I'll sit on top and hide behind the clothes. I hesitated for a moment, but we had no choice and agreed. I was small enough to fit in one drawer, so he put me down on the bottom one. He then pushed it toward the back behind his clothes and he sat on top, tucking his legs in. He put as many of his hung clothes in front of him, so he wouldn't be visible. A moment later the horde broke in and the drawer that blocked their path was pushed aside. They stormed into the bedroom looking for us and walked back and forth. I heard one of them stand in front of the closet door. It never opened or turned the door knob, it just stood there without moving. Seconds later it walked out and the other undead followed it out. Until this day I believe that whoever stood in front of the door and led them out was my mother. At least, I'd like to think so.

After seven minutes of silence Fred decided to check if they were gone. He whispered to sit quiet while he went out to check. He gently opened the closet door and found his room empty. The drawer was pushed behind the broken bedroom door and he could see an empty hallway. He stepped out from the closet and tip toed to the broken door. From inside his bedroom, he poked his head out and saw the living room empty. He took one step out into the hallway with the other foot still inside and leaned out to see if anyone was outside the apartment in the hall. He didn't see anyone or heard anything. He slowly tip toed to the front door and poked his head out again. He looked left, then right and saw an empty hallway. He ran back to the closet and pulled me out. "Time to go he said," as he carried me in his arms. "Where are we going?" I asked. "Somewhere safe," he replied. We softly made our way downstairs. Step by step and holding me close, Fred carefully walked down the carpeted stairs that emitted a squeaky loud noise.

In the hallway of the second floor, an undead tenant walked back and forth from one end of the hallway to the other when his attention was turned to the squeaky stairs above. The undead man with a hairy chest covered in blood, plodded towards the stairwell. Fred took a step back up applying a small amount of pressure on his foot so he wouldn't make a sound. The undead tenant trotted past the stairwell to the end of the hallway and Fred seized the chance. Fred quickly went down the stairs, and as he turned the corner of the second-floor, the top step let out an echoing creaky sound that caught the undead tenant's attention. The two made eye contact. Fred immediately raced down the stairs with me in tow. The tenant growled and gave chase. Fred reached the front door of the apartment building, turned around, pointed his gun sideways and shot the hairy chested undead tenant in the forehead. His head nearly exploded like a watermelon as it fell back. I screamed in horror. That was the first time I ever saw someone die, but it wouldn't be the last. Fred then opened the front door and we saw our neighborhood in total chaos. We saw people lying dead in the middle of the street. Neighboring houses were lit on fire, and gun shots rang from every direction.

Fred ran across the street to his drug dealer's house in hopes of seeking refuge. It was an old house made with cedar siding that was rotting. Its white paint peeled around the edges and the frame below the front windows were infested with termites. It had a pitchforked roof and a porch. All the windows around the house had black security bars and a security front door.

Fred banged on the door, "Open up, please!" he said loudly with panic in his voice. A tall thin black man with dreadlocks wearing a gas mask opened the door and pointed a sawed-off shotgun in Fred's face.

In downtown, Robbie caught up to his friends who were banging on the locked glass doors and pleading with the three security guards on the other side of the doors to let them inside. The security guards kept waving them away. Robbie called his sister Linda, the receptionist, to let her know that they were out front and weren't allowed inside. She instructed him to go around back behind the alley where she'd meet him at the emergency exit door. "Come on guys, my sister will let us in through the back," Robbie said in a low voice.

A man, who also tried getting in, stood close by the doors and overheard Robbie. He followed the group of teens and kept a far distance as to go unnoticed. Robbie went through the narrow alley and came to the door. He knocked three times and the door slowly opened. His sister, who had a security badge around her neck which gave her access to the building, smiled with relief and tightly hugged her little brother. Linda had taken on the role of his mother after their parents died in a car accident four years ago. It was date night and they were heading home after leaving a restaurant when a drunk driver took the red light and slammed into them. They died on the way to the hospital, but the drunk driver lived and only suffered a broken wrist with minor bruises. He was found guilty of intoxication manslaughter and was sentenced to thirteen years in prison.

Linda held the door open for Robbie and his friends as they hurried in. Flaco was the last to rush in. Just as the door was about to close, the man who had followed them, dashed toward the door and slipped his fingers through, catching it before it shut. He held it for a few seconds before gently opening it and poking his head in. Linda and the teens were gone, and the man stepped inside. He examined the hallway and looked up the emergency staircase which went up for several floors. The man who had a murderous look in his eyes was Chris, and he was making his way up the flight of stairs to Kari's floor.

Robbie spoke to Linda in a soft voice and told her about the horrifying events that he and his friends went through. His lip quivered, and he covered his face to hide his tears. "Henry's dead," he muttered. "He died in my arms and there was nothing I could do for him. I just left him." Linda held him as he cried into her shoulder. Sheena placed her hand on his back. "I'm so sorry about Henry," Linda said. "There was nothing more that you could have done for him. You had to leave. You had no choice, or you would have ended up like one of them too."

He wiped his tears and took deep breaths. "You're right," he said. "I'm glad you're okay sis."

"So what's the story here?" Joey asked.

"After the news broadcast, security decided to lock this place down. To keep everyone safe. They aren't letting people inside because of the virus."

"Are they letting anyone out?"

"Yes, we can leave if we choose to, but we can't come back in."

"Okay… well I told my friends that we could catch a ride with you back to our house," Robbie said.

"Of course," Linda replied.

"Oh my god, are you okay?" Linda asked Lily after she noticed the gash on her leg.

"Yeah I'm alright, just hurts a little. Fell off a bike trying to get here," Lily explained.

"Come on follow me, we have a small first aid kit in the break room behind the cafeteria," Linda said and helped her along.

"We'll get you cleaned up and wrap your leg. Then we can all leave."

On the eleventh floor, Kari sat at her desk and dialed Mikes phone again. He picked up on the third ring.

"Hello, honey?" Mike answered.

"Oh thank God. I've been trying to call you Mike. Are you okay?"

"Yes I'm fine love, are you okay? Do you feel sick? Do you have a fever? Cold? Or any of those symptoms?"

"No, I feel fine I'm just really scared Mike. Have you heard the news about the virus that's going around? They say it started at a warehouse in Hawthorne and I feared that you might have gone there. Where are you?"

"I'm in a police car right now, James is driving and we're on our way to you. There's a lot of traffic but we'll try and get there as soon as we can."

"A police car?! What are you doing in a police car? Are you under arrest or something?"

"Honey it's a long story. I'll explain later when I see you. I'm just glad that you're okay... Hello? You there?"

Kari stood up from her chair and noticed that her coworkers were coughing and sneezing. She grew worried that the virus had made its way to their office.

"Mike, there's something wrong here. Everyone's showing signs of the illness."

"Oh no, it's happening."

"I don't feel safe here. I'm getting out of here."

"But it's dangerous to go outside."

"Then I'll find some place to hide and wait for you. There's a janitor's closet down the hallway on the eleventh floor that's kept unlocked sometimes. I'll wait for you there."

"Yes, that's good. Take the phone with you and lock the door. I'll call you when I'm in the building."

"Okay, I'm going now. Please be safe."

"Okay honey, I'll be there as soon as I can. I love you."

Mike grew worried, and James could tell. James swerved through traffic with the sirens wailing. He would jump on the curve then swerve back into traffic when it was moving and floor it.

"Kari said people in the office look sick," Mike told James with a worried look. "We have to get to her before, before…"

James cut him off, "Don't worry, Kari's a tough girl and she's smart. We'll get there okay. Hang tight. Is she okay though?" James asked steering the wheel with both hands and a concentrated look. His eyes were wide open as he scanned the roads and checked his blind spots.

"Yeah, she's fine. She said she's going to hide and wait for us," Mike said hanging on to the ceiling grab handle.

CHAPTER 6

"Who the fuck is you!?" screamed a thin man with dreadlocks wearing a gas mask followed by the sliding motion of the pump on the shotgun he held at Fred's face. Fred stared down the double-barreled shotgun, "I'm Freddy, I buy from snails, I live across the street," he quickly replied. "My building is full of, of, of whatever the fuck those people are. I need help, please let us in."

"Shoot that motherfucker already and close the God damn door slim!" yelled another man from inside the house.

"Snails, that you? It's me, Freddy, from across the street. Let us in man please, I have my little sister with me."

"Step off this porch or I'll blow you the fuck off," the dreadlock man said in a fierce tone.

"We have nowhere to go, I'm begging you, please."

"You got five seconds motherfucka. Five… four … three…"

"I'm a loyal customer Snails. If I die out here, like a lot of these people out here, you won't have any customers left alive to buy from you.

The window curtain was pulled to the side and quickly shut closed.

"Let 'em in Slim," ordered the man from inside.

Fred rushed in with me in his arms. Slim, the tall man with dreadlocks, shut the door close behind us and secured all five locks on the door. Fred stood in the living room in front of a dark skinned, obese black man who sat on a worn down blue couch. He had big puffy cheeks, and small, narrow and obstructed eyes. By his looks, he seemed to have weighed almost three hundred pounds. His fat fingers, or sausage fingers as the kids at his elementary school would tease, held a gun rested on his lap. Eddy, or 'Snails' as he was called by, grew up in the same neighborhood as Fred. Both attended the same elementary school all the way up to high school, but never really were friends. They just knew of one another and said an occasional hello or nod whenever they would pass each other by. Fred hung out with the Hispanic gangsters, or bald headed cholos as they're often referred as and Snails hung out with the Crips and drug dealers. It wasn't until after high school that Fred started buying weed from Snails, ever since most of his gangster friends got arrested for dealing drugs in addition to other crimes.

"What up Freddy," said Snails. "It's the end of the world and you tryna' to get high?"

"Nah man, my building is filled with those... sick people. My mom, she uh, she ..."

"She's one of them," Snails interjected and nodded at the TV that showed live news coverage of people in the city attacking and eating one another.

"Yeah," Fred answered with watery eyes.

"My uncle Charles too," said Snails. "Tried to bite me. Slim here pushed him off me. I had to put him down. We took him out in the backyard. Take a seat, you're safe here. I got security bars on every window and security doors, front and back. They ain't getting in and if they do, we got something for they ass, right slim?"

"Fuckin' right," Slim replied holding up the shotgun with his right hand and an AK-47 with the left.

"Damn you got an AK?" Fred asked Snails.

"Yeah, got it from my connect last week. Dude hooked me up. Got some more handguns in the back too. I was gonna' sell them. But with all this crazy shit going on, looks like we may end up using them."

I sat on Fred's lap and kept staring over at Slim who was still wearing the gas mask. It freaked me out.

"This your little sis huh?" asked Snails.

"Yeah, this is Maddie. Say hello Maddie." I was scared of Slim and buried my face into Fred's chest.

"I think you scaring her with that mask Slim," joked Snails.

"Well, I ain't taking it off. They said the virus is airborne and if it is, I ain't getting sick as long as I'm wearing this," Slim asserted.

"Don't worry Maddie, he's uglier without the mask anyway so it's better if he keeps it on," Snails jokingly said. "Sorry about your mom. She seemed like a nice lady."

"Thanks. Sorry about your uncle. He was cool. He was funny and pretty smart," Fred remarked.

"Uncle Charles was something else boy. Yeah, he was smart. Always preaching about something. He's got a whole bunch of books in his room. The only reason he would turn on his TV in the room was to watch the news. You know he has stacks of dirty magazines?"

"Like porn magazines?"

"Yes, porno magazines. Who the fuck buys porno magazines these days? I asked him too, 'Unc, why do you still buy that shit when you can just go online and watch as much porn as you want for free? This ain't the nineties. He would say, 'cuz of the stories, they're fun to read and fun to imagine. I like reading. That's what's wrong with you damn kids these days, you don't read shit anymore. Don't educate your mind anymore. All you do is go online and be on that social media shit all goddamn day and night and post shit that makes absolutely no contribution to the growth and expansion of your mind. Teenagers in high school these days are still struggling to read at a junior high level. Damn shame, damn shame,' he'd say. And he would go on and on about it. I think he was just trying to change the subject of why he had so many damn dirty magazines. For the stories," Snails sarcastically said and rolled his eyes with a smirk. "Yeah right. Then why are all the pages stuck together Unc? Ha, ha, ha."

His laughter was amusing to watch. Fred laughed but not at Snails' stories or jokes but at the way Snails laughed. It sounded like an obese child giggling. His gigantic belly would move in a wave-like motion every time he laughed.

"He was funny," Fred said.

"Uncle Charles was comedy, man. Always cracking jokes too and saying some dumb shit. He was family, but I didn't hesitate to put a bullet in his head. And I'll do the same if anyone else tries to attack me," Snails told Fred with a stern look.

Fred nodded his head with comprehension. The awkward silence that followed was cut by live breaking news and Snails turned up the volume with the remote. Reporter Carolyn Zhen stood across the street from the warehouse of where the airborne virus outbreak began. Fred attentively listened to the reporter as she gave an account of a young man that was mauled by a group of large women minutes earlier. The cameraman zoomed in on the young man who lied motionless on the street in a pool of blood. His skin dangled from his upper body and face and most of his flesh had been eaten through. Organs and intestines were stretched out from his ripped open belly. His hands lay motionless at his side and then his fingers twitched. "Y'all see that?" asked Slim focusing in on the dead man. The man's head jerked and within seconds he sat up. He looked around and saw the camera man. The camera man zoomed in on the undead man's face. Fred along with everyone else in the living room gasped at the man's peeled off face and visible insides. The young man got up on his feet with all his organs and insides dangling, and rushed toward the cameraman. The cameraman recoiled in horror and ran backwards filming the incident. He tripped on the curve and fell on his back with the camera facing up to the sky. The undead young man caught up to the cameraman and jumped on top of him. He pinned him down and savagely took a chunk out of his neck. The cameraman bellowed in agonizing pain and although he was out of view, the audio of him being eaten alive was disturbing and difficult to listen to.

A loud pounding on the front door startled everyone inside and they turned their heads toward the door in terror. Slim got up to inspect and slightly opened the window curtain.

"Holy fuck!" Slim cried softly. "The whole God damn block is outside Snails. Come here, look at this shit."

Moving as fast as he possibly could, Snails slid from right to left and gave himself a push off the couch and waddled to the window.

"Muthafucka! You invited the whole God damn block, Fred!? Look at this shit, the porch is full of these motherfuckers."

A horde of the undead crowded the front porch and banged on the door to try and break in.

"They must have seen him come in!" Slim exclaimed.

Fred apologized, "holy shit, my bad guys I didn't see anyone follow me," he said peeking out the window.

"Alright well, we're safe here. We got the security door with five locks and I got security bars on every window so they ain't breaking in," Snails said calmly reassuring everyone's safety.

The lower rusty bolts screwed into the front window security bar loosened from the banging and pulling. The wooden frame around the windows that were crawling with termites had softened the wood over time. The small group of undead grew into a massive one. They banged on the bars and pounded at the door. The bottom screws fell out and the security bar was being held on by the top screws which were coming undone. One of the undead punched through the window and shattered the glass. I shrieked loudly at seeing a person's bloody fist through the window and Fred quickly picked me up to calm me down.

"Dammit!" Slim angrily said holding the shotgun.

"My ass they ain't getting in Snails!" shouted Slim. "That bar is about to get yanked off any minute now and then they'll come crawling in- through that window."

"Fuck these rusty ass screws man shit! And Fuck you too Fred for leading them over here," Snails shouted pointing his weapon at him. "I ought to shoot your ass dead for this."

"Chill Snails," Slim interjected. "We might need his help bruh. We gotta' secure this window now!"

"Alright, alright. Let's board up the window using one of these bedroom doors and we can secure the rest of the windows with whatever wood we have in here."

Snails brought out a bag of tools he kept underneath the sink. They used a hammer to undo the bathroom door which they would use to board up the window. Fred hammered in the nails while Slim and Snails held up the door over the window.

"We need more nails," Fred said hammering in the final nail.

"That's the last one," said Snails. "There's more in the garage where my uncle keeps the rest of his tools. But I ain't going back there."

"Why not?" Fred asked.

"Cuz' the side gate is broken and they may have busted through and if they did bust through, they're probably in the back yard. And if they are in the backyard, as you can clearly see, I'm not fast enough to run away from them which is why my ass is not going back there. You are."

"Me? Why me? What about Slim?"

"Mothafucka' I'm guarding the door! That's why!" Slim shouted.

"You got this Freddy. Don't all you Mexicans play soccer anyway? I know you fast," Snails remarked.

"Just because I'm Mexican doesn't mean I play soccer. Okay yeah, I *played* soccer when I was a kid, but I'm not that fast anymore," Fred said shaking his head.

"Well we're not going to draw straws here Fred and the longer we sit here, the more time we give them to keep pounding and break their way in. You want your little sister to get eaten alive like that cameraman? We need those nails!"

Fred sighed and rolled his eyes, "Is the garage door unlocked?" he asked.

In the back of the house, next to the kitchen, Fred stood in front of the door, mentally and physically preparing himself. "It's a straight shot to the garage, 'bout fifty feet or so from this back door," Snails said. They both looked out the back window to check for signs of the undead.

"Okay coast is clear. You ready?" Snails asked.

"No," Fred replied with a scared look.

"Okay good."

Snails opened the door, pushed Fred out and immediately locked the door. Fred instantly ran toward the garage at a speed he forgot he had. He opened the garage door and quickly shut the door behind him. He stood bent over, with his hands on his knees trying to catch his breath. *Warn me before you push me out like that, fat fuck,* he said to himself. As he stood at the door, he looked around the garage. It had one small window to the side, but it was still too dark to see. He turned the light switch on next to the door and made his way through the garage in search of longer nails. There were two tables toward the back of the wall with large power tools. Above the table were tools that hung from the wall and a shelf with tin cans and buckets. As he slowly walked toward the shelf, he tripped over a box next to a shovel and leaf rake that both fell over. The sound of the wooden handles hitting the concrete floor echoed through the garage. Fred squelched his face and froze. He stood quietly without moving a muscle and hoped that no one heard. He listened for any sounds but all was quiet. He proceeded toward the shelf and picked up the bucket looking for nails but it was filled with screws and bolts. He then grabbed the tin can. "Bingo," he said with a smile. The tin can was filled with nails. He walked back to the door with the tin can. He stopped at the door, took a deep breath and opened the door. Waiting for him on the other side was a stocky man whose face was covered in blood and his eyes were pale like his skin color. Fred got startled and dropped the can of nails. The stocky man grabbed Fred by the shoulders and lunged in to bite his throat. Both wrestled back and forth in the garage. They knocked over tools and bumped into the walls. Fred was overpowered by the man's superior strength. He was driven against the wall and knocked the hanging tools down. The sound of multiple wrenches hitting the floor made a loud noise that attracted five others of the undead that were by the front. They made their way through the side of the house. The hefty man pressed Fred against a workbench and inched closer to his throat. Fred desperately tried holding him back using all his strength. As he struggled off his back, he looked to his right and saw a long Phillips tip screwdriver on top of the workbench. He desperately tried reaching for it. He stretched his fingers out as far as he could and bumped the screw driver with his fingertips. He pushed the undead man up and slid his back toward the screw driver. The man got in closer to his neck. Fred gave one more stretch and with the tip of his fingers he rolled the screw driver toward him. The man had his mouth wide open and got close enough to Fred's throat that he could feel the man's cold breath on his neck. Fred picked up the screwdriver, roared in fury and ramed the screwdriver through the man's nostril up into his brain killing it as it dropped to the floor. "Fucker!" he yelled and kicked him in the head. He picked up the tin can and scooped up the nails scattered on the floor. He looked up and saw the undead approaching as they barged through the broken gate. Fred ran out the garage back to the house. One of the undead grabbed him by the arm and Fred kicked him off. Snails opened the door and fired his weapon as Fred rushed inside. Snails backed in and shut the door. "You got the nails?" he asked. "Barely," replied Fred holding up the tin can.

At the Insuracal building, Linda sat with Lily inside the break room and wrapped Lily's bruised leg while Robbie and his friends scoured through the cafeteria in search of food. Towards the back of the cafeteria, Joey found the lifeless body of a female cook lying on the red tile floor next to the freezer. She wore a white apron and black fishnet hair cap. He stared at her and examined her breathing, unsure if she was alive or dead. He bent down and shook her foot. She opened her eyes and the two stared at one another. Her bloodshot pale eyes filled Joey with terror and he slowly pulled back. She sat up and grabbed him by the arm. Joey yanked his arm and got free but she left deep scratch marks on his arm that bled. She got up and chased after him.

"Run!" Joey shouted as he hopped over the counter. They all met at the center of the cafeteria and ran toward the exit with Lily trailing behind. Joey fell back and threw Lily's arm over his shoulder. The undead cook lady leapt over the counter and ran after them groaning as she drew near. The group made their way up the emergency staircase while Joey and Lily followed behind. Her pace slowed them down and they were unable to keep up. Joey pushed the door open to the third level and ran down the hallway with Lily at his side while the others kept going up the stairs. At the other end of the hallway stood a man in a black suit and blue tie. His tattered suit was covered in blood and he growled fiercely at Joey. Joey opened an office door on his right and pulled Lily in. They ran through the small empty office toward the back and hid in the storage room. They locked the door behind them and turned off the lights. Joey felt dizzy and his breathing grew heavy. He sat and leaned against the wall frantically trying to catch his breath. Lily stood facing the door, quietly crying with hands in prayer held up to her lips. Several minutes went by without any sound coming from the office. They remained quiet inside the dark storage room.

"I think they stopped following us," she told Joey. "I don't hear anything. We should make a run for it. Do you think Sheena and the guys made it out? I bet they're hiding somewhere in the building. I know, I'll facetime her," Lily said and called Sheena. Joey's eyes were losing focus. The room was dark, and he could barely see Lily from the phone's glare. Her voice seemed distant. Joeys shirt was drenched in sweat and his breathing slowed down. His back rested against the wall but he kept losing balance. His eyes grew heavy. He blinked them open to try and stay awake. "She's not answering," Lily said in a shaky voice. "Oh God. Let me try calling my mom." The call kept ringing as Joey's body slowly slid down the wall and slumped over. The call went to her mother's voicemail. Lily wept as she held the phone, staring at the screen hoping for a text or call back. "Can you call your friend Robbie," she said through her tears. "I'll send Sheena a text."

Where are you? Lily's text message read as she hit send. The bright glare on Lily's phone cast Joey's shadow on the wall beside her. The shadow grew larger as he stood up and walked towards her. "Joey?" she called out looking up at the shadow. She felt his cold fingers on her shoulders and turned around. Joey's pale eyes stared back at her and he sunk his teeth into her throat and ripped out her flesh. Blood splattered on the wall as she screamed in agony. He forced her to the ground and gripped her by the head as she floundered on the floor.

Chris made his way through the long hallway in search of Kari and opened every door. He heard loud chaos coming from two doors down. He marched to the door and opened it. He found office personnel butchering one another. A woman held a man's internal organs and ate them. A man used a computer monitor to beat another man's head with it. He roared as he bashed it down on his head numerous times. The monitor cracked with every blow and blood spewed across the desk. Chris stepped in and checked every woman he saw that resembled Kari. People were running and others were fending off the undead and fighting for their life. Chris cautiously maneuvered through the chaotic office in search for Kari. An enraged woman with blood dripping down her mouth ran up on him. Chris pointed his gun and shot her point blank. He went through each isle reading the name tags on every cubicle. He found Kari's desk empty and stormed out back into the hallway. He dialed her phone.

At the other end of the hall, he heard a phone ring. The call was canceled after two rings, but he knew it came from inside the janitor's closet. He walked up to the door and grabbed the door handle when he was yanked by the arm. His attacker, an undead woman in her early forties wearing a pink top and black pants, fiercely held onto Chris and pulled him in close to her mouth. He grabbed her by the hair and flung across the wall. He picked her up and knocked her head against the wall repeatedly, chipping and breaking her teeth as her faced smashed against the wall. He slammed her head down onto the blue carpeted floor and stomped on her head until her brains splattered onto the carpet. He went back to the janitor's door and again was attacked from behind by another of the undead. Chris spun around, seized the undead man by his throat and pressed him against the wall. He held his gun under the undead man's chin, pointing it up toward its brain. He squeezed the trigger and blew a hole through the top of the man's head, covering the wall and ceiling with blood and pieces of brain. He walked back to the janitor's door and turned the handle. He heard more growls quickly approach behind him. He turned around and shot down two more. He looked around for any more would be attackers but didn't see any and redirected his attention to the janitor's closet and turned doorknob. He heard a low voice from inside call out, "Mike?"

From inside the janitor's closet, Kari unlocked the door and slowly cracked it open thinking that it was her fiancé Mike. She saw the gun through the small crack and smiled. "Thank God," she said and opened the door wide. She trembled. Her face turned to horror. In the blink of an eye, Kari's life flashed before her. She was taken back to the time when her father taught her how to ride a bike in their driveway when she lived in Texas; and to the day when Mike proposed to her on a gondola ride through the Huntington Harbour at sunset. Chris smiled at her, "found you," he said.

The next sound she heard was of a man who stood across the hallway and yelled out, "Chris!" At the other end of the hallway in front of the emergency exit door was Mike holding a fire ax. "MIKE!" Kari cried out looking over Chris's shoulder with tears rolling down her face. Mike charged at Chris with his ax. Chris' face grew red and furious. He stormed toward Mike. A small group of the undead stepped into the hallway and stood in between both men. The men took the fight out of the narrow hallway and into the office. Chris shot two down before running out of bullets. He used the butt of his gun as a hammer and smashed an undead over the head with it. At the other end, Mike buried his ax in one of the undead's forehead while kicking off another with his foot. The fight got pushed further inside the office toward the long windows that overlooked downtown. Chris fended off an undead using a chair as a barrier between him and the undead while Mike jumped on top of a desk and kicked a man across the face. He swung the ax down and struck the man on the top of his head. Chris slammed an undead woman's head into the corner of a desk then picked her up and threw her against the window. The glass shattered as she broke through and fell eleven flights. Her head splattered like a watermelon onto the sidewalk.

Other people in the office who hadn't caught the virus but were bitten by the undead began to turn. "MIKE!" Kari yelled out from inside the hallway as she struggled to hold off her undead co-worker. She kicked his legs out and hopped over him as he fell. He grabbed her by the ankle as she backed away. Mike jumped off the desk and ran back into the hallway. He swung his ax into the undead man's skull before he could take a bite into Kari. Suddenly, Mike got tackled from behind by Chris and was slammed up against the wall face first causing him to drop the ax. Temporarily dazed, Mike fell to his knees while Chris picked up the ax and swung it over his shoulder. Just as he swung the ax down to give Mike a blow to the head, an undead man jumped on top of Mike and got whacked on its back as Chris struck down. Chris furiously tried to dislodge the ax buried deep into the undead man's back so that he could strike Mike with it. He shook the handle side to side trying to wedge it out from the man's back who was on top of Mike trying to bite him. Mike laid on his side and was still in a daze. He tried to hold the undead man's head back who kept snapping its jaw like a starving animal. Chris stepped down on the undead man's back and yanked the ax out.

Just as he swung the ax over his head to strike again, Kari gave him a shove and knocked him off balance. Mike regained full conscious, rolled the undead man over and stomped its head in.

Chris took another swing, but Mike dodged the ax and tackled Chris, pushing him against the wall. Both men struggled for control of the ax and Mike head-butted Chris, breaking his nose which immediately started gushing blood. Chris was momentarily stunned and lost his grip of the ax. Mike snatched it from his hands and gripped the ax like a baseball bat. He swung the ax with all his might and missed by an inch as Chris ducked. The ax got stuck on the wall when an approaching undead from the other end grabbed a hold of Kari and opened its mouth wide to bite her in the neck. She threw him over her shoulder, a jiujitsu move she learned from Mike.

Chris immediately got up, grabbed the undead man by the head and rammed it into the wall. Mike managed to free the ax and swung it into the undead man's head almost striking Chris with it. Kari pointed to the horde of newly turned undead down the hall running toward them. "This way!" Kari yelled out and ran back into the office. Both men temporarily put their differences aside and closely ran behind Kari. Chris got in front and forcefully pushed an undead out of the way while Mike swung the ax over another undead woman's jaw. Kari led them into the mail room at the other end of the hallway which had an emergency door exit that led into the emergency staircase. The three entered the mail room and immediately shut the door behind them. Both men grunted as they put their weight on the door. Mike planted his feet and pushed with his back while Chris pressed forward with his arms using the weight of his chest. "Push!" yelled Mike as the undead pounded on the other side of the door. Kari got in between and helped to hold the door closed. Chris backed away from the door and Mike looked at him in disbelief. He couldn't believe he was about to leave them and slip out through the back door. Chris pulled a table away from the corner wall and slid it toward the door. "Kari step to the side and help me push this table to block the door," Chris said as he positioned himself to push the table against the door. "Mike, on three jump aside. Ready? One, two, three, go!" Chris pushed the heavy table against the door with Karis help and just as Mike got out the way, an undead man's arm slipped through the door and kept it from shutting close.

Chris and Kari kept pressing the table forward with all their strength. Mike picked up the ax and chopped the undead man's arm off. The bloody limb fell by his foot and the door shut. Mike pulled a metal file cabinet from the wall and pushed it against the table while Kari grabbed file boxes and stacked them on top of the table to add more weight to keep the door from getting pushed open.

"That should hold," said Chris as he placed another box on top of the table.

Mike took Kari in his arms and finally embraced his fiancé. He held her tight and she passionately kissed him while Chris stacked more boxes on the desk with a disgusted look.

"Are you okay? Are you hurt?" Mike asked as he examined her face with a soft touch.

"I'm fine," she replied in a trembly voice. "Just a bit shaken up with all of this. And him," she said and looked at Chris.

Mike approached Chris with a crazy look and ax in his hand.

"Try it mother fucker, come on," Chris said with his hands up ready to fight.

Kari got in between and diffused the situation by reminding them of the terror on the other side of the door.

"If we're getting out of here, we'll need each other's help. So please, let's not do this right now," Kari said pushing both men away from one another.

"Why'd you come here?" Mike demanded. "To hurt her?"

"If I wanted to hurt her why would I save her life back there you idiot?" Chris countered. "I'm here same reason as you are."

The pushing and pounding on the door amplified and Kari realized that they would soon push through.

"We need to leave now. Where's James?"

"He's downstairs helping others," Mike replied with his angered eyes fixed on Chris. "We had a long fight just to get up here. By the time we got to the front entrance, we found broken glass and blood everywhere. We had to kill the security guards who attacked us. They must have gotten infected somehow or by someone. Then we saw people running down the stairs to evacuate the building. James stayed behind to help them leave. I told him that I would come and get you and well… here I am. Now let's get out of here. No telling how many more of the infected are still inside the building so we have to move as fast as we can. Are you good to keep running?"

"Yes."

"Okay, are you ready?" he asked standing in front of the door exit.

"I'm ready," she replied and took in a deep breath.

"I'm ready too," Chris sarcastically said with a grin.

Mike rolled his eyes at him and pushed the door open. He grabbed Kari by the hand and they both made their way down the stairs with Chris close behind.

James patiently waited at the lobby when Mike and Kari came down the last steps.

"I knew you'd be okay," James told Kari as he greeted her with a hug.

"Mike told me what happened," Kari told James as they hugged. "Thank you for helping him get here."

"Of course, he's my brother. And who's this?" James asked.

"This is Chris," Mike answered at which point James aimed his weapon at him.

"It's okay partner, lower your weapon," Mike told James. "I'll take care of him later."

"HELP!" Screamed out Linda followed by gasping breath as she ran down the emergency staircase. He brother Robbie, Sheena and his friends were right behind her. Behind them was a horde of the undead chasing after them.

"Oh my God, Linda!" Kari cried out. "We have to help her."

James reloaded the shotgun he took from the police car and Mike stood next to him as he firmly gripped the ax while Chris and Kari stood behind them.

"Get down!" James shouted at Linda and the others as he pointed the shotgun toward the oncoming group of undead. He aimed and shot two down before pumping the shotgun and killing another. Mike swung his ax splitting one of the undead's skull in half. James and Mike held their ground in the middle of the lobby as they fought off the small pack of undead. Robbie and his friends joined in on the fight. Chris grabbed an undead and knocked her to the ground. Sheena used her bat and smashed an undead man's head open. Kari and Linda grabbed an undead woman by the hair and knocked her head against the reception counter repeatedly until she stopped moving. A few minutes later, the group finished killing off the last of the undead.

"You guys okay?" Mike asked as he pulled out the ax from an undead's forehead.

"Yes, thank you," Linda replied. Kari gave short introductions to Linda and her fiancé and Linda did the same with her brother and his friends.

"We were upstairs hiding in an office and heard over the radio that the military is here in the downtown Los Angeles area," Linda told the group. "Anyone looking for safety or medical assistance should make their way there. I think that's the safest place to be right now."

"I agree," said James. "Those helicopters we saw flying over us on our way here must have been the National Guard."

"Yeah, I think it's a good idea too," said Mike. "Let's go there. The streets are jammed up though. Seems like people are either trying to go there or evacuate the city, in either case, seeing as how traffic is really bad, driving is not an option. How far is the base?"

"It's about ten blocks from here. They set up at Grand Park," Robbie replied.

"Okay, we'll go with you guys. We'll stay close together but we all have to go quickly," James declared. "I'll take the lead, Mike, you guard the rear."

They prepared themselves for the short but dangerous journey. James led the group outside and just as he walked through the broken glass entrance door, an undead woman attacked him and bit his arm. James was caught by surprise, as the undead woman clamped down on his arm. Sheena screamed as Mike came around with the ax and hacked away at the undead woman's neck. He swung the ax again and chopped the undead woman's head off. It rolled toward Flaco stopping by his foot. He let out a frightful cry as he kicked it to the side. Linda and Kari tended to James' grave injury. His arm had a deep wound from the attack. They sat him down on the curve and used Jesse's belt as a tourniquet to stop the bleeding. James began to sweat.

"Come on partner hang in there," Mike told James. "You're going to be alright. Once we get to the base, they'll patch you up really good; so up on your feet Marine."

"I'm sorry brother, I'm not going to make it. I'll just put you all in danger."

"No James, we can get you to the base. You have to hang on," Kari pleaded.

"I'm sorry Kari, but it's only a matter of minutes before the virus spreads and shuts down my body. And then, well, I become one of them. I've seen it happen. I won't let myself hurt anyone of you."

"Guys we got to move!" Robbie shouted and pointed at the group of undead quickly approaching from down the street.

"They're coming!" Jesse shouted and pointed at another group of undead from inside the building.

"Go, get them to the base," James told Mike. "I'll hold them back for as long as I can."

"I can't leave you brother," Mike replied with watery eyes.

"I can feel it… I can feel it spreading all through me. Soon I'll be just like them and it'll be me trying to kill you. Having me around is far too dangerous. You have to go without me."

During their brief talk, Robbie had run to an abandoned yellow cab parked over the curb. He got in the driver's seat and drove it onto the sidewalk and parked it in front of the building entrance. He opened the gas cap and inserted one end of his bandana into the fuel tank and lit the other end on fire. "Let's go! It's going to blow!" Robbie shouted.

James and Mike hugged one last time. "I love you brother," Mike said squeezing James' hand. "Thank you for always having my back." James took a deep breath. "I love you too my brother. It was an honor to have fought along your side one more time. You take care of yourself and them." Kari teared up as she came over to say goodbye and gave James a quick hug and kiss on the cheek. Mike led the group off and they ran toward the military base while James walked the opposite direction toward the horde of undead down the street. Both men looked back at one another one last time before brushing off their emotions and getting back into the fight.

James made distance between him and the cab that was about to blow. He walked with the shotgun aimed at the crowd of undead and fired off three buckshot rounds before stopping to reload. Just as he loaded the last round, the yellow cab exploded and blew away several of the undead that were rushing out from inside the building. James kept firing until he ran out of shells. He swung the shotgun like a baseball bat with his good arm and knocked several of the undead over. He kicked, screamed and punched through the horde. He grabbed one and tossed it down and stomped its head in. Another undead grabbed him from behind and bit into his neck. Another undead man grabbed his arms and held on. He was overpowered by the massive body of the undead. They swarmed in on him like a group of killer bees.

In South L.A, Fred finished helping Snails and Slim board up the last window inside the deceased uncle's room. During their work, Fred noticed a small door above Uncle Charles' closet. *That small entrance probably leads to the attic,* Fred thought to himself.

"That should do it," said Slim hammering the last board.

"Hey Snails, if they don't give up and they keep trying to break in, is there a place where we can hide?" asked Fred.

"What'chu mean? They're not getting in. We just boarded up all the windows and reinforced the front door."

"I know, but I'm saying- what if? I mean, all that beating they're doing to the windows and doors, they just might break in. It's a lot of them out there and they keep multiplying."

"Stop trippin' Fred, they're not getting in. And if they somehow do get in, then we shoot them all down- okay?"

Fred stared at Slim with a blank expression and realized that Snails didn't really have a concrete backup plan. Before walking back to the living room, Fred examined Uncle Charles' room preparing a backup plan in his head, just in case.

"So what now?" asked Slim.

"I'm tired. So we sit here, quietly," said Snails getting comfortable on the sofa. "Maybe smoke some weed, watch the news for any updates and wait."

"I'm taking my sister into the room. Don't want her breathing this stuff in," Fred told Snails.

Fred grabbed me by the hand and led me into Uncle Charles' room and locked the door. "Sit here for a second little lady," he said and sat me down on the bed. He then picked up a chair and carefully placed it underneath the small door in the closet.

"Stay there Maddie. I'm just going to go up and take a quick look."

"No, don't leave," I said with a scared look.

"Oh no, I'm not going anywhere. I'm staying right here with you. I promise. I'm just going to take a look up into the attic. I'll be right here, really close, trust me."

He stepped up on the chair, pushed the small attic door open and pulled himself up. The empty attic had a low ceiling, filled with dust and spider webs. Across the attic was a small window, two feet above the old and dusty wooden floor. A thin stream of light shined through the gaps of the boarded window. *We can hide up here if we have to*, Fred thought to himself. *Maybe get up on the roof somehow and signal for help.* He climbed back down and put the chair back in its place. He then sat on the bed next to me and turned on the small TV. Local news channels only showed the emergency broadcast system alert with a rainbow-colored background. Other channels from cities like New York reported that the Governor of California had declared a state of emergency. He clicked through the channels and found another report of temporary shelters staffed with quarantine medical and public health officers from the CDC. He paid close attention finding a sense of hope and safety at the shelters mentioned in the news report.

A loud thumping noise was heard coming from the living room followed by shattered glass. Fred got up to investigate. "Stay here, do not come out understand?" he said.

"What's going on?!" Fred asked as he walked back into the living room. "Grab the AK underneath the sofa and get ready to shoot," said Snails while standing in front of the boarded-up living room window with his two guns pointed at the window.

"They tore down the security window bar and just broke the other window," Slim told Fred as he cocked back the AK-47 assault rifle and stood next to Snails. Fred rushed to get the weapon from underneath the sofa and pointed the gun. The banging on the boards grew fierce and the boards slowly started to inch off the window frame.

"The nails aren't holding!" screamed Fred.

"Well, why the fuck did you bring in these weak ass fuckin' nails you idiot!?" Snails yelled back.

"Hey fuck you man! Those were the only nails I found back there."

"Fuck me? Fuck you motherfucka!"

"Fuck you!"

Both men went back and forth exchanging insults before getting interrupted by Slim.

"Chill! Chill!" Slim yelled. "Look- the boards are coming off!"

Snails redirected his attention to the window and shot at it multiple times striking three of the undead on the other end of the wooden boards.

"That's not going to help," Fred told him. "You just made the board weaker by shooting at it. Now when more of them come, they're going to easily break through it and we don't have any more wood that we can use to board up the window."

Soon after more of the undead approached and started banging at the boards. Within seconds the board cracked and broke apart. All three men unloaded their weapons on the group of undead outside the window trying to push their way in. Several of the undead got struck in the head killing them for good, but others got hit on the torso and kept pushing through. Slim ran out of bullets and an undead girl jumped through the window, grabbing onto Slim's legs. Fred came around and used the end of his weapon to bash the undead girl's head. As he did, Fred had left the other side of the window unattended and let more of the undead hop and crawl in. He redirected his weapon at the undead inside and shot at them while Snails and Slim reloaded. As they reloaded, the group of undead multiplied outside and kept bashing at the windows.

An undead teenaged boy with facial skin dangling from the left corner of his chin jumped through the window and grabbed on to Snails' ankle and used it to pull himself inside. Snails shot at the undead teen but missed the head shot. The teen bit into Snails ankle which brought the heavy man down. The floor shook as Snails fell hard on his back. He let out a loud scream of pain with tears running down his eyes. The teen grabbed a hold of Snails' shirt and pulled himself on top of Snails' large belly. He bit into the gigantic flabby belly and tore out a large chunk of meat and fat. Slim yelled at Fred to help Snails as Slim kept firing his weapon. Fred pointed his weapon at the teen's head and pulled the trigger. Nothing was fired off. Fred ran out of bullets. The teen masticated and swallowed the meat as Snails lied helpless screaming in excruciating pain trying to push the teen off. Fred swung the weapon onto the teens head and bashed its brains in until it stopped moving. Having left the window unattended again to help Snails, more of the undead piled in. Slim kept firing but was unable to hold them all back by himself. Another female undead, a crack head that would always hang around the corner liquor store, crawled in and grabbed a hold of Slim. He kicked her off but another undead bit his inner thigh. Slim struck him with the weapon and knocked the undead off. He fired at them while backing away. He also ran out of bullets and decided to retreat. He limped toward the back, leaving Fred to fend for himself. Snails was passed out on the living room floor getting eaten by the horde of undead that had broken through the window. It would take a while before the group could get through their meal.

Seizing the opportunity to escape, Fred rushed inside Uncle Charles' bedroom, locked the door and pushed the wooden frame king sized bed towards the door to block the entrance. He picked up the chair again and placed it underneath the attic door inside the closet, stood on top and pushed the attic door open. He then picked me up from the bed as I cried hysterically with a stream of tears rolling down my cheeks.

"Calm down and listen to me," Fred said. "We're going to get out of here. We're going to go up into the attic. I'm going to put you inside first but you have to stay very quiet please."

"No, no, no, don't push me up there," I cried to him shaking with fear. He hugged me tightly and kissed me on the forehead.

"Trust me Maddie, I'm not leaving you. After I put you in the attic, I'm going to go up too, but you have to stay very quiet-shhh, shhh," he said with his finger to his lips. He wiped my tears and made a low shush to keep me from crying. Just then, the undead stormed past the living and furiously banged at the bedroom door. They heard my cries and the living room filled with the undead as they crawled in through the broken living room window. Fred picked me up and lifted me up into the attic. He then pulled himself up and closed the attic door. He crawled toward the boarded window with me walking next to him. The boards were old and eaten through by termites which made it easy to break off. Outside the window was a pitched roof that led towards the backyard. Fred broke off the small boards. He picked me up and carried me through the window and sat me down on the roof. "Do not move," he said with his upper body sticking out the window. He kicked his leg over through the window, but his jeans got stuck on a nail sticking out from the window frame. I pulled on his arm trying to help him come down. Above us, we heard the sound of whirling helicopter rotors get closer. Fred looked up and saw a military helicopter in the far distance. "Help! Help!" he yelled as he tried to set himself free.

He placed his hands down on the roof as he wiggled around and jerked his leg. As he kicked his leg back, his jeans came unhooked and he stumbled forward losing his balance. He tumbled down the side of the roof scraping his arms against the shingles. As he reached the edge, he pushed off the gutters and rolled to his side, stopping himself from going over. "Holy shit," he said to himself as he looked over the edge and saw a horde of the undead below with their hands raised up to grab him. He sighed and took a deep breath. The helicopter was only a few yards away now and quickly approaching. Fred scrambled back to his feet and went up the roof. He leaned forward occasionally using his finger tips for balance as he yelled up at the helicopter. "HELP!" he shouted at the top of his lungs. He waved his arms back and forth trying to catch their attention. The undead below moaned and growled louder as Fred shouted, but the helicopter flew right past us toward the downtown area. The undead below grew in numbers as Fred's shouting attracted more of them. He stood by the window, with me behind him, far away from the ledge. He hung his head and I could see the despair in his face. I wrapped my arm around his leg and leaned my head on it. He smiled at me and gently rubbed my shoulder.

Seconds later we heard another helicopter and saw one out in the distance. Fred picked me up, swung me over his head and sat me on his shoulders. "Look Maddie, a helicopter," he beamed and pointed. "Wave at it," he said and waved his arms wildly. "HELP!" he screamed out loud. The long beige transport helicopter that carried several Marines approached us and within minutes was hovering over us. A large gust of wind blew, and we squinted our eyes. The pilot talked over the speakers and ordered Fred to put up two fingers if he was not infected or bitten. Fred put up two fingers. "Now put up two fingers if the little girl is not infected or bitten," the pilot said. Again, Fred put up two fingers. A Marine in full desert camouflage combat gear opened the helicopters belly hatch and dropped a roped ladder. He placed one foot below the other as he climbed down the ladder. Fred and I looked up at him with our eyes squinted as the rotor blades spun above us. The Marine stepped onto the roof and gave Fred a quick inspection with a scanner that looked like a small tablet that was able to detect traces of the virus. I heard a beep and then he did the same with me all the while the Marines above kept their rifles aimed at Fred's head. The scanner beeped again and cleared us both.

"My name is Sergeant Mathers. Is she okay?" asked the Sergeant.

"Yes sir, we're fine. I'm so glad to see you," Fred said with a huge smile across his face. "Thank God you stopped for us."

"You're welcome. Is this your daughter?"

"No, she's my sister, Maddie."

"Hello Maddie, we're going to get you somewhere safe. Sir, please understand that we are on a completely different mission, one that does not include aiding civilians. But, we made an exemption and can take your sister to a safe place."

"You mean, you can take *us* to a safe place?"

"No, we cannot allow you onboard, I'm sorry. Only the child. You have to go back inside until help arrives."

"Until help arrives? You have arrived, what are you talking about?"

"Give me the child sir," the Sergeant said and reached for me.

"Get your hands off her!" Fred snapped back. The marines above had their scope on Fred ready to pull the trigger.

"Sir you have to understand, I'm all she has left. Our mother is dead, and it is swarming with them all around and inside the house. There is nowhere for me to hide and you know that help isn't going arrive. I will not leave her side. Please."

The Sergeant exhaled noisily. "Can you climb?" he asked.

"Yes," Fred replied with a grin.

"Alright then, let's go. You go first. My men will hoist you in. I'll hold your sister and follow as soon as you're onboard the chopper."

Fred climbed the roped ladder and was pulled up by the Marines inside the helicopter. Sergeant Mathers climbed up next holding me in his arms. They picked me up as soon as we entered the hatch.

"Glad to see you're okay," Sergeant Mathers told Fred as the Marines strapped me down onto a seat next to Fred.

"I can't thank you enough sir. I didn't think you guys would stop for us. I saw another one of these helicopters pass by so I waved at it and shouted, but it kept going."

"Yeah, they told us they saw the two of you up on the roof waving for help, surrounded by those sick people down there, so we stopped to pick you up. Glad we found you."

"So, where are you guys heading?"

"There's a base in downtown providing shelter and medical assistance, now that most hospitals are overrun by the infected. We're reinforcement sent to aid with security. But we're not letting just anybody in; only the non-infected. Which is why I scanned you, just to make sure you're not one of them."

"I saw that on the news earlier. Is it safe there?"

"It's one of the only safe places left in this city."

"Good. Well, we appreciate the lift over there. My name is Fred by the way."

"Sergeant Mathers, Gabriel Mathers," replied the Sergeant and firmly shook Fred's hand.

THE
END
IS
HERE

CHAPTER 7

Above an alley that stretched for several blocks were fire escapes attached to several long-standing buildings made from brick. The structures were used for commercial property of different sorts such as residential, warehousing and restaurants. The surviving group walked in between the buildings down an empty alley toward the park turned to shelter. Mike walked ahead tightly holding Kari by the hand. Linda followed closely behind. Next to her was her brother Robbie who held his girlfriend Sheena's hand followed by Jesse and Flacco who stayed alert for anyone that tried to come up behind them. Chris stayed far behind but close enough to keep his eye on Mike and Kari.

"You think Lily and Joey escaped?" Sheena asked. Robbie kept gazing at the graffiti art on the brick wall before being tugged on the hand by Sheena. "Do you think they escaped?" she asked again but he ignored her. He found it a difficult question to answer because he didn't want to accept the fact that their friends might be dead.

"Well do you?" she frustratingly asked.

"I don't know! I think so. Joey is smart and he's fast. I'm sure they got away."

"But why haven't they replied to our messages or answered our calls?"

"Maybe their phone's dead."

She looked down with a gloomy look, "she had a full battery. She always has a full battery."

Mike fell back a little to walk alongside Robbie. "Hey, uhh Robbie right?" he asked.

"Yeah."

"After this block, we keep going straight or cut a left?"

"Straight. We'll cut a left in two blocks. I'll tell you when we get there."

"Hey, have I seen you before?"

"I don't think so?"

"Were you in the Hawthorne area earlier this morning, skateboarding with your friends?"

"Yeah I was? Why?"

"Yeah okay, I thought I recognized you. You guys jumped in front of our van and you flipped my partner off."

"Holy shit, that was you guys? Wait, your partner, was he the bald guy that…" Mike nodded.

"Oh, wow. Honestly, we didn't see you guys turning. I thought you guys cut us off. Sorry about that and I'm really sorry about what happened to your partner. He was a brave dude. I lost two of my friends also. One of them, Henry, for sure he's gone. I saw him turn into one of them and then chase after me. My other best friend, Joey, I'm not certain, but… I think he's dead too. We lost him over at that building. I called him but he doesn't answer. My girl's friend, Lily, her too. She and Joey were both together when we lost them."

"Damn, I'm really sorry about your friends. It hurts, trust me I know, but there will be time to grieve for them and time for remembering them. Right now, we have to keep our heads in the game and get through this. Stay sharp and keep fighting as hard as you did back at the building. From here on we stick together, stay close to one another, and if we get into a jam where we have no other choice but to fight, then we get into a circle formation with our backs against each other and fight our way through. Think you guys can do that?"

"Yeah I think we can." Sheena also nodded her head.

"Ok good. Let your boys know also, please. We have to be ready, just in case. Thanks."

Mike looked toward the back and made eye contact with Chris.

"What?" Chris asked with arrogance.

Mike fell back and waited for Chris to catch up, so they could talk. Kari looked back, paused and stared at them with a worried look.

"I don't know what your deal is," Mike said, "or why you decided to pop up out of nowhere and go to Kari's job today, but I'm doing my best to keep my cool and overlook all of it, for now, so that we can all get out of this alive."

"For now?" Chris asked and laughed. "Tell me oh fearless leader, what do you mean with, 'for now'? What exactly is it that you think you're going to eventually do? Because whatever it is, I guarantee that you won't get out of this alive."

"You threatening me you son of a bitch?" Mike said and got in Chris' face. Kari walked towards them.

"I'm being realistic Mike. Look around you, death is everywhere. It's behind you. It's at every corner. It's staring you in the eye and it's about to grab you by throat."

"Hey, come on you two break it up," Kari said and pulled them apart. "Let's not get into this now. We've made it this far, so please let's just keep going."

"Keep a leash on him and everything will be fine Kari," Chris said with a smirk and kept walking. Mike stepped forward to get in his face again. "Easy," Kari said and placed her hand on his chest. "He's just being an asshole like he's always been. He has this way of getting in your head. You can't let him get to you."

"You're right," Mike said. "I won't give him the satisfaction."

She took his hand, "come on, we're almost there."

As night took over, the street lights and neon signs turned on. The Downtown Los Angeles area was in pandemonium. Vehicles were left abandoned in the middle of the road. Motorists drove in the opposite direction on a one-way street and caused traffic jams that caused several accidents. The roads were congested. Hot dog and taco stands were left abandoned with the meat left to char on the smoky grill. People fled from their loved ones and close friends after watching them revive from the dead and savagely attack. Bikes and electric scooters were scattered thought out the streets. Citizens flocked together as they made their way through the streets toward Grand Park seeking safety.

"Up here, turn left," Robbie told Mike. As soon as Mike turned the corner, a police officer covered with bullet holes, and a ripped and tattered bloody uniform attacked him. Mike pushed him up against the building and slammed the officer's head against the brick wall repeatedly and killed the undead officer. He squatted and dug through the dead officer's duty belt. "Here take this," Mike told Kari and handed her a fully loaded magazine. He then gave her his empty gun and asked her to load it.

"Okay everyone, let's get ready to run from here," Mike addressed the group by the side of the building. "Remember- stay close together. Don't forget the circle formation if we have to fight. Everyone Ready?" Robbie and his friends made a frown.

Linda had a scared look in her eye. Chris rolled his eyes. "Ok let's move!" he said and led the way.

It was nighttime and the full moon shined over the City of Los Angeles, illuminating its crowded streets with the lifeless bodies of her population; civilians and those in service such as police officers, fire firefighters, and emergency response lay dead in the street. Sirens, car alarms, and horns echoed from building to building. Road pavements were covered with broken glass from cars crashed into one another. Busy intersections blocked each other's path with oncoming cars that went in all directions of each lane. Thick black smoke spread through the air. Vehicles were engulfed in flames and buildings were ablaze. The air was thick and smelled of char. A corner liquor stores' windows were shattered, and its door hung from its rusty hinges. There was broken glass, scattered chips, gum, soda, and candy that covered the dirty white tile floor like carpet. Beside the entrance lied a knocked over yellow sign that read 'caution wet floor.' Next to it was a yellow bucket tipped over with spilled muddy red water and a broken mop. Thick red blood flowed out of the motionless bodies that lied beside one another. Like the girl with a hand chewed through to the bone or the man whose face was bitten off. He had chunks of meat dangling from his cheek. The blood from his face trickled down his neck and soaked his white t-shirt. A puddle of blood formed beside his waist. Within seconds they would turn into one of the undead.

Down the street, cries of pain and rage grew louder. "They're coming! Run!" screamed Mike. Several people that were heading toward the shelter bumped into one another. They pushed and shoved their way through the crowded streets to outrun the undead. A small bunch hid under vehicles, others ran inside stores, and cafes that were left unlocked. Mike and his group kept running toward the shelter. Saul the construction worker was hiding inside of a car when he saw Mike's group and decided to join them.

Hordes of the undead chased after the living and attacked them all through the city. As more of the living were brutally attacked and killed, the number of the undead grew. A small bunch of undead were feasting on a body when Mike and his group approached. Robbie used a black lug wrench and cracked an undead man's head with it. Mike swung his ax and buried it into an undead's skull. Kari stood beside him, firing off her gun. She shot down two more with accurate precision. Saul held his hammer tightly and saw one approach. An undead woman, with pale ripped open skin that dangled off her face attacked Saul and grabbed onto his shoulders. He pushed her off and knocked her teeth out with a swing of the hammer. He turned the handle with the claw facing outward and rammed it into her right eye breaking through the eye socket and into her brain. Chris got closer to the group and stayed within Kari's reach. He used a rod that he picked up on the street to fight off the undead, and constantly looked over his shoulder to stay within Kari's sight. Sheena swung her bat across an undead girl's face and put her flat on her back before busting her brains. Flaco and Jesse used their skateboard as a shield and maneuvered through the group.

The group pushed forward staying close together during the chaos of the night. Two blocks away, the shelter, protected by emergency barricades and barbed wire fence surrounding the entire park, was shutting down due to an inundation of people seeking refuge. People surrounding the gates pushed their way up to the front crushing those already standing at the front. Several individuals, healthy and the sick, screamed and shouted, pleading to be let in. "Help us please!" shouted the rowdy crowd. Others shouted vulgar profanity at the guards who stood on the other side of the barricades. Marines posted above the guard towers stood ready with machine guns pointed at the hostile crowd. Several transporting helicopters flew in with reinforcements. The angry mob rattled the fence and attempted to climb. "Get down or you will be shot," Sergeant Leonard firmly warned over the intercom. Toward the back of the crowd, some of the ill coughed, sneezed and vomited irrepressibly. Spectators gasped and screamed at the sight of the ill succumbing to the infection as they died and came back to life. The spectators ran toward the front and shook the fence with even more aggression.

"It's starting," Sergeant Leonard told his commander above the guard tower with large searchlights focused in on the crowd below. The commander scanned the area with binoculars and saw that some of the civilians were plagued with the illness. He watched as people held their stomach in pain and threw up blood. He observed some of the undead attack the people toward the back. He spoke through the walkie talkie and ordered his snipers to take out any of the infected before coming back to life. The snipers used a scope attached to their rifle and navigated through the mass of people, looking for the infected or anyone lying on the floor. They adjusted the scope while positioning the cross hairs in the middle of their target and pulled the trigger once they found a victim. The snipers shot down anyone who showed symptoms of infection. The scared and angry mob climbed the fence ignoring the sharp barbed wire above. Sergeant Leonard repeated his orders to get down, but the mob kept climbing. "Lethal force will be used on anyone attempting to break in," he warned again. "If they reach the top, open fire," the commander ordered Sergeant Leonard. Mike and his group reached the shelter and found a large mass of bodies swarming the gates.

"Oh my god," said Kari in dismay as she observed hundreds of people encircling the gates. "Mike how are we going to get in?" she asked. Survivors pushed their way forward, shoving the weak aside and climbing over them. People were trampled over and crushed to death. Those who made it to the front climbed up the fence ignoring the warning overhead. "We have to get in or we'll die out here," Robbie told Mike pointing to the group of undead and the disease-ridden individuals standing amongst the large crowd.

Machine guns at the towers echoed through the park as Marines tore people down from the fence like a chainsaw cutting down trees. "Remove yourself from the fence and go back home," Sergeant Leonard ordered the massive crowd of people over the intercom. "There is no more room inside!" he shouted. "And we are not allowing anyone else to enter the gates. Leave or we will keep firing." The crowd grew louder with cries for help and terror.

"We didn't come this far," Mike said and grabbed Kari by the hand. "Come on," he shouted to the group and led them through the crowd toward the front gate.

A few miles out in the distance, the last of the transporting helicopters flew toward the shelter. A sizable portion of the infected died and came back to life, attacking several of the healthy civilians trying to enter the shelter. Before long the shelter was surrounded with more of the undead. Snipers and guards manned at the machine guns shot at the undead but failed to stop the rapidly increasing number of infected from coming back to life. They abandoned their search of anyone showing signs of infection and began to shoot at everyone standing close to the front gate, slaughtering innocent people, piling bodies on top of each other. Mike and everyone that followed him stood together and fought off the undead. A teenager in a gray hoodie with a bloody face grabbed Chris by the arm. Chris pulled away and grappled with him in circles. A few feet from him was Mike swinging his ax away. Chris noticed he had his back turned and seized the opportunity. He shoved the undead teen onto Mike and the teen fell onto Mikes back. They both tumbled forward and fell to the ground. The undead teen rolled over on top of Mike. He lunged in for his neck, but Mike stuffed his face and pressed his thumbs deep into his eye sockets. The teen kept up with his attack even after Mike gouged his eyes out. A second later the teens head was split open like a canoe from a single gunshot. Kari shot the kid from two yards away. Mike pushed him off and as he got back on his feet, he saw Chris running away and lost him in the crowd.

Jesse ran over to help his friend Flaco. He tackled down a bald heavy-set undead man but was soon overpowered by the man. Robbie, distracted with ramming the lug wrench through an undead's skull, heard Jesse's cries for help who was on the ground kicking and screaming while being eaten alive by the bald heavy-set man who ripped off a large chunk of Jesse's neck. "Noooo!"

Robbie loudly cried as he helplessly watched his friend get torn apart by a group of undead.

The chopping sound of helicopter rotor blades cutting through the air grew louder as it approached the shelter. Inside the helicopter were Fred, myself, Sergeant Mathers and his unit of marines.

"My God is that the shelter?" asked Fred looking down at the gory mayhem surrounding the shelter.

"It was. It's out of control now so they've been ordered to close it down. Looks like you'll be the last of the civilians to go in," Sergeant Mathers replied.

The Sergeant looked down at the crowd of people fighting for their lives against the growing number of undead. He aimed his rifle and fired at the undead, protecting the healthy civilians. With the telescope mounted to his rifle, he zoomed in on a small group moving together and fighting against the undead. He zoomed in closer with his telescope and noticed a man wearing an officer's uniform. He followed the officer to protect him from harm. The officer in blue uniform swung his ax at an undead's face then turned to his side and swung again at another undead.

"Mike?" the Sergeant murmured as he zoomed in on the officer with an ax. "Stop the helo!" Sergeant Mathers ordered the pilot. "Hover over that small group and keep it steady. Men," he addressed his unit, "I want all guns focused around that small group and take out anyone that approaches them."

"But they're as good as dead sir," the pilot contested.

"That man down there was a marine who served with me during the Iraq war in '03. He is my friend and fellow marine and we are not leaving him behind do you understand?"

"Yes sir," the pilot replied as he maneuvered toward Mike.

Mike prepared to swing his ax at an oncoming undead when its head was blown off from a shot that came from above. He stood astonished at the sight of the undead's headless body on the ground and wondered where the shot came from. He ducked and thought it was the marines shooting into the crowd. He looked up at the helicopter and saw his old friend Sergeant Mathers providing cover from above. Mike was surprised and overcome with joy. Sergeant Mathers' unit fired at the undead who gathered around Mike's group.

Robbie was enraged over the death of his close friend Jesse and decided to pursue the undead man that killed his friend. Mike yelled at him to get back in a circle formation and signaled at Sergeant Mathers above to assist Robbie. Sergeant Mathers signaled back at Mike to move his group to the side of the shelter where they can pick them up.

"Go to the side and wait for me there," Mike told Kari. "They'll provide cover from above."

"Where are you going?" Kari desperately asked trying to keep him from leaving as she held onto his arm.

"I'm going after Robbie. Go, I'll catch up."

"Please help him," Linda cried.

"Don't worry, I'll bring him back in one piece. Now go!"

Kari and the others made their way to the side of the shelter keeping their heads low with their eyes squinted to avoid flying debris generated by the helicopter. Sergeant Mathers opened the helicopters belly and threw down the roped ladder. He swung his rifle over his shoulder and climbed down roped ladder followed by his unit to provide cover for Mike and his group.

"Form a single file line," ordered the Sergeant. Sheena went first, followed by Linda and the rest. He scanned them one by one, letting the climb once the scanner cleared them.

"I can't leave without my fiancé!" Kari shouted at Sergeant Mathers.

"Where is your fiancé?" he asked.

"He went after the kid with long black hair."

"Does he have a blue uniform on?"

"Yes."

"Then your fiancé is my good friend Mike. Don't worry Miss, I'll bring him back, that's my word. But please I need you to climb up and get in the helicopter now."

"Please bring him back to me," Kari said to the Sergeant with watery eyes as a she held on to the ladder.

Sergeant Mathers and five of his troops moved together as one through the crowd shooting down undead after undead. The Sergeant got attacked from behind, but quickly threw the undead over his shoulder in a karate move and shot him in the head. He continued to press forward with his rifle pointed searching for Mike.

"Let's move out marine!" Sergeant Mathers shouted at Mike five feet away from him.

Mike, who held Robbie's arm over his shoulder to help him walk, smiled and hugged his old friend Sergeant Mathers. "God am I glad to see you brother," Mike told him.

"So am I amigo. Your fiancé ordered me to come get you, so let's not keep her waiting."

"She's in the helo?"

"Waiting on you," Sergeant Mathers replied with a nod.

"Thank God bro, thank you."

Robbie limped to the chopper with Mike's help, when Sergeant Mathers' unit stopped and aimed their weapons at Robbie after noticing his limp.

"Whoa, whoa, he's not infected!" yelled Mike shielding Robbie. "He got hurt, but he's not infected Mathers."

"Stand down!" ordered the Sergeant.

They lowered their weapon and the Sergeant scanned Robbie. "He's clear," he said. "Let's move." They made their way back to the helicopter which hovered over the shelter. A Marine on board opened the belly hatch and dropped the rope ladder. Mike fixed his foot on the first step and climbed up the ladder. The other Marines followed him up and Sergeant Mathers climbed last.

Mike reached the top and the Marine extended his arm and pulled Mike in. Kari stood by the open hatch and threw her arms around Mike as he climbed in. "I knew you'd come back," she said and kissed him on the lips. "I said I would," he smiled. He looked around the helicopter and smiled proudly as he saw everyone seated on the red foldable troop seats. He was happy to see that they all made it on board safely. His cheerful mood quickly disappeared at noticing the person seated at the far end of the helicopter. Strapped down on the last seat by the rear door ramp in bloody clothes and a torn button up shirt was Chris who looked at Mike with a loathing stare. Mike charged down the aisle and pummeled Chris with his fists. The Marines pulled Mike off Chris and restrained him as Mike furiously yelled for them to release him.

"I'm going to kill you, you son of a bitch!" Mike yelled as he got dragged away kicking and screaming. Chris, with a busted bloody lip, looked astonished at Mike's outburst and stayed strapped to his seat. "What the hell is your problem?" Chris yelled out to Mike as he wiped the blood from his mouth.

"Don't play stupid with me! You know exactly what you did. You threw that kid onto me hoping that it would kill me. That it would eat me or get me infected so that you can get rid of me. Why is he on this helicopter?" Mike demanded and then turned his anger toward Kari. "You were there. You saw what he did. Why would you let him board the helicopter Kari?"

Kari was shocked after hearing what Chris had done and of Mike's accusations. "I didn't see him do that Michael, I swear," she said. "If I knew that he did what you say, then I would have killed him myself." Linda spoke up in Kari's defense and told Mike that she was with her the whole time and didn't see Chris shove anyone on to him.

"Alright, alright, enough!" Sergeant Mathers interjected. "I didn't see what happened Mike, but I believe you. But what I will not allow you to do is murder someone on my aircraft. You understand? We'll deal with this matter later. Right now, I need all of you seated and buckled in. And you, stay your ass right there until I say so," the Sergeant ordered Chris. Mike took a seat on the opposite end of the fuselage eyeing Chris who stared back with an evil grin. Kari sat next to Mike and held his hand. The Sergeant took a seat and introduced them to Fred and I.

"Fred, looks like you'll have some company," the Sergeant said. "This is my good friend Mike. Mike this is Fred. We picked them up and saved him from a horde just like the one below us about an hour ago."

"Hi Fred, nice to meet you," Mike said as polite as he could, still fuming over Chris. He shook Fred's hand before strapping in. "You were saved by a good man here Fred. Which I forgot to thank you for Gabriel. Really though, thank you for saving us down there. So, what's the plan?"

"The plan is to check you all in to a safer harbor," the Sergeant replied. "As you can see, this area is no longer safe. It's FUBAR. In a moment, we'll fly out to the Naval Station San Diego where everyone will be safe -until we can get the situation back under control. For now, no one can go back home until all of Los Angeles is a virus free zone and we don't know when that'll be. I'm sorry to say, but for now, the NS San Diego is home. But there, you all will be safe and protected. There's plenty of food and housing accommodations."

Mike leaned in closer to Sergeant Mathers seated beside him and asked in a low voice, "Okay straight up, what's next?"

"Straight up brother," speaking in all seriousness Gabriel replied, "I don't know. You know how these things play out. We're on a need to know basis and right now all I need to know is that NSSD is our next planned course of action. From there, my best guess is we'll have to wait on what the CDC has to say about all this. Maybe they'll find a cure? Of course, if they do, they'll have to figure out how this whole thing ever started to even begin developing a cure, but that'll take a while. So really who knows?

We'll have to stand by and wait. But once I hear something, I'll make sure to give you a briefing. But I'm glad to see that you're doing okay. How's James by the way?"

"He's gone," Mike replied. His throat hardened. The thought of James' death was always at the back of his mind but during his struggle for survival he hadn't the time to reflect on it until the Sergeant brought it up. "He helped us get this far, but he got bitten and decided to stay back. Went out on his boots."

"Jesus, man I'm sorry to hear that. I know James was a good friend to you and a good man. May he rest in peace."

"Thank you."

"Well look, hang tight, we'll be leaving soon."

"Thanks again Gabriel, I appreciate you stopping to help us. If it wasn't for you, I honestly don't know what would have happened to us down there."

"Of course, we're brothers of the core. We look out for each other, right?"

"Oorah!"

Fred studied Mikes face and his uniform. He leaned up to Mike, "You a customs officer huh?" he asked.

"Yes," Mike replied.

"I've seen you before."

"Really? Where?"

"The warehouse in Hawthorne – Worldin Logistics."

"Yeah… yeah, I've stopped in to inspect freight a couple times before. In fact, I was there earlier today with my partner. That's where we first encountered the infected."

"Yeah no wonder you look familiar. I remember seeing you before. I work there, in the warehouse."

"You do? Do you know what happened?"

"Yeah… I do. I caused this. This is all my fault."

CHAPTER 8

"This is all my fault, my fault. It's all my fault," Fred repeated while sobbing with his face buried in his hands. I placed my tiny hand on his head trying to comfort him. I was saddened by his breakdown and felt the urge to cry. My lip started to quiver, as it usually does right before I'd burst into tears, but for a little girl, I was really brave and held them in. I know that the burden of the world rested heavily on Fred's shoulders, like Atlas from Greek mythology, who was condemned to hold up the sky for all eternity. Fred wanted nothing more than to crawl in a hole and die.

Below us, was an ongoing brutal and chaotic scene of soldiers at the gates firing into the crowd of both the living and the undead. It wasn't long before the number of people grew too large for the National Guard to hold back. The amount of force that was garnered by the undead and the living as they pushed and rattled the gates broke them down. A swarm of people, both living and dead, stormed through the torn down gates and destroyed any hopes of survival for those already inside.

Deafening red alarms sounded off to alert of the breach. The living rushed inside begging for help while the undead pounced on anyone with a pulse. Bodies riddled with bullets were scattered throughout the encampment. Shrieks of pain and terror reverberated from one end to the other. A soldier with fleeing courage abandoned his post once it got overrun with the undead. He was chased down like a frightened deer running from a pack of wolves and was taken down by the ravenous horde. They tore him to shreds and fought for his remains. It was a bloody scene for everyone on board.

"Sir, this LZ is no longer safe. We cannot land," said the pilot as he hovered over the landing zone.

"We won't," Sergeant Mathers replied. "It's bursting with them now. Get zone three on the radio and ask if we're clear to land."

Fred sniffled and looked outside. "We aren't landing, are we?" he asked wiping his tears.

"No, it doesn't seem like it," Mike replied looking out the window. "This place is crawling with them. God help those poor people."

"Where do you think we'll go from here?" Kari asked Mike.

"My guess, another place like this. One that hasn't been breached of course."

The pilot tried to communicate with zone three, but there was no response. "I repeat zone two has been breached," the pilot said over the radio. "We are requesting permission to land -over." Silence fell over the radio for the next ten seconds. "I repeat. This is pilot Gilhem aboard the O-two chinook carrying a crew of eight along with numerous civilians. Zone three has been breached and I am requesting permission to enter and land –over." Dead silence fell on the radio again and the pilot looked at Sergeant Mathers with an uneasy look. "I don't think zone three is operational anymore sir," despondently said the pilot. "Do we have enough fuel to get to SD?" Sergeant Mathers asked. "Negative sir," the pilot replied as he looked at the fuel control panel. "The nearest place where we can re-fuel is at the Hawthorne Municipal Airport which is approximately 30 miles from here. We can make it."

"Then proceed."

"Fred, what did you mean when you said that this is all your fault?" Mike asked leaning in. Kari looked out the window as the helicopter flew over the havoc circulating the city. She watched the city go up in flames with sirens blaring as its soundtrack accompanied by the cries for help below. Fred hung his head low and hesitated with giving his shameful explanation.

"Fred? What did you mean by that?"

"At work… there were these hazardous barrels," Fred recounted in an unsteady voice.

After catching the words "hazardous barrels" Sergeant Mathers' attention was quickly turned to Fred and he got closer to listen.

"I was driving the forklift and I had some documents on my lap. As I was driving down the warehouse, they just flew out of my lap and I got distracted and drove into the dangerous goods area. That's when I punctured holes in one of the barrels. It started leaking a weird smelly liquid."

Sergeant Mathers' eyes widened with curiosity and an intense look settled on his face. As Fred kept talking, the Sergeant clung to his every word.

"We called the fire department and once they arrived, people at work started getting sick and killing one another. I think it started with one of the truck drivers who touched the barrel. Later on, the cops showed up. One of them shot at one of those, those things and hit one of the barrels. It caused an explosion and that's when the smoke started coming out from the liquid. I *think* the smoke is what's causing people to get sick, die and come back to life. No… I'm sure of it. If I hadn't punctured holes in that barrel none of this would have ever happened. No one would be dead. Not my mom, not…" Fred's eyes teared up again and he bit his tongue to keep from breaking down.

"Fred, I need you to tell me exactly where you work," Sergeant Mathers firmly ordered him. Fred wiped his tears and took in a deep breath, "at …a warehouse, in Hawthorne."

"In Hawthorne? Okay good. What's the name of the building? What streets?"

Fred provided the Sergeant with all the information while Mike stared at Sergeant Mathers with curiosity. His look concerned him and he began to wonder what actions the Sergeant might be planning in his head. A few minutes later, the helicopter approached the landing strip of the small air field illuminated with red flashing lights. At the edge of the airfield was a little shack with a gas pump in front and an abandoned small black helicopter.

"Alright, everyone listen up," Sergeant Mathers shouted. "We're going to land at this airfield and refuel the tanks. The pilot along with the co-pilot will stay here to refuel and make sure this place is safe while the rest of my men and I go on quick mission. You are all to stay here until we come back. We shouldn't take long, just hang tight."

"What quick mission?" Mike asked as he pulled him to the side.

"I cannot say amigo you know that," replied the Sergeant.

"But you said we would be going to SD?"

"And we will, right after we come back."

"You're going to that warehouse, aren't you?" The Sergeant gave him a serious stare almost confirming Mike's question but remained silent.

"What are you guys hoping to find? It's too dangerous out there. If Fred is saying the truth, then this is ground zero. Where it all started. Lord knows how many of those sick people are out there. Besides you don't have any protective gear. What about the fumes? What if you guys get infected?"

"Look, we are at ground zero which is precisely why we must do this," the Sergeant replied as he loaded a magazine into his rifle and chambered a round. "The warehouse is within walking distance from here. And don't worry, we'll be fine. If the virus didn't infect any of us by now, there's no way it'll harm us anymore. Here, take this." He gave Mike a fully loaded firearm, "stay inside and keep everyone calm. Most importantly, keep your cool," the Sergeant said and directed his eyes over at Chris.

The wheels on the helicopter touched ground and everyone's fears were elevated as the helicopter shook. There was no telling who or what was outside. The coast was clear for landing and there were no signs of *them* but that didn't ease everyone's nerves. It didn't ease Robbie's concern for the wellbeing of his girlfriend who tightly held his hand. It didn't ease Fred's concern for my wellbeing. It didn't ease Mike's concern for Kari and everyone else aboard the helicopter. Even the Sergeant was gripped with fear, although he didn't show it. He stood tall and was ready to fight. Ready to die on his boots. He never feared an enemy before, but this enemy was unlike any other. This enemy wouldn't stay down after getting pierced with bullets. It kept coming. And worst of all, it wanted to devour you alive. Not the way Sergeant Mathers would like to die. A warrior's death would be more fitting, but this? This was subhuman. A barbarous type of death. But as Carl von Clausewitz said, "Courage, above all things, is the first quality of a warrior." A quote the Sergeant memorized and would live by. A quote that would shake away his fear and put him back into the fight ready to stare death in the face no matter how it was served. He opened the ramp and pointed his weapon as the ramp lowered and ordered the troops out with him following behind, scanning the area.

As the minutes dragged on, everyone nervously sat and waited for the Sergeant and his troops to return so they could take off and get to the safe zone as promised. They whispered amongst themselves careful not to raise their voice and attract any unwanted attention from whatever may have been lurking outside. The pilot and co-pilot were outside the helicopter and worked quietly to hook up the fuel pump to the helicopter. Mike opened a small storage unit strapped down next to the cockpit and brought out bottles of water. He handed them down to Kari and she passed them down to everyone else. Saul got up from his seat with a bottle of water in hand and walked to Mike. "I wasn't sure if you wanted me to give one to the guy next to me, so I came to ask," Saul said looking back at Chris. "Him?" Mike asked with disdain jerking his head at Chris. "No, fuck him. He doesn't get anything from me."

"I thought so. Glad I asked. My name is Saul by the way."

"Nice to officially meet you Saul. My name is Mike. Glad you made it out safely with us. How did you end up in downtown anyway?"

"I work in construction and was working at a new building there. That's when it all started for me. I managed to escape the building alive, thank God, and that's when I ran into you guys. And yourself?"

"It's a long story Saul. But like several of those poor souls back there, we heard the broadcast of a shelter close by in downtown, so we made our way there seeking refuge. That's when we saw you and a couple others on the street trying to do the same. And well the rest is history. Now here we are. And here we wait."

"For how long do you think? And where did they go?"

"I wish I knew. I just hope they come back in one piece and soon. I would love to know what the hell this mission of theirs is, but it must be important enough for them to walk there and do it."

"Yeah I guess it is. This is crazy. All that's happened. Seems like the end is near and we're just waiting for our turn to be judged."

"I wouldn't go so far as to say all that Saul. I'm sure there's some type of scientific explanation for all this and everything will get worked out, eventually. Try and stay positive. Let me introduce you to my fiancé. This is Kari."

Saul shook Kari's hand who was seated close to the cockpit. Saul took a seat across from her and introduced himself to Fred and asked about his story. Everyone who had not met Fred or knew how he came to be on board the helicopter quieted down and listened as he shared his frightening tale. Kari became emotional and cried after hearing of our mother's fate. Mike stood over Kari massaging her shoulders while she wiped the tears off her face. Chris who remained at the back of the helicopter in his seat also listened in, periodically giving Mike and irritable look.

"I was in the park hanging out and skating with my friends," Robbie said holding Sheena's hand. "That's when Sheena came and told me about what was going on. After that, we walked to my sister Linda's job to get a ride home." His friend Flaco sat beside Sheena with his head hung low. He thought about his friend Jesse who minutes earlier was killed by the undead. "He died protecting me," Flaco softly said and burst into tears. Robbie got up from his seat and sat next to Flaco. He put his arm over his shoulder. "I know man, it's okay, it's okay," Robbie said and shed a tear. "They're all together now. In heaven. Skating in a park where there are no rules. Where you can freely grind all the rails and never fall. Where you always land all your tricks." "And you never break a bone," Flaco said back with a grin. "Yeah dude," Robbie chuckled.

"Can I share my story now?" Chris said aloud with his hand raised. "Of how that man stole the only thing that has ever mattered to me. That woman's love," he said pointing at Kari.

"You shut the hell up Chris. Right now!" Kari furiously said and pulled on Mikes arm to keep him from getting into another fight with Chris. There was a loud thump on the side of helicopter that alarmed everyone, and Sheena let out a scream. She quickly covered her mouth. "What was that?" she whispered in a trembly voice.

"It's probably just the pilots outside," Robbie whispered back with his ear pressed against the side of the helicopter. Multiple shots were fired outside which gave Robbie a jolt and Sheena gasped. The shots stopped and the next sound we heard was of a man wailing in pain. "Oh god, they're here," Linda cried. The sounds of growling and shrieks outside terrified everyone on board. Loud banging on the cabin door located on the right side of the aircraft startled everyone and they jumped up from their seat. Mike cocked the gun and walked in between everyone down the middle isle toward the door with Saul, hammer gripped in hand, behind him. Chris got up and took a few steps back bumping into Mike. They both gave each other the evil eye. "Get the hell out the way," Mike said.

"Let me in! Mike! Its Mathers! Hurry-Open the door. Hurry!" screamed Sergeant Mathers with fear in his voice. Mike unlocked the hatch and opened the lower part of the door which was more than three feet above the ground. He looked down and saw the Sergeant below him shooting his weapon in multiple directions. Mike grabbed him from the vest and pulled him in with Saul's help. "Close it!" the Sergeant yelled from his back as he tucked his legs in. A horde of the undead stormed at the door and got their hands through the door before it could shut. Mike fired his weapon while Saul swung his hammer wildly. Hands reached up from the bottom of the door and soon multiplied in numbers. Chris tried closing the door as Mike and the Sergeant kept firing. Saul put the hammer down and helped Chris. They grabbed the door handle and pulled on the door. They grunted and huffed as they forcefully pulled the door up and locked it.

"What happened!?" yelled Mike as the loud thumping spread around the helicopter.

The Sergeant was panting, "there were too many of them," he replied while refilling his front pouch with extra ammunition. He reached over Mike to grab another vest from above the door and handed it to him. "Put this on," he told Mike while the thumping on the plane steadily grew louder.

"Where are your men? Where are the pilots?" Mike demanded.

"They're dead, Okay! They're all dead," replied the Sergeant in a strong tone. "I had to put the pilots down myself when they tried to attack me. It's just us now, trapped in here with no pilots and no way of leaving here. So, I need you to gear up and get ready to fight."

Chris smirked once he heard that the pilots were dead. Everyone else panicked. Linda clasped her hands and started praying. Flaco nervously looked at Robbie as he held Sheena's hand. Saul gripped his hammer. Kari was next to Linda and saw her praying. She thought it a good idea to join her in prayer and closed her eyes. A thought flashed through her head and she opened her eyes and looked over at Chris.

"I knew this was a bad idea. I knew this would happen," Mike said strapping on the tactical vest. "What the hell did you go do out there that got all your men killed Gabriel?"

"Following orders," the Sergeant replied.

"How many of *them* are out there?"

"The whole damn city," replied the Sergeant in a hopeless voice. The helicopter then rocked and the noise level of the undead increased twofold with hundreds more making their way from every street corner. "We're totally fucked," Robbie said. Sheena gasped and tightly hugged Robbie. The growling and rocking of the helicopter intensified. "I don't want to die," Sheena whimpered into Robbie's chest.

"Alright everyone, stay calm and move toward the front of the helicopter," said the Sergeant. They all moved toward the front of the aircraft as directed and huddled closely. Chris stepped back but then quietly stepped forward again to ease drop on Mike and the Sergeants conversation.

"God dammit Gabriel, enough with the bullshit," Mike angrily said in a low voice as they stood at the back of the helicopter. "No more of this 'I need to know basis bullshit'. Come on man, it's me, tell me. What the hell where you guys doing out there?"

The Sergeant looked at Mike, then looked away. He shook his head and stayed quiet. "Dammit man, we might all die here, and I need to know why," Mike demanded looking at the Sergeant in the eye.

"Alright, alright, I'll tell you. I was ordered to collect samples of the liquid from the barrels."

"The barrels that exploded? Why?"

"Because the liquid itself holds the key to a cure."

Mike was flabbergasted. "How do you know that?"

"Because we've known about the barrels all along. The government has known about it for a very long time and kept it a secret. Since WWII to be precise. When they found out that the Russians had spies working here in the U.S and tried to get it for themselves, they ordered that the barrels be transported out of the research facility as 'normal' cargo to fool anyone who might be a spy. The barrels were to be transported to a regular shipping and receiving warehouse and later be hauled down to San Diego for further development. We just never knew what warehouse because the transporting truck driver along with the warehouse dock worker who were paid off to receive the load were found dead the next day. We suspect that the Russian spies killed them. When I overheard Fred talking about the hazardous barrels, I knew this would be the warehouse where they were transported to.

"Jesus. Why the fuck would they allow a dangerous chemical with the ability to wipe out the world be transported so carelessly like that?"

"They didn't know what the chemical reaction to fire would be. Testing and further research was never done. It never got approved by the CDC until recently. They had no idea that if mixed with fire, the smoke would become deadly and ultimately turn into an airborne virus and cause all of this, this damn mess."

"But if you knew from what Fred said, that the barrels exploded and there was nothing left, why go back there?"

"Because I also know that when the barrels were transported, they were transported along with a small locked metal box. In that metal box were two test tubes filled with the liquid from the barrels. They were to be kept in a freezer that the warehouse holds on one of their docks."

"Did you find it?" Mike excitedly asked. Gabriel nodded and patted his side pouch affirming a success to his mission.

"That is why we went out there and that is why we need to fight to survive so that we can get these test tubes to San Diego where they can work on finding a cure. Whatever happens Mike, know that these tubes are more important than both of our lives. Do you understand?"

"I understand Gabriel. But moving forward, no more secrets. Be transparent with me. And we'll get those tubes to SD one way or another. Which brings me to my next question. How are we getting there or anywhere for that matter if our pilots are dead?"

Outside of the helicopter, a mass army of the undead had the aircraft surrounded. Their thunderous grumbling and continuous thrashing to the helicopter was heard from several blocks away. Some of the undead climbed on top of the helicopter and bashed the top of the aircraft with their fists. They pounded with so much force that their hands broke and bled, but that didn't stop their determination in trying to break in. All of us inside were shaken with fear. We bunched together and Linda prayed for the undead to stop. "Dios, todo poderoso, salvanos," she prayed in Spanish. Flaco jumped at every booming thump. The helicopter would shake as the horde of undead violently battered the helicopter. Mike and the Sergeant could see out from the circular windows that the body of the undead had grown in size. They knew that it would be an impossible fight to break free of. They feared that it could possibly be their final moments.

"We can throw a grenade outside and make a run for it?" suggested Mike.

"Too risky," the Sergeant replied. "The fuel pumps are outside and we could *all* blow up."

"What if we create a diversion, that would allow the rest to escape?"

"Possibly. If someone runs out and leads them away. But that person would get mauled the very moment we open that door. Not only that, it's a risky move opening that door. We got lucky when you opened it for me, but now there's more of them. A lot more," he said with his face up against the window.

As they pondered for a solution, the thrumming sound of the aircraft's turboshaft engine powered on followed by the rotor blades winding up. They looked at one another in disbelief and rushed toward the cockpit. Seated in the pilot's seat and buckled in was Chris flipping switches overhead and preparing to lift off. "I suggest you all take a seat and buckle up. It's about to get a little bumpy," Chris said.

"What the hell are you doing?!" Mike screamed at Chris and pointed his gun. Chris followed the barrel of the gun between his eyes down to Mikes arm and up to his face. "What Kari saw in you is beyond me," Chris said shaking his head in disappointment. "You're as dumb as you look. All the pilots are dead, except for me, and right now you're pointing your gun at the only hope of getting us out of here with an itchy finger on the trigger? Sergeant please order this man to lower his weapon and take a seat. Or better yet Mike, why don't you just go outside and clear us a path huh?"

Chris pushed Mike's button with his quick wit and Mike firmly pressed the gun against his forehead. "He's licensed!" Kari quickly shouted from the back as the rest of the group observed. "He knows how to fly Mike. He got his license years ago."

"That true?" asked the Sergeant standing by the co-pilots chair. Chris nodded his head and strapped on the pilot's helmet. "I own a company that manufactures parts that go into the turbine engines of this helicopter. It's my business to learn all there is to know about these types of aircrafts. What kind of owner and business man would I be if I wasn't familiar on how to operate one? A very stupid one. So yes, I have a license and I renew my license every year. In fact, last year I learned how to fly a similar helo like this one. This is the new CH-47F is it not? This aircraft is equipped with CASS, Common Avionics Architecture System, a system that uses commercial standards. In addition to its upgrade, it comes with a fully integrated digital cockpit management system. Hell, with all the new bells and whistles, this bad boy can practically fly itself. But you need me to operate it. Now, are you going to let me fly us out of here or not?" Chris asked Mike as he stared at the gun in his face and then looked back up to Mike. The Sergeant put his hand over Mikes weapon and lowered it.

Saul walked into the cockpit with a bottle of water and handed it over to Chris. Saul turned and looked at Mike as he walked back to his seat but quickly looked away. "Alright everybody in your seat now and fasten your seatbelts," ordered the Sergeant. "I'll stay up here with him," Sergeant Mathers told Mike and patted him on the back.

"I don't trust this guy Gabriel, keep an eye on him," Mike replied unfolding the troop commanders jump seat in the center companion way just behind the cockpit. The Sergeant jumped in the co-pilots seat and fastened his seatbelt. The others were ecstatic when they heard that Chris was going to pilot the helicopter. The rumble and vibration in their seat was pure bliss. Linda clasped her hands in prayer and thanked the Lord for the miracle he had presented to them in the form of Chris and his ability to fly the helicopter. Chris pulled on the thrust control and the rotor blades began to make a slapping sound as the helicopter lifted off the ground. The Sergeant was uncertain of Chris' ability to fly. He sat with a nervous look and held on tight. He was comforted once he saw Chris doing a good job and in control of the helicopter. The helo ascended perfectly without any shaking. The Sergeant's nerves had calmed.

Blood splattered onto the windows and the side of the aircraft. Limbs sprang out from the top as the rotor blades at the front and back of the helicopter sliced through the undead that had climbed on top of the aircraft. Although not the person he would have picked to save the day, Mike was relieved that Chris flew them out of there safely. He didn't express it, but he too was in a jovial mood. He and his fiancé Kari were safe again, and that's what really mattered to him. So, for the time being, his anger took a ride in the backseat, but he knew not let his guard down nor turn his back on Chris. He put on a pair of headphones that were hanging next to his seat to communicate with the Sergeant.

"Hey Gabriel, does he know where we're heading?"

"Yeah, he's got the coordinates," replied the Sergeant pointing at the moving map display.

"Good. So, what else do you know about this virus?"

"Well from what I learned after discussing it with a doctor at the CDC, the virus or lethal agent as she described it, was originally created with a mixture of drugs, like alpha-PDP or commonly known by its street name 'Flakka'. The physiologic effects of Flakka lead to a psychotic state characterized by a surge of violence and increased strength, loss of awareness, loss of reality and surroundings. The virus has other chemicals and substances that I can't even pronounce. But they all work together to shut down all cognition and leaves you in a predatory state of mind where hunger is your only driving force. As far as why they don't die except with a bullet to the head, beats me."

"The Flakka substance would explain why they're so fast and strong. Do they ever slow down? Or eventually die?"

"Well if they keep feeding, then no they won't slow down. Like a regular person. The food you eat gives you strength and energy. If you don't eat, you grow weak. Same works with them. As far as eventually dying? Yes, once you destroy the brain."

"The cure. Will it treat all of the people already infected?"

"It'll treat the people who got infected from breathing in the virus. The infection will be reversed and in time and with proper care, the person can go back to being normal. But if you got bitten, then the possibility of getting cured is very slim. Only twenty percent. Now, say someone got infected from a severe bite wound and is missing a limb, or if your body is riddled with bullets and are somehow still walking, then no. You'll just completely collapse and die as soon as the treatment enters your body."

"And how exactly is it supposed to enter the system. I don't see these…*beings* lining up waiting to get a shot."

"I'm not a scientist Mike. I don't know. I just know what info they tell me. That's for the people at the labs to figure out. I just know we have to get these tubes there before it's too late."

"What do you mean too late?"

"I've been informed that every base and military encampment is getting overrun with the undead. Military reinforcements are unable to come to anyone's aid. They're dealing with their own matters at hand."

"So, we're on our own."

"Yes," replied the Sergeant with a solemn expression that covered his face. "Mike, I am sorry to have to tell you this, but the lab is located inside the naval base and is currently swarming with the undead. Over ninety percent of all naval and military personnel are dead and only a few remain guarding the labs."

"Gabriel are you telling me that the 'safe' Naval base where we are supposed to go to is no longer active?"

The Sergeant nodded his head, "Affirmative. I am sorry I didn't tell you sooner. I was told when we landed to refuel. There is no safe shelter for us to go. Not anymore."

Mike looked back at everyone on board and faked a smile at Kari who smiled back. The news disheartened him. *How can I tell Kari and everyone else that they have nowhere to go*, he thought? In addition to that, the place where they were headed to was surrounded by the undead. We had just left hell and were flying right back into it. It seemed like a never-ending nightmare. One that Mike wished he could wake from, hug his fiancé, and go back to sleep in the safety and comfort of their bed. The thought of his bed and being warm wrapped under the blankets alongside Kari suddenly crossed his mind. He looked at Kari again and tried to keep a cheerful face, but his eyes couldn't hide the truth. He looked despondent and Kari knew something was wrong. They've come to recognize each other's facial expressions very well as most couples do overtime and she stared back at him with a concerned look on her face and with eyes that were asking him what was wrong? Mike hid his distressed look with a wink and a smile.

The thrumming sound of the helicopter blades roared through the air as the helicopter headed south toward San Diego shadowing the packed freeway with empty cars that were left abandoned by the people who decided to flee on foot. Other vehicles were occupied by the undead who were locked inside.

Saul looked out the window and saw all the cars below. He remembered being stuck on that freeway for Memorial Day weekend when he and his friends packed his friend's truck with plenty of alcohol to last a week and backpacks stuffed with an extra pair of underwear and socks, deodorant, toothbrush, and shirt. Not to mention the box of condoms that no one ended up using that unlucky weekend. All his friend's faces raced through his mind. His last memory of them was making a toast and watching a soccer game. He closed his eyes to keep the tears in as he remembered their laughs and the possibility of never seeing them alive again. I thought of my mother and I'm sure Fred did as well. I imagine he he wished to have seen her face before walking out the door to go to work that morning. He wished he could have given her a hug and tell her I love you Ma. He wished he could have said thank you for every warm hug, every hot meal, every pair of shoes, roof over our head and the unconditional love that you gave me. He would give anything to see her warm smile and hear her comforting voice one more time. I know because I wish for all of those things.

Flaco thought about his parents who were both at work. His father was a mechanic and his mother worked at a hospital as a custodian. During the day, he tried reaching them, but neither would answer their phone. He thought about the rotisserie chicken with Spanish rice that his mother cooked the day before. It was his favorite meal. They all sat down in the living room table and had Sunday night dinner together as they normally would every Sunday. His dad made it mandatory to save that day, so they could sit together and talk. It was the last time they were all together. Robbie hugged his girlfriend Sheena as she sobbed. She thought of her parents and hoped to see them again. She hoped to contact them once everything was settled and got back to normal. She thought of her best friend Lily and clung on to hope that she was still alive and would someday get to see her again. But in the back of her mind, she knew Lily was dead as much as she didn't want to accept it. Linda had a smile on her face as she glanced over at her brother Robbie. She was happy to have her brother next to her. Kari thought of her parents and prayed that they were safe in the comfort of their home back in Dallas, Texas. Her dad owned a rifle and that gave her somewhat of a small relief to know that he would be able to protect themselves if necessary. She glanced over at Mike and thought of what he might say when she tells him he would be a daddy.

That morning after he left with James for work, she took a digital home pregnancy test and the results read Pregnant. She wanted to tell him at night when they would go over the reception list, but of course the day's events wouldn't allow for that anymore. She waited during the whole day and night for the right moment to tell him, but it never came. Not until the good news of a haven in

San Diego surfaced. Once situated there, she would sit him down and finally tell him.

"We're almost there," Sergeant Mathers told Mike pointing at a large five story white building in the middle of a small town surrounded by an army of undead. The roof was wide enough to land on and had an entrance on the roof. "On the roof, there's a basement-hatch style entrance with a code. But there's a problem," said the Sergeant.

"Which is?" asked Mike.

"Every level of the building is armed with guards... or at least was. The first level stopped reporting to level 2 shortly after the outbreak. Minutes later, level three stopped reporting to level four, and finally level four stopped reporting to level five. And well I'm sure you can just imagine what happened to level five. We lost all coms with them. The only communication I get on my radio is from the labs down below the basement which is where we have deliver the tubes. There's an elevator on level five that will take us down with an access code, but the problem is, that the elevator is on the other side of the building. Once we gain access through the roof, we will have to run down a flight of stairs to level five and then down the hall to the other end of the building to get to the elevator. Do you see the problem with that?"

"That there are a countless number of the undead roaming level five since all of the infected most likely ran up to the top level to keep feeding on the last remaining survivors?"

"Exactly. We'll be facing all of level 1 thru 5. I can't do this alone and now that my squad is gone, I'll need all the help that I can get. We must get these tubes down to the lab at ALL costs. Copy?"

"Yeah… roger that," Mike hesitantly replied with a heavy breath. "Dammit! Do you have any more bad news that you'd like to share with me Gabriel? Or are you saving it for when we are in the actual moment?"

"I'm sorry amigo, that's all the bad news I have. But if there's more, you and I will be the first to find out."

Mike shook his head. He knew he had to go with Gabriel and somehow get to the elevator. But he also knew that it was a suicide mission. Every level had an army of the undead made up of lab technicians, scientists and other government personnel roaming the halls waiting for their next meal. Although they had weapons, it wouldn't be enough. If the armed guards at each level couldn't stop the undead, what chance did they have? He stared down in deep thought then looked toward the back of the helicopter and focused his attention at the six-barrel rotary minigun mounted on a folding tripod secured onto the back of the ramp door.

"We'll lure them out," Mike said.

"How?" asked the Sergeant.

"We'll position the tail of the helicopter close to the edge of the building and lower the door ramp. You and I will man the gunner, secure someone with a rope tied to the helicopter and have them run out to open the roof door, run back to the helo and when the undead start chasing after that person, you and I will shoot them down. Specially with that minigun back there. It can shoot two thousand to six thousand rounds per minute. This will give us a fighting chance in getting to the elevator to take us down to the labs and deliver the tubes."

"I like that plan Mike. We'll need a volunteer to open that roof though. And they better be lightning fast."

CHAPTER 9

As they approached the flat roof top of the building, the Sergeant went over the plan of action with Chris while Mike looked for a volunteer. He stood up in the front of the aisle and addressed the group. They were all seated and looked up as Mike began to talk. He didn't sugar coat any of it nor did he hide the fact that they had nowhere to go now. He revealed to them that the initial plan to fly to a secured station in San Diego was terminated. They all gasped in shock after hearing that the once safe and secure station in San Diego was no longer standing and that everyone was dead. Linda buried her face in her hands and began to weep. Kari became panic-stricken with worry painted on her face. Mike tried calming them and shared his plan. He delighted their disheartening mood when he explained to them that they had a key element to help finding a cure. He quickly went over the plan in detail and made it clear that whoever volunteered could possibly die.

"And you need to be fast, really fast," Mike said with a serious face. "I know that I'm asking a lot," he said looking at everyone directly in the eye. "But if we don't get these test tubes down to the lab, then the world we know will cease to exist. We have to act now. So please anyone?"

The group stared back at one another wondering who would volunteer. Flaco felt at ease. He was the slowest of them all. There was no way could he run back to the helicopter in time before getting attacked by one of the undead. Linda felt the same. She was a bit husky and wasn't wearing running shoes to begin with. She knew she was out of the equation. Sheena looked at Robbie hoping he wouldn't volunteer. "My leg is busted, but I can try," Robbie said as he tried getting up.

"I'll go," Fred confidently said and stood up. "I'm probably the fastest one here anyway. Besides, I'm the one that caused all of this, I might as well be the one that helps to fix it."

"Fred, you understand that if you manage to get away but get bitten, we have to put you down. We can't risk the lives of everyone else in here."

Fred nodded, "I understand. I wouldn't want to put anyone in harms way, especially her," Fred said looking down at me. "Can you promise me, that if anything were to happen to me, you'll take care of Maddie? I'm the only family she's got. Please promise me that you will take care of her."

"You have my word Fred. I promise to always take care of Maddie," Mike said and firmly shook his hand.

Fred kneeled in front of me. I remember like it was yesterday. He brushed my curly hair away from my face and looked me straight in the eye. "Hey little lady, I need to go and help them now. I'll be gone for a little bit but while I'm gone, I need you to be a big girl and behave yourself okay?"

"Will you come back?" I asked with a worried face.

He paused, unsure of how to answer. A knot in his throat formed. He coughed to clear it. "You remember the cartoons you were watching this morning with the superheroes?" he asked and I nodded. "I'm going to be a superhero and help save the day. But, what I'm going to do is very dangerous and I might not come back. If I don't come back, this man Mike, he will look after you. He's a very good friend of mine and he's a good person, so please be nice to him."

My lip started to quiver, and a stream of tears began to roll down my small round pink cheeks. I leaned in and hugged him tightly around the neck. I squeezed with all of my might so that he couldn't leave. "No, I don't want you to be a superhero," I said in a loud trembly voice. "I want you to stay here with me. Please don't go Freddie."

Fred held me tight and a tear escaped his eye. "Five minutes to approaching the roof," the Sergeant said as polite as he could from the cockpit as he looked on.

"I know sweetie," Fred said and sniffled. "Believe me I want to stay here with you too, but I have to go do this. I will try my very best to come back, but if I don't, know that I love you very much and so does mommy. We will always love you and watch over you. Now be a good girl and always do the right thing.

Oh, and remember, boys lie. I love you." He gave me a kiss on the forehead and one last hug before walking away. I screamed his name with tears bursting from my eyes and reached out for him. Kari who was seated next to me, picked me up and sat me in her lap to calm me. Fred walked toward the back of the aircraft wiping away the tears from his eyes.

A gust of wind blew across the roof as the helicopter approached and Chris maneuvered the aircraft into position. The Sergeant strapped a vest onto Fred and buckled one end of a strap to the vest and secured the other end onto a tie-down ring on the overhead of the troops seat. Mike did the same and strapped on his harness. Once Fred was secure, the Sergeant gave Mike thumbs up and Mike pushed the button that lowered the door ramp as the helicopter hovered over the edge of the building. Once the ramp was lowered, Mike sat on the edge of the ramp in front of the minigun, examined the ammunition cartridge belt and prepared to fire the weapon. Sergeant Mathers, also strapped down, stepped onto the edge of the ramp with Fred by his side. Fred slowly stepped forward and trembled with fear. His heart was racing as he looked over the edge. Using the headphones on the helmet, the Sergeant guided Chris as Chris hovered closer to the edge of the building. He flew the helo close to the edge of the building to make a quick jump off the ramp onto the building.

"Okay, remember the access code is 5-6-5-7," Sergeant Mathers told Fred in a loud voice. "The noise from the helicopter will have already attracted them, and they will most likely be at the roof door, so once you lift open that door, run your ass back here as fast as you can. You'll be strapped onto the safety harness in case we have to fly up. If we have to lift off, just jump off the building. The harness will keep you from falling and we'll reel you back in. Mike's ready to cut them down with the minigun once they start running out that door and I'll be here with my rifle in case any of them get past Mike's fire. Don't look back, just keep running toward us, we got your back. And when you run, make sure to run along the side, this way you're not in our path as we shoot them down. Got it?"

Fred shook his head and gave thumbs up. "5-6-5-7 right?" Fred asked.

"Yes, you got this Fred!" the Sergeant shouted back and patted Fred on the shoulder. Mike looked up at Fred with his hands steady on the trigger and gave him thumbs up. "Godspeed!" Mike shouted. Fred gave Mike the thumbs up, inched a little closer to the edge and turned to look back at me. The tears in my eyes kept rolling down as Kari held me in her lap. The others on board still strapped to their seats tried to hide their solemn faces with a supporting smile. Fred waved me goodbye and smiled. He turned around, looked down at the edge of the ramp, took in a deep breath and jumped off the ramp onto the building. The sound of crushing gravel rolled from under his shoes as he quickly walked up to the middle of the roof to open the door. Upon arriving, he took a knee and looked back at Mike seated at the gunner position, steady with both hands on the minigun ready to fire and so was Sergeant Mathers who stood at the ramp with his rifle pointed at the door. Fred looked back down at the electric panel next to the large metal door and punched in the code, 5-6-5-9. A flashing red light and beep sounded off. *Ahh c'mon man,* Fred thought to himself. *5-6-5…7?* he punched in the code. This time a green light flashed followed by the sound of a metal lock release. He smiled for a second before it quickly ran from his face. He realized that the dreadful moment was now upon him. He grabbed the door hatch, took three deep breaths, turned it counter clock wise and pulled it up.

An army guard with foggy eyes and pale skin pushed the roof door wide open and let out a terrorizing grunt. Fred was startled, jolted backward, and fell on his butt. The undead guard threw himself onto Fred but before he could bite, the Sergeant fired a single shot into the guard's head killing it. "Run!" shouted the Sergeant. Fred scrambled to his feet and a horde of undead rushed out from the roof door. Instantly rat-a-tat-tat the minigun roared and echoed inside the aircraft as Mike squeezed the trigger. Bullet casings clinked as they bounced off the floor and rolled down the ramp. Limbs and torsos were cut in half as the undead pushed their way out through the door. One by one they all fell as bullets pierced through their bodies. The Sergeant kept his weapon aimed towards Fred's back making sure no one ran up behind him and saw Fred running as instructed. He ran to the side avoiding Mikes fire and started getting closer to edge of the building. Just as he was two feet away from jumping onto the lowered door ramp, Fred was strongly yanked. His legs flew up in the air and he fell on his back. The long strap secured on his vest had wrapped around a vent pipe which pulled Fred to the ground. An undead guard who Mike had cut in half with the minigun used its arms as legs to scuttle towards Fred. The Sergeant aimed at its head and squeezed the trigger but missed hitting the roof. As Fred sat up to get on his feet, he blocked the Sergeants view and the undead guard latched onto Fred's back. Fred huffed and reached for his back to throw him off. The guard threw his head back and caught Fred's hand, biting him on the wrist. "Fuck!" screamed Fred in a painful voice. "God dammit!" yelled the Sergeant as he took aim at the undead guard who clung to Fred's back. Fred swung his body from side to side trying to shake the guard off. The guard's guts swung side to side and his spleen dangled from its open lower torso as he hanged on and swayed with Fred's vigorous swings. "Turn around!" shouted the Sergeant at Fred so he could get a clear shot. Fred heard and spun around bringing the undead guard's head into view. The Sergeant pulled the trigger and shot the guard in the head. The guard's torso dropped to the floor. Just then Mike's ammunition ran out and the undead kept rushing out of the roof door, running straight at Fred. He was down on one knee and miserably examined the bite wound on his wrist. Blood trickled down his fingers. He slowly rose to his feet and stumbled toward the helicopter. The undead came within reach and the Sergeant ordered Chris to fly up. "Jump!" Mike yelled at Fred as the helicopter began to ascend. Fred looked behind him and saw the horde of undead inching closer. He staggered to the edge of the building. He looked straight down with terror, closed his eyes and jumped.

As he went over the building, the undead followed him over the edge. They swung their arms out trying to catch him. Bodies splattered by the side of the building with their arms stretched out toward Fred as they flew down. An undead guard who was stationed at level five and wore a blood stained beige camouflage uniform, grabbed onto Fred's ankle. Mike reloaded the minigun as the Sergeant aimed his weapon at the guard that hung onto Fred. Chris adjusted the throttle and pulled back on the stick as Fred swung from side to side slamming into the windows on the side of the building. The Sergeant could see that Fred started to cough. His eyes were blood shot red and started changing color. His skin lost color and turned pale. The Sergeant aimed at the guard's head and fired. The guard released his hold on Fred as the bullet struck him on the side of the head. He splatted as he hit the concrete floor. Fred, with a heavy-eyed look stared up at the Sergeant and began to unstrap his harness. He undid the first buckle and struggled with the last one. He mustered his strength and got it to release. As the buckle came free, he fell six feet down onto the roof by the edge of the building. Mike kept a steady aim and fired the minigun at the undead who kept running out the roof door. Fred laid on his side, curled up in a fetal position as the virus spread through his body. His shirt was soaking with sweat. The minigun stopped rotating once the last of the undead ran out from the door.

"Alright Chris, bring her down," said the Sergeant. Mike unbuckled his strap and the Sergeant did the same. He loaded his weapon with a full magazine and Mike reloaded his pistol. As Chris lowered the helicopter onto the roof, Mike walked over to Kari and knelt in front of her. With tears in my eyes I looked up at him and asked, "where's Freddie?" Mike looked up at Kari with a regrettable look on his face. "He went to go be a hero Maddie. And I'm going to go help him," Mike replied and then looked back up Kari. Her face was gloomy, and her eyes pleaded for him to stay. She feared that Mike would never come back. "I'm coming back honey, I promise you," he told Kari while gently squeezing her hand.

"You have to," Kari replied. "We need you, the three of us." He looked confused at her remark and then she took his hand and placed it over her belly. He looked up at her with wide eyes, "you're pregnant?" he asked in shock.

Chris had just walked out from the cockpit and stood there watching them waiting for Kari to answer Mike's question. She nodded her head, "yes, I found out this morning when I took a home pregnancy test. I wanted to tell you tonight at home but then with all that's happened, I never found the right moment. So, you see, you have to come back to us because this baby will need a father. I'll need my husband and you promised Fred that you would take care of Maddie."

Chris squinted his eyes and clenched his jaw. He looked down with an angry face and slightly shook his head. He walked toward the back feeling scorned and stood near the ramp looking out at the dead bodies scattered over the roof of the building.

The Sergeant walked to the side of the building and kneeled by Fred's body. "I'm sorry amigo," he said and put a zip tie around Fred's wrist. "I don't want to put a bullet in your head because you don't deserve that. What you did took a lot of guts and you deserve a medal for valor. What I can do is spare you and hope that someday the people down in this building work on finding you a cure. But I can't leave you up here to harm anyone so I'm tying your arms and legs. I'm going to leave you here by the side of the roof, out of sight, but I'll come back for you. You did good Fred. Thank you."

Mike wrapped his arms around Kari and gently squeezed her. She placed her soft lips onto his and their tongues swirled around one another. He gently placed his hands on her cheeks, "I promise that I'll come back to you. I promise you that this baby will grow up with his father and you will grow old with me by your side as your husband and Maddie will be looked after," he said. A tear rolled down her cheek and she smiled back at him. "*His* father?" she asked and chuckled. "I think it's a she."

"Whatever it is, it's a blessing and I'll be by your side when it's born. I love you honey."

"I love you too," she replied and sniffled. They gave each other one last kiss before he turned and walked toward the ramp. Mike stopped to talk with Saul. He instructed Saul to close the ramp door once he and the Sergeant were inside the building. Just as he walked out of the helicopter he shoved Chris outside with him. "You're coming with us," Mike ordered Chris. "The hell I am," Chris contested.

"I am not leaving you here alone with her and my baby," Mike told Chris as he got in his face. "So, get your ass moving or I'll splatter your brains on this roof like the rest of them." Chris looked at Sergeant Mathers who stood beside the helicopter and the Sergeant simply shrugged his shoulders. "This is absurd," Chris said and rolled his eyes as he walked toward the roof entrance. "Stay in between us," the Sergeant told Chris as he walked ahead with Mike following behind Chris.

The three men pulled the bodies of the dead away from the door. Limbs and torsos were scattered around the door. There was an upper torso blocking the door and Mike asked Chris to grab one arm, so he can grab the other to lift it off the door. As Chris pulled on the arm, it detached from the socket. "Oh Jesus," he said repulsed by the bloody limb. He dropped it and gagged. He felt the vomit rise to his throat. Just as he was about to put his hand over his mouth, he looked at his bloody hands and squinted his face with disgust. He took in a deep breath and swallowed his vomit. "Shake that shit off," the Sergeant told Chris as the Sergeant helped remove bodies from the entrance. "When we get inside, be prepared for anything. We still don't know how many of them are in here. Once we get to the elevator, we'll have to punch in another code, 4-3-3-4. This will open the elevator door that'll take us down to the labs. You guys ready?"

Chris shook his head no and Mike nodded yes. The Sergeant lifted the metal hatch door which emitted a creaky sound. The Sergeant used the hand rail and climbed down the flight of metal stairs to level five. Chris and Mike followed behind him. "Mike, you sure it's a good idea to bring him down with us?" the Sergeant whispered at Mike at the bottom of the stairs. They both looked back at Chris who was standing by the staircase. "If we need to evacuate for any reason, he's the only pilot we have left."

"I don't trust him with Kari on board. And what if he decides to take off?"

"Kari's got a gun, right? She can fend for herself. And she damn sure won't let him fly out of here without you."

Mike nodded in deep thought.

"You win, okay. Is that what you want me to say," Chris said looking at Mike. "She loves you and is having your baby, so congratulations bud', you win. You don't have to worry about me anymore or what you think I might try and do. She's happy and deeply in love with you. I see that. As much as I hate to admit it, she'll never look at me the way she looks at you. Besides, I'd never put Kari in harm's way, especially now that she's expecting. But the Sergeant's right, we don't know what's down here and if we have fly out of here, as I recall you two don't even know what switch to flip, nor does anyone on board that aircraft. I shouldn't be down here."

"Alright," Mike said. "I'll walk you back up and have Saul open the door for you. Gabriel, hang tight."

Mike and Chris went back up the stairs and opened the roof door. Chris stepped out first and Mike followed closely behind. As they began to walk, Mike stopped and called to Chris, "Hey."

Chris turned around and Mike punched him square on the chin. Chris' legs buckled and he fell to his knees. "That's for shoving that kid onto me back at the shelter you asshole," Mike said standing over Chris with his fist clinched. "And as much as I'd like to beat your ass up and down this roof, we'll call it even."

Mike signaled at Saul who looked out through the window of the helicopter to open the ramp door and let Chris in.

"Ow?" Chris said from his knees trying to compose himself. He planted his foot and stood up with a dazed look. "Even-steven," he murmured back and wobbled toward the helicopter. Mike watched as Chris staggered up the ramp. He waved at Kari who was standing by the door ramp. She waved back and smiled.

Mike went back into the building down the stairs where the Sergeant stood waiting for him. "All good?" the Sergeant asked. "Yeah, we're even-Steven," Mike replied as they made their way down the long hallway with walls made of cement that were painted white. The dusty dome shaped lights that hung above casted two shadows of the men who treaded quickly but silently on the polished concrete floor of level five. There were metal doors with an electronic proximity reader with keypad attached to all doors every ten feet and an elevator at the end of the hall. Toward the end of the hall by the elevator was another staircase to the left which led to the lower levels. Both men feared that an attack by another horde of undead loomed around the corner. Sergeant Mathers put up a fist to signal stop and turned to face Mike. "Cover the staircase," the Sergeant whispered. "I'll punch in the code."

They moved toward the elevator and stopped at the corner wall that lead to the staircase. The Sergeant poked his head out and checked if anyone was by the staircase. He scanned the floor and as far down the staircase as his eyes could see. It was empty. He signaled Mike to move forward and stand guard by the wall while he walked up to the elevator keypad lock. He punched in 4-3-3-4 on the silver buttons and a greenlight flashed. He looked at Mike and gave him the thumbs up as the silver elevator doors opened.

Three undead soldiers who were stuck inside the elevator rushed out as soon as the doors opened. The first soldier caught the Sergeant by surprise and bit him on the neck. The other two attacked Mike. The Sergeant pushed the undead soldier off and Mike fired his pistol at his attackers. He shot one at close range and struck him in between the eyes. The Sergeant fired his rifle and shot his attacker in the chest and forehead. Mike shot the legs right under his other attacker. As the undead soldier fell to the floor, Mike shot him in the head. Three more undead soldiers were racing up the stairs as they grunted and made loud footsteps with their boots. Mike slid against the wall and into the elevator. "Get in!" he shouted. The Sergeant stood by the staircase and fired off his weapon with one hand and reached into his leg pocket. He pulled out the case that held the tubes and handed it to Mike. "Take it!" he shouted back. "I can't go any further amigo." Mike noticed the blood dripping from his neck and realized he got bitten. "Dammit Gabriel!" he screamed at the Sergeant with a disheartened face. "You got this Mike," the Sergeant said with a heavy breath. "I'll hold them off. Godspeed brother." "Godspeed

Gabriel," Mike said as the elevator doors closed shut. He heard the rifle firing off followed by a loud scream.

The elevator was wide with stainless-steel panels and blue carpet. The numbers on the elevator button panel lowered from five to one and the elevator stopped. Suddenly a voice was heard coming from the intercom. "Identify yourself," the voice said. "I'm Michael Monreal," replied Mike. "I have the original chemical agent with me," Mike said holding the container with test tubes up to the camera fixed to corner of the door.

"Unload your weapon, empty the chamber and place it down on the ground behind you. Get down on your knees and place your hands behind your head, lock your fingers, and cross your right leg over your left," the voice firmly commanded. Mike did as he was told and placed his gun toward the back of the elevator. "From here we will control the elevator to take you down to Biosafety Level-Four. Once the elevator doors open, you are to remain in this position whereupon an officer will scan you for infection. If you are infected, you are to be executed immediately. If you are clear, turn over the tubes and await further instructions. Do you understand?"

"Yes," replied Mike from his knees looking up at the camera. The elevator lowered and passed biosafety levels one through three.

At stopping on level four, the elevator doors slid open and waiting outside were five armed men wearing blue positive pressure protective suits. They pointed their fully automatic assault rifle directly at Mikes head while a woman with green eyes wearing the same suit stepped to the side and scanned Michael with a black machine that looked like a small tablet with a touch screen on the front and a body scanner on the back. Mike nervously tried remaining still as she scanned him up and down. The machine beeped once with the words 'CLEAR' written in green displayed across the screen. Mike sighed with relief and took in a deep breath. "The tubes please?" the woman asked as one of the armed men handed her a small yellow plastic container with racks inside to accommodate the tubes. Mike handed her the case. She took it to a table across from her where the labs were stationed and opened it. She pulled out the tubes and carefully inserted them into the container and cautiously walked them to her laboratory. "Miss?" Mike gently said while still on his knees in the elevator. She stopped and turned back, "Doctor Hayes" she replied. "Doctor Hayes, will this help to create a cure for the virus?"

"Walk with me," she answered. He got up and started walking with her down the large white facility. Mike looked around as he walked alongside the doctor down the hallway with overhead lights. There were small stark white rooms to his left. You could see through them from the hallway through the one-way mirror, similar to what you see in police interrogation rooms. To his right were labs with see through walls. The armed men followed behind them.

"First let me commend you on risking your life to get these tubes down here," the doctor said with container in hand. "I am sure that it was not easy."

"No ma' am, it was not. We lost good men in retrieving these tubes and have been through a lot today just to get them safely down here. In fact, a good friend of mine, Sergeant Gabriel Mathers just gave his life upstairs to ensure the safety of these tubes."

"I am deeply sorry about your friend Sergeant Mathers. But I thank you for what you have done. Rest assured, it will not be in vain."

"Doctor Hayes," Mike said. "How long have you been working to find a cure? And exactly how will these tubes help in curing the ill and terminating the already … undead?"

"Well, while I cannot tell you how long we have been working on the vaccine nor get into details about it, what I can say is that thanks to you, we now have the original chemical agent needed for preparing the first antivirus and/or cure. We know that the antivirus will combat the illness that plagues millions of people. Once the vaccine is introduced into the body, it'll provoke the immune system to create an antibody to fight and kill the infected cells. In time, the immune system will then begin to heal itself and of course with proper medical treatment, a person should fully recover within weeks. As for the ones who got the infection from a bite wound, they're chances of recovering are minimal. It is hard to determine when or if we can ever find them a cure. But at least we now have what's needed to conduct further research in creating a vaccine for those misfortune souls."

"I see. And how will you get this cure out there?"

"With the help of the American Red Cross and other humanitarian organizations, we can start vaccinating people immediately. Now, if you'll excuse me, this is my lab and we have work to do. But you are welcomed to stay here."

"Thank you, Doctor, but I have my people with me. They're on the roof, inside of the helicopter. Can you let us stay here? Please."

She gave him a harsh look. "My fiancé is on board, she's pregnant. And there's a little girl on board too. She's the sister of a brave man that died helping us get inside this place. Along with a few kids, teenagers to be exact. Please we have nowhere to go."

"Alright," she said standing by the doorway of the lab. "If you can bring them down safely, you're all welcomed to stay. For a little while that is. Until we find you a more suitable location."

"I appreciate that, thank you."

"The guard behind you will accompany you back up and assist you with getting them here safely." She redirected her eyes to the guard standing behind Mike, "make sure and scan each one of them."

"Follow me," the tall guard said to Mike as he led him down the hall. The guard stopped in front of a metal door and punched a code on a keypad lock. It beeped and the guard pushed the door open. He took a step to the side and held the door open for Mike to walk through. The lights were off and it was dark. Mike was suspicious and hesitated for a second. He had no choice but to enter. As he stepped inside the sensor was activated and turned the lights on. Mike was standing in a weapon room. To his right was a rack of assault rifles. To his left, a wall of hand guns. The metal drawers beneath the guns held magazines and boxes of bullets. Directly in front of him was a table with a metal case on top of it. Mike was eager to open the metal case. He took a step forward and turned the door latch.

Inside were three rows of grenades and a grenade launcher on the bottom shelf.

"Gear up," the guard said. "Take whatever you need." Mike grinned and grabbed two grenades and stuffed them in his pocket. He grabbed the assault rifle with ten magazines.

"Let's roll out," Mike said to the guard as he walked out the room. They proceeded toward the elevator. The guards inside the security room located next to the elevator operated a computer system that controlled the elevators. They opened the doors and

Mike stepped inside with the guard beside him. The doors closed shut and the elevator went up. "Expect close contact as soon as the doors open," Mike said as he pulled the hammer back on the riffle. "I'll take the staircase on the right, you watch our twelve." The guard pointed his rifle at the door and got ready. Mike held his rifle with both hands ready to fire. He looked up at the elevator digital number screen as the numbers went higher. As the elevator passed level four Mike pointed the rifle at the doors. The guard took in a deep breath and the elevator came to a stop on level five.

The doors opened and they could see an empty hallway. The guard stepped forward with his rifle pointed and an undead guard attacked him. Mike fired his gun and shot the undead guard in the head. "Move!" Mike said and pushed forward. Four of the undead were roaming the staircase to the right and one of them was his friend Sergeant Mathers. Mike hesitated on pulling the trigger and the guard fired his rifle striking the Sergeant in the head. A horde of the undead came racing up the stairs from level four. Mike reached in his pocket and pulled out a grenade as the guard kept firing. "Grenade," shouted Mike as he threw it into the staircase. They took cover by the wall beside the staircase and felt the roar of the explosion. "Alright let's move," Mike said through the smoke and ran down to the end of the hall toward the staircase that led to the roof.

They got to the staircase and ran up the stairs. Mike opened the roof door and stepped out. A smile came over his face when he saw Kari looking through the window of the helicopter. She smiled joyfully. Saul lowered the door ramp and Mike eagerly waited for it to lower. Once down he walked up to her and she wrapped her arms around him. She kissed him and buried her face into his chest to hide her tears of joy. "I told you I'd be back," he said.

Mike devised a plan to finish off any of the undead still wandering the building. With the help of the guard and Saul, they carried the minigun down to level five and placed it on the floor in middle of the hall. Mike sat on the floor and pointed the heavy gun at the other end of the hallway where the staircase led to the lower levels. Saul screamed out loud and made noise. He banged on the walls with his hammer. The guard stood next to Mike with his riffle to help shoot down the undead. Within seconds a small horde of undead guards and personnel came rushing up the stairs and toward the three men. The minigun let out a piercing echo as it rotated. The ammunition belt clinked as the bullets boomed out of the barrels. The guard fired his rifle. A group of undead created a bottle neck at the hallway and Mike threw a grenade. They hit the floor as the grenade exploded killing the small bunch of undead. The small battle was over in less than four minutes and they cleared out the entire building making it safe for everyone.

We took the elevators down below the bio-levels where some of the guards used to sleep. Almost all of them died during the outbreak so there were plenty of bunks to choose from. I asked for my brother every day, and every day they would say, "he's fighting supervillains and can't come right now."

Later that day, Mike went up to the roof and found Fred tied up by the corner of the building. He had a pallid face and growled at Mike, occasionally snapping at him. Fred had turned into one of the undead. Mike figured that the Sergeant perhaps left Fred alive and tied him up in the hopes that someday there would be a cure for him. Mike didn't let anyone know, especially me. Not until years later when I was old enough to understand. With the doctor's permission, Mike brought Fred down to the lab and placed him in quarantine. They took extra measures and hog tied him. They placed a black mask over his face and carried him inside of a holding cell. They kept him alive with the intent of using him for biology lessons, medical training, experimentation with other drugs and vaccinations. When a cure was finally discovered, he regrettably, was not cured but his aggression levels and predatory state had decreased which was a huge step toward finding a cure for others like him.

A military operation was drawn up by surviving commanders to get the cure into the hands of the people. It was called Operation Zoe, Greek for life. Small armed forces would fly in a helicopter here to our building and pick up large batches of the vaccine and then carry out their deadly mission. It took some time and a lot of casualties, but in the end, they achieved their objective.

Slowly people started to rebuild and bring life back to how things were before UD-Day.

Mike and Kari got married and adopted me. Kari gave birth to a healthy boy, James, named after my father's friend who died heroically on UD-Day. Saul went back to working construction as head manager and even gave Robbie his first job right out of high school. Sheena went off to college in Alabama and ended her relationship with Robbie. Flaco joined the gym and went to community college to learn software engineering. Linda started her career in insurance as a claim's assistant, thanks to my mother Kari who put in a good word. After two months of giving birth, my mother quit her job at Insuracal to stay home and raise my brother James and I. Doctor Hayes, the woman credited for creating the vaccine hired my dad to be head of security, so we moved here to San Diego. My father still works here as head of security and we see each other every so often. Sometimes we'll have tea upstairs in the café lounge area. As for Chris, he moved his business operations to San Francisco. There he fell in love with his young accountant and married her a year later. Eight months later he filed for divorce after coming home early from a business trip and finding her in bed sleeping with her co-worker. Karma, I suppose. You may run from it, but one day, it'll catch up to you.

And well, that sums up the story of who I am. I am a product of all the events and the people that have come and gone in my life. They have shaped me in some way and created the person you see today.

Fred, I know you really can't understand me. Our sessions, which I hoped would have sparked some sort of reaction, really haven't done much. Every day after sharing a bit of my story, especially the parts that included you, I studied your eyes and facial expression hoping to see something. Hoping to see some sort of light coming from your eyes or an understanding. Just a tilt of your head would give me hope. But all I see is a cold blank stare. I suppose these sessions were for me more than anything. They have given me the chance to tell you things that I've been wanting to share with you. Things about my life and of my accomplishments. Which leads me to the next topic that I want to share with you. We have a cure! Our tireless work has created a vaccine that will finally put an end to the Strike Down Law. With this vaccine, no child will ever have to live in fear of being executed again. I've named it Andrew's Vaccine. I hope that you're proud of me big bro. I dream of the day when we find you a cure; you'll wake up, smile and recognize me. I dream of the day I get to hear you call me little lady again and hug me. In time I know we'll get there. Now, with this new vaccine, we're closer to finding you a permanent cure, more than ever before and when we do, I hope you'll remember some of the things that I've shared with you. I also want you to know that my father Mike, kept his promise to you. He along with my mother Kari, did their absolute best to give me a wonderful life and upbringing. They love me as one of their own and have always treated me equally with my brother James. I love you Freddie. But not to worry, this doesn't mean I'll stop coming by to see you. I'll still say hi every morning and talk to you. Maybe one day, I'll tell you about my first girlfriend in college. That was an interesting chapter. I have to go now. I'll see you tomorrow hermano, adios.

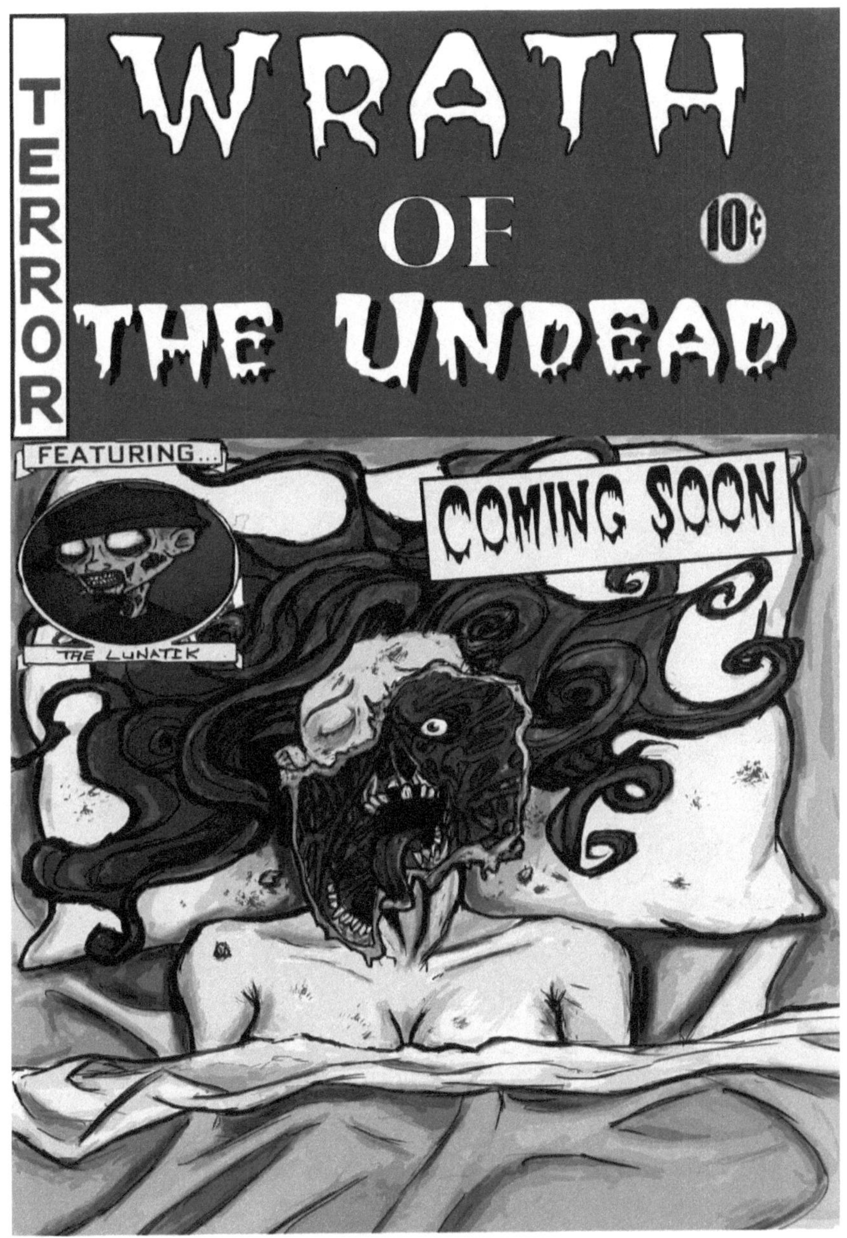

TERROR
WRATH
OF
THE UNDEAD
10¢
FEATURING...
THE LUNATIK
COMING SOON

ERIC MORENO
WRATH OF THE UNDEAD

About the author

Horror was deeply rooted in me at an early age. As a child, like most, I was terrified when watching horror films (bless my mother's heart for allowing me), but I couldn't close my eyes for fear of missing out on a scene where the monster would show up. But as scared as I was, I actually enjoyed the thrill, the fear. Weird? Maybe. Now as an adult, I get to write my own horror stories and share them with other like-minded people. I hope someone will enjoy it as much I have enjoyed writing it.

The idea for this book started fifteen years before the book was published. It began while working in a warehouse. As I hopped off my forklift, something sparked an idea. At that very moment, I wrote one full page, typed it up at home later that evening and saved it to my computer. But I never did anything with it. Fast forward eleven years later after graduating college and earning a Bachelor's degree in Business Management, while cleaning out my computer, I found that page, read it and was impressed by it. I felt it was so good that I had to keep writing. And so, I did. Every day after work, I went home and typed away. It was my hobby. Before I knew it, I had chapters of it and decided to make a book out of it. Four years later, I published this very book you hold in your hands. This is a true testament that through hard work and dedication, anything is possible.

ERIC MORENO

www.ingramcontent.com/pod-product-compliance
Lightning Source LLC
Chambersburg PA
CBHW050235110726
47898CB00007B/2157